AS MAGI
AS THE S

are the many beasts and beings who populate
these pages, each of their stories a unique
holiday gift to be opened and read not only
at Christmas but the whole year round.

"A Compromised Christmas"—He had
wanted to honeymoon on a warm beach, she
beside a cold Scottish loch. But neither could
have foreseen the magic that awaited them
when they compromised for the sake of
love. . . .

"I'll Be Home for Christmas"—They'd abandoned the city for the inheritance of an isolated farmhouse, but no one had told them
just how strange a country they were ventur-
ing into. . . .

"The Blue-Nosed Reindeer"—In an age of
satellites and heat-seeking missiles Santa
needed a reindeer with a nose as keen as
radar—for without him the presents would
never get through. . . .

CHRISTMAS
BESTIARY

FANTASTIC anthologies from DAW Books:

DRAGON FANTASTIC *Edited by Rosalind M. Greenberg and Martin H. Greenberg. With an Introduction by Tad Williams.* From a virtual reality watch dragon to a once-a-century get-together of the world's winged destroyers to an amazing little dragon of the home-grown variety, here are swift-winging fantasies by such talents as Alan Dean Foster, Mickey Zucker Reichert, Esther Friesner, and Dennis McKiernan.

HORSE FANTASTIC *Edited by Rosalind M. Greenberg and Martin H. Greenberg. With an Introduction by Jennifer Roberson.* Here are magical tales for anyone who has ever wished to gallop off into the sunset. From a racer death couldn't keep from the finish line to a horse with the devil in him, these are original stories by such top writers as Jennifer Roberson, Mercedes Lackey, Mickey Zucker Reichert, Judith Tarr, and Mike Resnick.

CATFANTASTIC I and II *Edited by Andre Norton and Martin H. Greenberg.* For cat lovers everywhere, two delightful collections of fantastical cat tales, some set in the distant future on as yet unknown worlds, some set in our own world but not quite our own dimension, some recounting what happens when creatures out of myth collide with modern-day felines.

THE NIGHT FANTASTIC *Edited by Poul and Karen Anderson.* Let Poul Anderson, Ursula K. Le Guin, Isaac Asimov, Alan Dean Foster, Robert Silverberg, Fritz Leiber, and a host of other fantasy masters carry you away to magical realms where night becomes day as the waking world sleeps and sleeping worlds wake.

CHRISTMAS BESTIARY

Edited by Rosalind M. Greenberg
and Martin H. Greenberg

DAW BOOKS, INC.
DONALD A. WOLLHEIM, FOUNDER
375 Hudson Street, New York, NY 10014

**ELIZABETH R. WOLLHEIM
SHEILA E. GILBERT
PUBLISHERS**

Cover art by John Howe.

Introduction © 1992 by Stefan Dziemianowicz
A Compromised Christmas © 1992 by Jennifer Roberson.
Karaoke Christmas © 1992 by Elizabeth Scarborough.
The Raven Teaches the Professor A Lesson © 1992 by
Jack C. Haldeman II.
The Rocking Horse Christmas © 1992 by Barb Jernigan.
The Abominable Snowman © 1992 by Laura Resnick.
A Bird of a Different Color © 1992 by Blake Cahoon.
Christmas Seal © 1992 by Jane Lindskold.
In This Season © 1992 by Harry Turtledove.
A Web for Christmas © 1992 by Karen Haber.
Babe and the Christmas Tree © 1992 by Lawrence Schimel.
Of Dust and Fire and the Night © 1992 by Barry N. Malzberg.
I'll Be Home for Christmas © 1992 by Tanya Huff.
Birthnight © 1992 by Michelle M. Sagara.
Ox and Ass Before Him Bow © 1992 by Mark Aronson.
Fate © 1992 by Kristine Kathryn Rusch.
The Last Sphinx © 1992 by Barbara Delaplace.
The Best Laid Schemes © 1992 by Jack Nimersheim.
The Gift of the Magicians, With Apologies to You Know Who
© 1992 by Jane Yolen.
The Blue-Nosed Reindeer © 1992 by Mike Resnick.

DAW Book Collectors No. 895.

First Printing, November 1992

1 2 3 4 5 6 7 8 9

CONTENTS

INTRODUCTION

by Stefan Dziemianowicz

The bestiary is a literary subgenre that enjoyed its greatest popularity in Europe during the thirteenth and fourteenth centuries. Its origins, however, date at least as far back as 2 A.D., purportedly to ancient Greece. The prototype of all bestiaries, the *Physiologus,* was a compendium of forty-eight stories written by an anonymous author. Each of the selections was told in the form of an allegory derived from the natural characteristics of a real or imaginary plant or animal (including the phoenix and the unicorn). Although the stories of the *Physiologus* were tied to biblical texts (in fact, the book's nearest rival in circulation was the Bible) and intended to provide moral instruction, today we might look upon this text as the first collection of fantasy tales.

Although translations and adaptations of the *Physiologus* abounded in early medieval times, one is not likely to run across a copy in the modern bookstore. The reason for this seems fairly straightforward: We live in a more sophisticated world than our forebears knew, and no longer depend on myths and superstitions to guide us down the correct path of moral conduct.

In truth, though, the bestiary is still very much with us today in the form of fantasy literature. One can trace a line of descent from the *Physiologus* to some

of the most distinguished and beloved works of imaginative fiction of the past century: Rudyard Kipling's
The Jungle Books, Edgar Rice Burroughs' *Tarzan of
the Apes,* George Orwell's *Animal Farm,* J. R. R.
Tolkien's *Lord of the Rings* trilogy, Richard Adams'
Watership Down and *The Plague Dogs,* and John
Barth's *Chimera.* In fact, a reader from the Middle
Ages might find himself overwhelmed by the variety
of imaginary creatures that have been added to the
bestial register since his time: the leprechaun, the
pixie, the gremlin, the troll, the hobbit, the wendigo,
the werewolf, the vampire, and the golem are just a
few representatives of folklore and mythology from
around the world that have become a part of fantasy's
literary legacy.

The regard in which we hold the fantastic bestiary
is evident from the symbolic association some of its
members have with traditional holidays. In America,
for example, we still count on the instinctive wisdom
of the groundhog to forecast the approaching Spring,
while the rabbit and the turkey have become folk em-
blems of, respectively, Easter and Thanksgiving.
Christmas is a feast day particularly rich in beast lore,
ranging from the attendance of the ox and the lamb
in the traditional Christian manger scene, to the par-
tridge of popular song, and the folk myth of one very
specially-endowed reindeer. But the overwhelming
majority of fabulous beasts do not owe their renown
to a particular holiday or season. Thus readers of this
Christmas Bestiary will find the traditional animals of
Christmas lore mingling with some of their less traditional brethren.

To better prepare you for the winter's tales to come,
we present herewith a field guide for Christmas beasts.

Abominable Snowman: Reputedly half-man and
half-ape, the Abominable Snowman of the Himalayas

was once presumed to be the fabled "missing link" of the evolutionary chain. He stands taller by several feet than the average human being, is covered from head to toe by a dense thatch of fine body hair, and possesses extraordinary strength. Although the legend of the Abominable Snowman, or yeti, is kept alive by the Sherpa tribe that inhabits the valleys of Nepal, it parallels the legend of Sasquatch, or Bigfoot (so named because it leaves a footprint one-and-a-half feet in length) of the American Pacific Northwest. Some have proposed that Bigfoot is just an American cousin of the yeti who crossed the Bering land bridge during prehistoric times.

Basilisk: Also known as the cockatrice, the basilisk is a small snake of Libyan origin supposedly born of a cock's egg that is hatched by a serpent. A fierce killer whose name translates from the Greek as "little king," its breath is said to scorch grass and burst rocks. Its gaze is fatal, but can be turned back upon it with a mirror. It is also vulnerable to the venom of the weasel and the crow of the cock. A basilisk's dried skin is prized for its power to repel snakes and spiders, but the reckless adventurer who tries to kill one with a spear will find its venom preternaturally endowed with the ability to travel the length of the spear and destroy its attacker.

Dragon: The dragon is a beast of variable shape and disposition. A serpentine behemoth, it is frequently portrayed as bat-winged, fire-breathing, and sometimes possessing many heads and/or lion's claws. Although dragons can be found in the mythologies of many different cultures, beneficent representations tend to be Asian in origin. In China, for example, the dragon is a symbol of power, fertility, and heaven (the yang that balances the yin of Chinese cosmology). In Western culture, the dragon is almost always associated with paganism and portrayed as evil: Satan appears as the red dragon of the Book of Revelations and adopts a dragon's shape to fight his losing battle with St. George.

Elf: Although divided into two classes, the light and the dark, elves are generally mischievous but possess great magical powers that can be used either benevolently or harmfully. Benevolent elves coexist peacefully with man; some cohabit in human dwellings where they cause beer to brew, bread to rise, and butter to churn. Their less benevolent kindred steal milk from cows, destroy cattle, and abduct unbaptized children from the cradle. In Scotland, fairies of short human stature are called elves. At the North Pole, elves are diligent workers with a fundamental respect for work deadlines; one is said to have grown up to become Santa Claus.

Fairy: Fairies are kin to the jinn of Arabic legend and the nymphs of Greek mythology. Depicted as an intermediate species between men and angels, and thought by some to be subdivided into many classes, including brownies, pixies, leprechauns, and hobgoblins, fairies can range in height from several inches tall to full human scale. Although they prefer to live near forests or under hills, they are not completely remote from humans. Some fairies marry human lovers, but under such proscriptions of fairy law that the marriage is invariably doomed to fail. Fairies sometimes substitute changelings for human children or spirit adults away to fairyland and encourage them to eat and drink there, after which there is no returning to mortal realms. Fairies are generally not malicious, but rather mischievous like Shakespeare's Puck.

Golem: Legends of the golem arose from Jewish folklore of the Middle Ages. The golem is a homunculus, or human effigy, often fashioned from virgin clay of a mountainous region. He can be endowed with life through the inscription of God's name on a piece of paper attached to his forehead or inserted in his mouth. Upon removal of the paper, he becomes deanimated and sometimes crumbles to dust. Golems make good protectors and servants, since they are mute and very good listeners. However, they can take orders too literally with disastrous results. The legend of the golem of Rabbi Judah Low ben Bezulel of Prague is thought to have inspired man-made monster tales such as Mary Shelley's *Frankenstein, or A Modern Prometheus* and other stories of animated simulacra.

Mermaid: Mermaids, and their male counterparts, mermen, have the head and upper torso of a human and the tail of a fish. Sometimes called sirens or lorelei, mermaids have a particular allure for men. The depiction of a mermaid as constantly holding a mirror or comb became an emblem of female vanity in the Middle Ages. It is said that if a man can steal these tokens from her, the mermaid is bound to him until she recovers them and returns to the sea. Mermaids are thought to have magical and prophetic powers. Their mesmerizing song can lure mortals to death by drowning, and their appearance to sailors at sea is thought to portend a shipwreck.

Ox: Cultures as different as the Egyptian, Assyrian, Babylonian, Greek, and Roman revered the ox as a symbol of strength and forbearance. The most famous of all American oxen is Babe, whom folk hero Paul Bunyan rescued from his plunge in Tonnere Bay during the Winter of the Blue Snow and who from that point on retained his blue discoloring. In some folktales, Babe's rambunctious energy inspires two cryptic dreams which his master eventually interprets as indicating that he should cross the Canadian border to start the American lumber industry.

Phoenix: Although its legend is thought to have originated in the Orient, the phoenix is closely associated with the Egyptian sun god Ra. It is a unique, heronlike bird with gold and red feathers, that reincarnates itself every 500 years by building a pyre from boughs and spices and setting it afire. A new phoenix arises from the ashes to start the cycle again. The imagery of the phoenix resonated with the beliefs of many ancient cultures: Egyptians depicted it as a symbol of immortality, Romans stamped it on coins as an emblem of the Eternal City of Rome, and Christians saw in it the allegory of the resurrection and life-after-death.

Pixie: Pixies are a less attractive offshoot of the fairy family, suspected by some of being the souls of Druids or unchristened children. They favor England's West Country and dress entirely in green. Pixies generally delight in misleading travelers, particularly those who neglect to carry a cross or a piece of bread, and they have been known to leave those whom they truly dislike stranded in bogs and swamps. Some ride horses at night in a circle to create fairy rings, and persons unfortunate enough to step with both feet inside one can become their prisoners.

Raven: Ravens initially were white in color until Apollo's pet raven bore him grievous news that infuriated the god and made him turn upon the messenger. The raven fared no better in Jewish folklore, where it was condemned by Noah for questioning his command to fly out to see if the flood waters had receded. Although the raven was allowed to make amends by bringing food to the prophet Elijah, St. Paul the Hermit, and St. Anthony, its secondary function as a guardian of the dead generated Satanic associations that persist today.

Reindeer: Although native to North America, reindeer are more commonly associated with the North Pole where they coexist peacefully with the few men they meet. They generally work best at pulling sleighs in teams of eight and respond well to alliterative names. Special members of their species have an unerring sense of direction. It was once thought that the red-nosed reindeer was a unique biological offshoot until other color variants were found. No one even questions that they know how to fly.

Sea serpent: Sea serpents describe a broad class of creatures ranging from the humongous leviathan to the squidlike kraken. Generic sea serpents move through the water by turning their bodies into undulating humps that often are spotted by human observers who invariably are not carrying a camera at the time. Legends of a sea serpent living at the bottom of Loch Ness near Inverness have persisted since the sixth century A.D.

Sphinx: Before it was immortalized as one of the seven wonders of the world and revered for its great wisdom, the sphinx—which possesses the body of a lion, the head and breasts of a woman, and sometimes wings—was the scourge of humanity. In its best known legend it prowled the high road outside Thebes where travelers were forced to answer its famous riddle or be eaten: "What animal is that which at the morning goes on four feet, at noon on two, and in the evening upon three?" Only Oedipus offered the correct answer, "Man," after which the sphinx dashed herself on the stones below.

Spider: Spiders are the children of Arachne, who challenged the goddess Athena to a weaving contest. So splendid was Arachne's tapestry that Athena tore it to pieces, whereupon Arachne hung herself in despair. Out of remorse, Athena changed Arachne's noose into a cobweb and Arachne herself into a spider.

Unicorn: One of the oldest and most pervasive figures of all folklore, the unicorn has a legacy that extends back to 400 B.C. Traditionally, the unicorn has the body of a goat or horse and, in the middle of its forehead, sports a single horn with talismanic properties. A solitary creature, the unicorn is elusive and can only be captured by a virgin. In this capacity, it has been interpreted by different cultures as a symbol of either purity or lust. Variant versions of the myth have the unicorn discovering that the woman is not a true virgin and impaling her on its horn, or submitting to a virgin and being killed by the hunters who used her as bait. The latter version is often interpreted as an allegory of Christ's meekness and murder.

And there you have the foundations for this *Christmas Bestiary:* fantastic tales of magical creatures for that most magical of seasons.

A COMPROMISED CHRISTMAS

by Jennifer Roberson

"Jane," he said. Then, when she did not answer; when she did no more then go on walking as if she didn't hear him, or as if she chose *not* to hear him (though that wasn't Janeish at all), more emphatically: *"Jane!"*

And Jane turned, clearly startled, dark brown hair curling this way and that in the thin, constant drizzle— a "soft day," she'd called it happily, claiming it was an Irish saying—(and wasn't he sick of hearing of Irish this and Welsh that; and now Scotland, to boot)—and stared at him in surprise, as if it did not occur to her that *he* did not care for the drizzle, or the day, and most particularly their destination.

"What is it?" Jane asked, pausing long enough in her single-minded striding for him to catch up.

And then he felt ashamed, because despite the cold-born blush in her cheeks and the bluish-pink hue of her nose, she was patently unconcerned about the miserable weather conditions. In fact, he thought suspiciously, she appeared to *glory* in them.

"Jane," he said more gently, not meaning to squash her spirit, "honeymooners *are* supposed to walk as a couple. You know, like in the cruise and resort commercials—hand-in-hand in the sunset against a tropical backdrop." In fact, he wanted nothing more just now than to *be* on one of those cruise ships in the Caribbean somewhere—even in the Bermuda Triangle, for Crissake!—if it meant they might be warm and dry instead of cold and damp.

But Jane had picked Scotland.

In December.

On Christmas Eve.

Jane laughed, expelling a rush of vapor like a dragon blowing smoke; in fact, he harbored suspicions that she had practiced for that very reason. "Oh, Joe, I'm sorry. Am I neglecting you?"

Yes, of course she was. She had struck out along the track like an Amazon—or whatever such a woman might be called in Scotland; he doubted it was an Amazon; weren't they Greek, or something?

He laughed a little himself, dismayed to hear how hollow it sounded; he didn't really want to mimic a pettish child. "It's only I'm not as fit as you," he told her, sending forth his own plume of dragon's breath. "I lead a pretty sedentary lifestyle, after all . . . writing ads doesn't prepare you for hiking into the wilds of Scotland."

Jane blinked. "The wilds? This? The road is right *there.*"

And so it was: a two-lane blacktopped road all of four or five feet away. So close, in fact, he might have suggested they at least walk on level asphalt to improve their footing rather than beat their way through a thin trickle of track hedged by tangled strawberry and blackberry bushes. In fact, he *had* suggested they rent a car in Inverness, but Jane had wanted the bus; now they had forsaken even that for foot-power.

So, no, he supposed it wasn't really the "wilds," not *truly* the "wilds," but it was close enough for him. "Jane—"

But she cut him off by stepping close, very close,

and made him temporarily uncognizant of the damp, the day, the destination, by kissing him.

Joe kissed her back, thinking inconsequentially of Judy Garland and ruby slippers; if he tapped his booted heels together, would Scotland go the way of the Emerald City? (Please?)

No. Scotland remained. So did he.

Jane punched him lightly. "It's not so bad. This is not Glencoe, after all, and I'm not making you climb the Devil's Stair. This is only a bit of a stroll—"

"A *stroll*!"

The light died out of her face. "Oh, Joe, it's really not that much farther."

A single step more was altogether too far for his peace of mind. But he had humored Jane, compromising, giving in to her crazy dream of honeymooning in Scotland, even though *he'd* wanted the Caribbean cruise, or maybe Hawaii—

"It's so beautiful," Jane said. "Just look around, Joe."

It was cold, and damp, and depressing. He was a man for sidewalks and multilevel parking garages and skyscrapers without a 13th floor—even if there really *was* a 13th floor and they just called it something else.

Scotland was Jane's idea. December had been his, and Christmas, *before* he'd known about Scotland. "Jane—"

Gray eyes were bright and hopeful. "Don't you think it's romantic? The air fairly *reeks* of romance!"

The air reeked of rain lacking the odors of oil, gasoline, human waste. He smelled dirt and stone and tree. It was not an aroma he knew; it was *certainly* not an odor he equated with romance.

But romance had brought them here; he did love Jane.

Joe smiled. "I suppose."

She caught his gloved hand in her mittened one, tugging him close to her side. "It's not so much farther," she said. "I promise."

"We can't stay long," he warned. "I don't want to miss the last bus back to Drumroll."

Jane's laughed kited joyously. "Drumnadrochit!" she cried. "Not Drumroll, or Drummer Boy—just Drum-na-drock-it. And I don't care if we *do* miss the bus; we'll just walk back."

He'd been afraid she'd say that. "One-way on foot is enough, Jane. We can climb all over your castle if you insist, but I want to *ride* back to town."

She arched a dark brow. "And all the way back to Inverness?"

"My God, yes! I don't want to walk to *Inverness*."

Jane laughed and tugged him along. "No, no—I don't want to walk that far, either. I only meant you sounded as if you're sorry you're here at all."

Well, yes. He was. "I know you've always wanted to come to the British Isles, sweetheart, but there is such a season as summer even in Scotland." He grimaced. "I think."

Jane shook her head decisively. "That's when all the tourists come."

"Possibly because they don't like the cold and wet any more than I," he chided gently. "I'm a warm-blooded mammal, after all—"

"And so am *I*, but this isn't so bad!" She pulled him along without respite. "For heaven's sake, you're swathed in layers of wool and down . . . it must be like a sauna in there." She snagged his parka zipper and made as if to pull. "Let me see—"

He caught her hand and grasped it, squeezing her fingers into immobility. "No. I don't want to be any colder than I already am."

"This isn't the North Pole, Joe. It's not *that* cold. And the drizzle's not much more than a mist."

"Do you know that in Australia right now it's summer?"

She laughed. "Yes. But why do what's easy? I wanted a honeymoon I could remember forever."

"I'd remember Australia," Joe said. *And the Caribbean. Hawaii. Any number of warmer places.*

"I didn't want to do what everyone else does. You know—like a cruise." Jane grimaced, bending blackberry out of her path. "Those sorts of things always seemed so *sterile,* somehow."

Joe thought she might have selected another descriptive word and gotten her point across as effectively. "I know lots of people who have had perfectly good honeymoons on board a cruise ship."

"Any of them still married?"

"Well—" He sighed. "No."

Jane laughed. "You see? Scotland is good for the soul."

"I doubt Scotland has anything to do with whether a marriage survives."

"No," Jane agreed. "That has to do with making compromises." She cast him an eloquent smile. "I know you didn't want to come here, Joe. Thanks for humoring me."

And so she made it all right without effort, which eased him a little in the matter of his temper. The stress of writing ad copy to deadline for multimillion dollar accounts didn't leave much room for compromise. Jane seemed to understand it. She made life easier.

He pulled her close, kissed her ear through tangled damp hair—Jane had left off her woolen hat (so the clean Scottish air would clear the city fog from her head, she'd said)—and told her he loved her.

"Me, too," she said, predictably; but it was a comfortable predictability. Then, "There! You see? Urquhart Castle!"

Ur-cut, she called it; not the Ur-cue-heart *he'd* called it the first time, when he'd seen the name in print; when he'd looked up in a travel book just where Drummer Boy was and the castle on the loch. Not *lock*—lochhh, with a breathy gargle in the throat. Or so Jane said. She had an ear for such things.

He had an ear for a jingle, a catchphrase, a *hook;* Captain Hook, they called him, in the early days before imminent burnout sent him running away from long-legged blondes in sleek, burnished sports cars to a serene, uncomplicated young woman who worked contentedly in a library and read historical and fantasy novels in her spare time.

Jane was—*different;* that's what his friends told him, verging on condescension, touching on implication without committing themselves. And she was, and he loved her for it; he supposed to her *he* was different. And so she had, in her very Janeish way, undertaken to overhaul his spirit, to restore his equilibrium and his priorities in life.

In *Scotland,* of all places!

Urquhart Castle, perched on the edge of a loch: piles of brickwork, a tower, a few open-air rooms, some grass-swathed mounds. As castles went, he supposed it was better than most, because much of it remained fairly intact; or so Jane had read out of a guidebook. Very romantic indeed, if your idea of romance was huddling up in goosedown, nylon, and wool, wishing for a ceramic heater—except at Urquhart, in Scotland, there were no outlets, and he didn't have his converter, either. It was back in the hotel in Inverness.

A muffled motorized roar behind Joe caused him to swing around in his tracks. "The bus!"

Jane spared it a passing glance. "So it is. But we're not even there yet, and I want to spend some time soaking up the atmosphere . . . we'll just walk back later."

Atmosphere. Joe sighed. He envisioned himself in a warm, packed pub swilling stout with the natives, or maybe Glen Fiddich, or maybe even plain old brandy; *something* to warm his bones!

The bus crept on by them, turned off the blacktop onto the gravel next to the entrance gate, and waited.

Bastard, Joe thought. *He'll wait long enough to tease me, then roar off just as I make up my mind.*

Oblivious to the bus, Jane dragged him on through the untenanted gate—no fee due in December, Joe decided; not even the Scots were foolish enough to hang about waiting for romantic-minded Americans (on Christmas Eve-day, no less!) and down the gravel pathway toward the stone piles of Urquhart Castle. Joe could not believe anyone ever actually *lived* in such a place, but he supposed at one point in time there were roofs over the rooms, and fires, and lots of wool kilts and plaids and sheep. Anything to cut the chill.

"Scotch," he muttered. "This is why they invented it."

"Come *on,* Joe!" Jane urged him into a faster walk. "You say you're not in shape—well, this is a way to get *into* shape!"

"Climbing around a pile of old rocks?"

"Joe." Jane swung to face him. He stopped short even as she did, so as not to step on her boots. "Joe, you're an advertising copywriter. You sell *dreams,*" Jane said earnestly. "Can't you see what this is all about?" She thrust out an encompassing hand. "This is history, Joe. It's a million miles away from yours or mine, but it belongs to real people, people who lived and died protecting this loch. *Look* at it, Joe. Can't you imagine the walls whole again, and the roofs? Can't you make believe the people live again inside these walls, looking eastward across the loch for the Christmas Star?"

"No one was here when the Christmas Star appeared—*if* it appeared; there's some doubt as to that—"

Jane cut him off. "I didn't mean at *that moment*, Joe. I meant other people like you and me, just starting out, standing here on the banks of the loch painting pictures against the sky—"

Joe grinned, hooking an arm around Jane's shoulders. "I'm just an old fuddy-duddy who's cold and wet and thinking about taking you to bed instead of climbing all over a ruined castle."

"Castle first, bed later."

He arched eloquent brows. "Makes a man wonder about his place in your scheme of things."

"My scheme of things is perfectly normal," Jane retorted. "Since you're no' a braw, bonny Scot wi' naught bu' a kilt o'er his ballocks—" she grinned as he winced, dropping the thick Highland burr, "—I doubt you're much interested in stripping down here in the wet grass during a cold Scottish sunset."

"No," he conceded, shivering.

"Then we'll do the castle first, bed later." And she was off like a dog just let free of the lead, darting to the tower. "Joe—come *on*."

Dutifully he came on, just as the bus behind began its laborious about-face on its return to Drumnadrochit.

"Bastard," Joe muttered.

*   *   *

Eventually, Jane gave in to his pleas to stop investigating each and every single stone—all of which Joe said were absolutely identical and therefore not worthy of her continued scrutiny—and sat down with him on a wooden bench (not a relic of Urquhart's era, but a modern convenience placed there for tourists; Jane disliked the anachronism) to stare across the loch.

Jane sighed and leaned close. "All it wants is a clansman on the hill piping down the sun. Maybe *Amazing Grace,* or an old Christmas song. A Gaelic Christmas carol."

"All *I* want is a warm bed, my wife in it, and a lock upon the door." The drizzle (mist?) had at last let up, but the temperature was no warmer; in fact, Joe was convinced it was colder than ever. "We could freeze out here."

Jane snuggled a little closer. "No. Not really." Her head tilted against his shoulder; rain-curled hair tickled his cheek. "We'll start back soon; the walk will warm us up."

"Then let's go ahead and—"

"Not yet. A little longer."

"I'm getting hungry, Jane."

"There are crackers in my pocket." But she didn't move to fish them out. She stared across the rippling waters of the loch, gray as her eyes. "I feel it in my bones. History, Joe. I can almost hear the cannon fired to fend off invaders there in the loch—"

"What about me?" He set his lips against her ear. "Hear this?"

Jane stiffened. *"Joe."*

It was neither a shout, nor a cry, nor a blurt of shock. What it was, he decided, was a whisper of sheer fascination. *If I could get that tone across in an ad—*

"Joe, *look.*"

Joe looked. And laughed; but softly, so as not to hurt her feelings. "It's just a log, or marsh gas."

"I don't think s—"

"Come on, Jane, you can't expect me to believe that *we'd* see Nessie when all those scientists never could track her—*it*—down."

"Joe—"

"You spent too much time at the Monster Museum, Jane."

"*Shut up, Joe!* Just look!"

He shut up. And looked.

Marsh gas. What else?

Jane's breath was audible: a long, low sigh of infinite wonder and satisfaction.

No, Joe declared to the Inner Hairy Man. *I'm not seeing ANY of this.*

But he was. He just *was,* despite his disbelief, despite his skepticism, despite evidence to the contrary; far more evidence against than there was *for;* after all, there was no such thing as a Loch Ness Monster.

Jane whispered his name. Joe didn't answer.

It was a long, slow, seductive roll, a displacement in the water; paler gleam of pale winter sun on loch-painted scales, dozens and dozens of scales, glistening like crystals, like diamonds, like black Australian opal. Water ran from a glossy pearlescent hide (skin? coat?) as it lifted itself to the surface: undulant spine (spine?) and a condescension of snout. It (he? she?) blew water from delicate flaring nostrils as Jane had blown dragon breath, then broke the surface with more than snout, feeding into the sunset a long, fluted head, then burgundy-colored throat, then the swell of serpent shoulders clad in filmy pewter-hued gauze, a gossamer web spun between the delicate birdlike bones that unfurled from against the body to catch the setting sun. It was sea-horse, dinosaur, dragon, a kraken of Loch Ness, rising like a whale to taste the death of the day.

I don't believe th—

Expelling spray and wind, the monster turned and blew eastward a mournful, eerie call (a winding horn? the belly-deep moan of a lion announcing the commencement of evening?) on the pale, fading edges of a day transmuting itself to dusk.

An elegant beast— and then Joe shook himself, laughing silently; to append such a term to a *monster*! "Here be dragons," he muttered, voicing the warnings on ancient maps.

The sun dipped low in the west. In the east, against deepening dusk, a new light was born, as if dawn came too quickly. A single point of light far brighter than manmade illumination, or a trick of the sun off metal. And a brief, brilliant burst as if it spent itself too quickly, then paled away into smoke. Only the burned edges of light danced in the corners of Joe's vision.

The beast-call came again. Then the ribbed gossamer webbing folded itself against damp-dappled scales and the massive serpent body slid beneath still gray waters.

"Jesus Christ," Joe whispered.

Tears shone in Jane's eyes. "I think—that was the point."

"Jane—" But he broke it off. For the first time in his life there were no words in his mouth, to disparage or deny; to condescend with glibness. There was only a terrible wonder, a consuming comprehension that he had witnessed—magic? Or maybe miracle.

From the hill behind them, hard by Urquhart Castle on the shores of Loch Ness, came the faint drone and wail of bagpipes played very softly, like the low moaning tribute of loch-beast to Christmas Star.

Joe didn't turn to look. To do so doubted the moment, and that he would not risk.

His wife leaned harder against him. "Merry Christmas," she whispered.

KARAOKE CHRISTMAS

by *Elizabeth Scarborough*

(With thanks to Rusty Wilson and Tom Lewis)

Tulu followed the people pod from the time it entered her territory until it blew up. Many boats entered her domain, but she had sensed something about this one from the time its shadow first appeared overhead, the throbbing of its engines sending vibrations down past her and for miles around her through the sea, so that fishes scurried out of the way and the sharks came zipping along, eager to dine on anything the ship might leave in its wake.

Including Tulu, if she wasn't firm with them, which fortunately for them, she was. The silly things would eat *anything,* including canisters of deadly poison and burning liquid, including paint cans and clear filmy bags that tangled the breathing apparatus and choked one to death. As a daughter of King Poseidon, Tulu was obliged by her noblesse to care for his subjects. Being a princess of the oceanic kingdoms was not merely an honorary position, especially not these days. There was so much to protect her subjects *from.* Although lately she and her sisters had been talking it over and had decided they felt much less like princesses and more like the charwomen of the deep.

Davy Jones' locker was now filled with the trash of the landlubbers, much of which Tulu had gathered

27

herself, netting the larger pieces or collections of the smaller and hauling them away to be buried in the sea bottom in the less inhabited places. Sometimes she entertained the fantasy of asking Melusine, the sea witch, for legs so she could gather all of the trash the two-legged had dumped into the sea and deliver it personally to some of those tall many-windowed dwellings clustering along the shore like so many lemmings.

It had been so much easier in the old days, when one had only to sing sailing ships onto the rocks, drown the sailors, and wait for the wooden and canvas ships to rot. Nowadays, she and her sisters had pretty well given up music except for their own entertainment. They'd never be heard over the racket that went on aboard something like the pod just ahead of her.

*   *   *

Randy Watson gave his strings one more down-stroke then shook the neck of his Fender axe as if the thing had gotten wet from the exertion of his playing. Fat chance. Other than "Jingle Bell Rock" and "I Saw Mommy Kissing Santa Claus" Christmas carols were a little hard to jazz up. He just played electric guitar. He was *not* Mannheim Steamroller. This was the last time he'd sign on a Liberian ship for the Christmas Cruise.

He and the four other Americans aboard were wholly responsible for being the Spirit of Christmas Present to a ship mostly full of U.S. tourists spending their life savings on having the Christmas of their dreams, as the brochure advertised.

He felt a little better, taking his bow, when the entire loungeful of people stood up clapping, though he didn't kid himself that his music actually deserved a standing ovation. The Leibowitzes were Jewish, for Pete's sake, and weren't likely all that enthused about Christmas carols, but he had been able to point Mrs. Leibowitz toward the best place to buy fine native-made baskets and to show Mr. Leibowitz where he could get his camera repaired ashore before the ship departed from Port Placide. And there were the honeymooners—Sylvia and Fred Ottermole-Sorensen, whose problems with getting a jacuzzi to themselves he had straightened out with the steward. Mr. and Mrs. Adams, from Rosedale, Missouri, were beaming fondly up at him as they clapped, as if he was a favorite son, and their nubile teenage daughter Rosalie, whom he had rescued from the advances of a drunken and lecherous crew member, gazed at him as if he was carrying a sword and shield instead of a Fender and wearing shining armor instead of a tux.

He'd led lifeboat drills, narrated travelogues, used charades to help untangle language barriers between crew and passengers. He'd also helped set up the Christmas tree and had led the decorating, had taken the caroling group from cabin to cabin, and hidden presents in his cabin. Very much against his own better judgment, will, and taste he also took his turn running the bingo games, a chore all of the entertainers hated. In his role as self-appointed ship's social worker, Randy had managed to steer Bennie Matarelli away from the ship's rigged gambling tables and toward other entertainments, to the eternal gratitude of the rich and well-preserved Mrs. Matarelli.

After the performance Randy worked the room a little, just to keep everybody in an up frame of mind. He generally collected his fair share of presents at Christmas, in the form of nice tips slipped into his hand, under his door, or onstage. He also tended to get too many drinkable tips this time of year and it was this excess of Christmas spirits that drove him down three flights of stairs onto the promenade deck, seeking fresh air. Trying to give up smoking in this business was useless. You inhaled cigarette, cigar, and pipe fumes with every note you sang and every word you spoke. Some of these folks had never *heard* of the Surgeon General, it seemed.

At nearly two in the morning, on a cold windy night, the deck was empty except for himself and the crewman cleaning the toilets, clattering his mop and bucket at the far end of the deck. Randy turned his collar up against the wind, crossed his arms and stood by the railing for a moment, letting the howl of the wind echo his lonesome mood. This trip would have been a lot more fun if the other entertainers—Win Jones, a depressed comic in his forties and The Amazing Armstrong and His Lovely Assistant, Lisa, a man-and-wife magic act—had been more sociable. There were no available or desirable women aboard, at least none who were even partially detached from coupledom, so it was basically all working at being charming to passengers with no one in particular he wanted to charm. The Liberian and Italian crew members spoke no English and had no free time, since they worked sixteen hours a day. Besides, they were a pretty funky lot, even compared to U.S. swabbies. American guys sometimes went to sea because their dads had done it and their granddads, or because they thought it was a romantic way to make a living, or because they'd done sea duty in the Coast Guard or the Navy and liked it, so you often got guys with some kind of standards and ideals mixed in with the riffraff. The crews on these foreign liners tended to be guys with no choices, no lives beyond work, and no work but the ship. Even if Randy had shared a language with them, he wouldn't have known what to talk about. They didn't have a lot in common.

Navy-blue clouds raced across the black sky like teenagers thronging to a rock concert. Whitecaps erupted and disintegrated on the swells and the ocean drummed on the ship's hull.

Despite the cold, Randy stood there for a few moments looking into the nighttime sea, watching the multicolored reflections of the Christmas lights strung along the railings and rigging on the wind-torn water.

He felt comfortable being lonely here. The ocean was a place made to absorb all the tears you could manufacture. He'd had enough of those liquid tips to be a little maudlin tonight and even though he didn't like country and western, he crooned to the waves a few bars of "I'm so lonesome I could die," and thoroughly enjoyed feeling sorry for himself. Pretty soon he was belting it into the wind with lots of appropriately anguished gestures, high on his own melodrama.

*   *   *

Tulu surfaced to scoop up a load of liquor bottles tossed overboard from the bar. That was when she heard him. A voice singing as she liked to sing, but a different voice and a different song. The voice was fine, deep, strong and—masculine. Though there were, of course, mer*men,* only the women sang, although these days, not many of them felt like it. But Tulu delighted in the sound of her own voice carrying across the waves, that is, when she could hear herself above engines, chatter, jet planes taking off from the decks of aircraft carriers, bombs, horns, and blaring, purposeless noise that competed with the roll and roar of the ocean even during storms. Quite frequently, the

noise won the competition. But tonight the sea was
calm, only one ship was in sight, and its engines, thun-
dering through the deep, were less noticeable when
she poked her head above water. She could easily hear
the man over them.

". . . I could di-i-i-ie," he sang, and Tulu thought,
Yes! and caught the melody as he started the refrain
again, her voice blending with his in perfect harmony.
Dying was precisely what mers always had wished for
the human occupants of ships, especially by drowning.
Tulu knew this and felt it showed the proper spirit on
the part of the singer to summon her with such a song.
Not that she was the one who was supposed to *be*
summoned, but it was significant contact of the right
sort, involving music and dying and was much closer
to her traditional purpose than the uninspiring chores
she and her sisters had been doing lately. Tulu was
an old-fashioned sort of siren and the man's voice
sounded as sweet to her as the distress bells of ships
on the rocks or foghorns during a storm.

She swam closer, guided by the voice, until she was
nearer to the vibrating hull of the giant ocean liner
than she had ever been in her life. This close, she
realized that the engines were not so loud, that their
racket had been magnified by the waters. So close,
she could hear the man very well. She joined in enthusiastically again, for once not staying hidden or
keeping back. The colored lights aboard the vessel
twinkled magically in the water and spotted her face
and arms with glows of pink, coral, and blue, red,
green, and gold and glittered off the wet scales of her
tail with a shimmering iridescence. She had never felt
more beautiful. This was what her life was supposed
to be about, she felt, gazing up at the man and singing
with all of her heart. He saw her, he heard her song,
he would listen, the ship would follow, and it would

be just like old times again. She preened herself, flip-
ping back the long strands of her coral-red hair and
swimming ever closer. The voice trailed off into a
question mark of amazement. She stopped singing,
too—she didn't know the man's songs but had been
following along with the melody. Before she could
start one of her own alluring tunes with the magical
lyrics in the old language, he started in again, his voice
a little less steady and sure of itself, "Jin-gle-bells—"
he began hesitantly, testing. He was waiting for her
to join him!

"Jin-gel-bells—" she sang too, and with a flip of her
tail was right below him.

*   *   *

Randy thought maybe he was in bed after all, having an unusually vivid dream. He had been just kid-
ding around, singing to the sea, when he heard the
soprano join him. "Watson, ol' boy, your hearing's
going," he told himself. "Has to be a weird echo or
maybe one of the women onboard who just *sounds* as
if she's out there." That was when he tried a different
song, to let her know he was onto her. But her "Jingle
Bells" sailed back up to him, faintly accented and dis-
torted by the wind.

Then something moving against the waves caught
his eye. It was definitely some kind of creature and
when it came within the glow of the Christmas lights
off the starboard side, a beautiful half-nude woman
with colored stars twinkling in her long red hair was
singing up to him, smiling and beckoning.

"Oh, my God," he said, "Hang on, Miss," and
loosed a life preserver and flung it down to her. She
looked up at him, laughing, jumped up, twisted at the
waist, and dived, hands, arms, head, hair, impres-

sively bouyant bosom and—tail, through the life ring
and back up again.

She shook her hair back, laughing, and sang up,
"Jin-gel bells," again.

"A *mermaid*? Get a grip!" Randy said to himself
then looked around to see who had put her up to this
trick, who was laughing at him from the other decks.
He was alone. And he knew damned good and well
he had never seen this girl before. He would have
noticed. Definitely. "Well, okay then, a mermaid. I
guess," he said, gulping.

He then did the only reasonable thing he could
think of under the circumstances and sang, "Jingle all
the way," at something a little less than full volume.

"Jin-gel alla way," she sang back, gleefully patting
the waves with her tail.

"Oh, what fun it is to ride—"

She repeated his line in perfect harmony, her voice
the perfect complement to his, magnifying and ampli-
fying his best notes with the underpinnings of her
chiming, honeyed tones. He called down to her,
"Hey, want a job? I could use a partner!"

She smiled and shook her head and began what
promised to be a very pretty song, except that they
started passing a cargo barge at the same time on the
port side and the noise drowned out her words.

He cupped his ear and tried to hear her, but to no
avail. Her words were lost beneath the rumble of two
engines and the rising wind. Still, he didn't want to
lose contact. She was a mermaid, after all. He couldn't
let her go just like that. She was the only good-looking
lady for miles and miles and he had to hear more from
that magnificent set of pipes.

She shook her head in disgust and dove beneath the
waves again. He stood on deck bracing himself against

the wind, wondering if she had ever been there, then slowly turned back toward the stairs and his cabin.

In the morning he thought he'd dreamed her. They docked in Sydney that morning—last shopping stop before Christmas—at 7 A.M. and he regretted the time he'd spent hallucinating the night before when he could have been sleeping.

He played tour guide in the Sydney Harbor and helped Mrs. Matarelli find a genuine kangaroo to photograph and gave Rosalie a boomerang lesson, but by and large the passengers didn't keep him too busy in this English-speaking port, where the currency was easy to figure out and the objects on sale were familiar. So he did a little more of his own Christmas shopping and sent his niece the koala bear that played "Waltzing Matilda" and his mother's dogs each a wombat bounce toy. He still hadn't found anything for his mom, however. He grabbed a cab, found a shopping center, but didn't see anything he wanted for his mother. She already had all of the standard Australian gifts at home. He wished he had sent her a lei from Honolulu earlier in the month when the ship docked there, since she always liked fresh flowers. He finally settled on a Plumeria bath set and a beach towel with stylized tropical flowers surrounding a pool. He grabbed another cab and got to the post office just after it closed.

"What's the rush, mate?" the cab driver asked him.

Cab drivers were unusually friendly and sane in Sydney, as opposed to others of their calling in other major cities in the world.

"Nothing now," Randy told him. "I'll take care of it in the morning. Just trying to get a Christmas present to my mom at the last minute."

"From the States, are you?"

"Yeah."

"Havin' a nice vacation?"

"Actually, I came in on the *Idi Amin*. I work on her."

"Sailor, eh?"

"Entertainer."

"Oh, hey, that must be excitin'. Lots of wild night life an' that."

"I wish. If there is any, I'm pretty much it," Randy said. He hadn't realized until then that he was depressed, but he was. The mermaid, if there had *been* a mermaid, was the first wild or exciting thing that had happened to him in a long time. "Well, say, that's tough. Tell you what, mate. I'm off in a bit. Stick with me and I'll take you to this pub I know. It's music night tonight. That'll give you a laugh."

"That's nice of you," Randy said, and meant it. He appreciated somebody being willing to show *him* a good time for a change. Later on, when they arrived at the pub, he was somewhat less grateful. "Music night," it turned out, translated to "Karaoke night."

Having held his job at sea for the last five years, Randy had heard of the phenomena, but so far had escaped having to witness it.

His cabbie was more than willing to demonstrate. "I allus get here ahead of the crowd, y'know, to warm up like," he told Randy. "But you could try it first." He handed the portable mike to Randy. "See, you just sing into it like this—"

"I usually play my guitar when I sing," Randy told him.

"No worries. What you want to sing? Let's see 'ere, we got all the Beatles' selections, Broadway shows, Neil Diamond's greatest 'its, and a lit'ul special collection of Yuletide favour-ites."

"Jingle Bells," Randy said at once, the song very

much on his mind since his encounter with the mermaid.

"Right you are. Just press this lit-ul button 'ere you see an' Bob's yer uncle."

The battery-operated recorder that went with the battery operated microphone didn't accompany him with anything as wonderful as the mermaid harmonies, but it did provide standard instrumental accompaniment, played at a fairly good tempo for most voices. Randy sang two choruses, his voice filling the pub as well as it usually filled the ship's lounge. "Amazing," he said with a sort of horrified admiration, which grew even more horrified as the evening progressed and he saw first his cabbie, then an awesome number of the customers who crammed into the pub, warbling pop hits, Broadway tunes, and Christmas carols the whole damn night.

He had a whole lot of beer in self-defense, which was probably what weakened his resistance enough to ask Brian the cabbie if he knew where the machines could be bought.

"Oh, sure," Brian said. "I'm thinkin' of gettin' one for meself to practice-like. I'll take you round there tomorrow if you like. What time shall I pick you up?"

"How 'bout eleven or so?" he asked. He knew he was nuts. But the passengers would *love* this. He knew they would. His mother would love it too. So he thought he'd buy one for her, try it out on the passengers, which might just get him off the bingo roster if it proved successful enough (though he was pretty sure he was creating a monster even beyond the terrors of bingo), then give it to his mom for a late Christmas present.

Brian the cabbie picked him up the next morning and took him to the music store, where the salesgirl was young and reasonably lovely and wore a miniskirt.

He told her what he wanted and she said in a fetching accent, "Oh, but we've something much better than what they've got in the pubs. Here's one that's all bat'ries and it comes in its own little waterproof case *with* your choice of three cassettes included in the price, just the thing for wooing off the reef or yachting parties."

It was also quite a bit more than he had meant to pay, what with the pound being so high against the dollar, but when he explained to her that he was single, a musician working on board a cruise ship, she hooded her eyes and pretended to shuffle through papers. He saw her calculating his age, degree of success, and net worth as she sighed and let her shoulders and everything below them sag. She assessed him wearily, daring him to disappoint her again, and said in an offhand voice, "I suppose you'll be wantin' the professional discount, then?" He nodded and before he had further time to think about it, with a whole ten per cent off (which made it only 90% more expensive than he could afford) he walked out of the store with it with the little-sisterly blessings of the salesgirl.

So, whether inspired by miniskirt, Christmas spirit, or plain and simple masochism, when the *Idi* sailed on Christmas Eve, Randy and the new karaoke machine sailed with it, along with an extra set of batteries, a Christmas gift from Brian the cabbie who stood by his cab at the dock waving and yelling, "Hey, Randy! Hey, Jingle Bells, mate! Bon voyage, now, and Happy Christmas! Kiss the island gals for me."

Randy waved good-bye, laughing, and turned back to talk to his returning passengers, but the girl he was thinking of wasn't exactly an *island* girl.

*   *   *

Tulu knew good and well that a cruise ship didn't spend more than a couple of days in any given port. She watched the shipping lanes closely, wondering if she'd see, and more importantly hear, the man sing again. She'd told her sisters about him and they claimed she was falling into the traditional trap.

"Crabs, Tulu," Noee said, wagging her finger admonishingly, "don't you know that if you fall in love with one of the humans, they chop your tail in two and you lose your voice and you end up beaching yourself somewhere in despair? Last one did that they poured metal over her and set her in the harbor in Copenhagen."

"I'm not in love with him," she insisted. "And he's not so much a human as—well, a bass. Basser than me anyway. And I know I could have lured him, I really could have. He was *very* interested. If only that cargo barge hadn't come by, I'd have had him hooked, liner, sinker, and all."

"You been inhaling glowing sludge from strange metal barrels, girl?" Nini asked. "Take a break from garbage patrol for a while. Papa says he's been feelin' a big storm comin' up, give us all a stir-up. That'll make you feel better."

As she watched the ocean that night, she felt the storm too, in the way the waves played catch with her, tossing her from one crest to another while she tried to stay on the surface. The hot wind dried the saltwater on her shoulders between one wetting and another and the sky was roiling and angry.

The landlings on board the cruiser would have known if they were decently in touch with the real world but no, they cut through the waves with their big engines, their noise louder than the wind and roaring sea, their lights piercing the darkness of the clouds. You couldn't have seen the stars for all of those colored lights even if the sky had been clear.

When she first saw the ocean liner, she stood no chance of being heard but she followed along, picking up garbage and disposing of it, biding her time until later, closer to the time when she had seen the man before. She really didn't think he was apt to forget her so easily. Humming to herself, she practiced the song she would sing for him.

* * *

The people on board *did* notice how much rougher the sea was, and they were pretty unhappy about how it was ruining their Christmas Eve. The captain and first mate drank heavily during dinner while toasting everyone in Sicilian. Later, when those passengers who weren't busy throwing up their turkey dinners showed up for the special Christmas Eve bingo session, the cards kept sliding one way and the pieces kept sliding the other way and they had to give up. The presents under the Christmas tree likewise slid all around the lounge with the roll of the ship and the ornaments fell off and smashed.

"My isn't this exciting," Myra Matarelli said to her husband. "Our first Christmas at sea. The grandchildren would enjoy this, wouldn't they?"

"The grandchildren wouldn't believe we'd come all this way just to get away from them and be seasick on Christmas Eve," her husband said. "Hey, Randy, how about we get up a game of poker?"

"I don't think so, sir. Same problem there as with the bingo," he said. "Tell you what though, I think I've got just the thing."

When he produced the battery-operated mike and cassette player preloaded with a cassette of Christmas favorites with the musical tracks produced to sound like big-name bands, Rosalie rolled her eyes and said, "God, Randy, *not* Karaoke."

"Sure, it's fun," he said, bringing his acting skill to bear to infuse his words with enthusiasm. "Come on, Rosie, what's your favorite carol? It's Christmas Eve, ladies and gentlemen, let's make a joyful noise!"

Rosalie snorted with disgust and lurched out of the lounge and onto the rolling deck. For a short time, however, before the storm became really bad, the karaoke provided some entertaining moments. Mrs. Matarelli flirted outrageously with Randy while singing, "Let it Snow," and the seventy-year-old Mr. Norwood's impersonation of Mick Jagger singing "White Christmas" was not to be missed. But then the door flew open and a ton of water splashed in along with the purser. The 12-foot Christmas tree fell over with a crash of lights.

"Everyone to cabins," the purser commanded in a very unfestive voice, just before he fell into the toppled Christmas tree.

By the time Randy and Win had helped the passengers back to their cabins, the wind was hurricane force and the seas were pounding the hull and licking at the promenade deck. Randy, whose cabin was on D deck below the promenade deck, tossed the karaoke bag on the bed and rapidly changed out of his soaked tux and into jeans, a turtleneck and an Irish fisherman's sweater his mother had knitted for him the previous Christmas. He had a bad feeling about this storm and he understood that the sweaters made bodies easier to identify. He put on his oilskins over his clothes and lay down on the bed, trying to pretend that storms at sea didn't scare the living daylights out of him.

He'd felt lucky when he was assigned an outside cabin, since crew members usually didn't rate one, but now, watching the water swirl over the portholes, making his cabin wall look like rush hour at the laundromat, he wasn't so sure about his luck. He rolled over on his side and wedged his head between his pillow and the karaoke bag, but a tapping at the porthole startled him into looking back. A strand of Christmas lights blinked at him briefly, then were extinguished by a wash of water. But not before he'd seen the white face and flowing hair of a woman beckoning from the waves.

*   *   *

To Tulu's way of thinking, the weather was fine for romance. In driving rain and howling wind, she could cut through the waves, finding her way by the flash of the lightning, without risk of being seen.

The cruise ship wallowed in the waves, and she grinned broadly when the big engines stuttered and stopped, their roar replaced by the din of the storm.

She knew nothing of mechanics, engineering, or electronics, but she could see from its position in the water and from the sounds it was no longer making that the ship that carried the singing man was in trouble.

She didn't much care what happened to it, except that there'd be a lot more litter to haul away. The people could be—what was their word—recycled—via the fishes. It was the rest of the ship that would present a problem. But she'd be dealing with that for several years, at least. Right now she wanted to find her singing partner. He could come with her when the ship sank. She might even take him to shore, if he really insisted.

Lights shone from the shiny transparent membranes lining the sides of the ship. She swam up on the curling waves to look through the ones on the lower deck but didn't see him. However, some of the shiny things didn't have lights in them. She reached up and grabbed the string of colored lights dangling from the railing above and pulled them over the nearest darkened cold transparent pane. The lights tapped against it and she saw a figure all covered in yellow rain clothes turn to gape at her. She recognized him at once!

"Jin-gel bells," she sang to him, to lure him out to her. "Jin-gel alla way."

About that time voices hollered from up above her, feet ran across the deck, and two orange life rafts full of terrified but determined sailors dropped into the foaming water on either side of her.

*   *   *

Randy smelled the smoke the minute he stepped out into the hall, and heard the shouts and pounding footsteps of sailors racing up the gangway. His mermaid had been trying to warn him! The ship was in real trouble and he'd need to help calm the passengers. Good thing he'd grabbed the karaoke bag— they'd liked that, maybe it would help distract them while the captain and crew loaded them into the lifeboats.

But through the lashing waves and the spray of water dashing into his eyes, he saw that he and the passengers were going to need more than the karaoke machine. Because, by the time he reached the rail of the promenade deck, the ocean below was filled with departing orange life rafts containing most of the crew.

"Hey, you bozos, get back here!" he screamed into

the wind. "This is mutiny! I'll report you to the captain."

Then the wind quieted, building itself up for another blow, and in the relative stillness he heard the captain's voice ordering someone to row.

"Oooh, shit," he said to the wind, watching the shiny rafts disappear into the darkness. Suddenly, below him, the mermaid's lovely but now somewhat irritated voice sang insistently, "JIN-gel BELLS, JIN-gel bells."

He looked down into her anxious face, her wild red hair whipping back in the wind. Bells, bells. Of course. He had to ring the bells. He blew her a kiss and hollered, "Thanks for reminding me, sweetheart," and broke the box containing the fire ax, setting off the alarm. He wasn't sure what the fire ax was for unless it was for cutting the ropes to lower the life rafts, and thanks to the cowardly crew, that was now impossible. He wished they could have left at least one, which would have allowed entertainers the opportunity to be cowardly as well, should they be so inclined.

As it was, he wasn't sure what to do next, tie himself onto something or throw himself overboard and hope to be picked up. He was still engaged in a rapid mental argument with himself about it when the door to the hold suddenly banged open and Win Jones, the Amazing Armstrong and Lisa emerged coughing and sneezing just ahead of billows of black smoke.

Randy rushed to slam the door behind them, and felt the pressure on the door as something beneath them boomed, the concussion shaking the entire ship, which suddenly developed a starboard list that sent them sliding toward the rails and brought Randy eye to eye with an alarmed looking mermaid.

Poor kid. She looked worried to death. Best thing

to do was keep her busy. He slipped the karaoke machine's waterproof bag from his wrist. "Look, honey, why don't you use this thing to entertain the troops while we go round them up." If anything would take the minds of a shipload of passengers off drowning, seeing an authentic mermaid singing Christmas carols into a karaoke mike would probably do the trick. Besides, he didn't need to be burdened with any more stuff than necessary.

He hooked his arm over the middle rail, his knee around the support, and used his hands to open the bag and pull out the mike. Oddly enough, his hands didn't shake and he didn't feel particularly panicked, probably because part of him—the dry part, deep inside of his oilskins—thought that this *had* to be some bizarre nightmare. If not, he just hoped he survived to put on his resume that on his last voyage, he had coaxed a local mermaid to join in the lively shipboard songfests. . . .

He flipped the switch for her, hoping he wouldn't electrocute them both, and handed her the mike. "Sing into this, honey. The tape will keep winding." He felt for the button through the bag and punched it and the tape started a complex synthesized arrangement, waiting for vocals. Fortunately, he had not let go of it as her fingers grasped the machine because the mermaid started violently, her tail slapping the water in alarm, when the music began vibrating in her hand, but he said, "No, no, it's okay, remember, 'Jingle Bells'? Just sing . . ." and he began.

"Hey, Randy, what the hell are you doing? Come on, bud, we got to get these folks to the lifeboats," the Amazing Armstrong called to him.

"Yeah, yeah, I'm coming," he called back. The mermaid looked at him with eyes that had no whites, that were all blue-green iris with pupils like deep blue wells in the middle. He didn't even know whether she spoke English, so he hefted the bag and her hands out of the water, putting her little webbed, faintly greenish hands, around the mike on the outside of the bag. "Keep it dry, sweetheart—you don't want to get shocked. And just keep singing like you did for me. Okay? Now, I got to go help get these folks up top. Okay? Sing now—Jingle Bells—"

He kept singing as he crawled away from her and heard her singing, jerkily at first as she recovered from her amazement at her amplified voice, then more lustily, so that he could hear her all the way as he made it to the outside staircase and onto the upper decks, where passengers were already pouring from their rooms, confused, frightened, and shouting.

* * *

In all of her years in these waters, Tulu had never been so amazed by anything as she had been by the gift her singing partner placed in her hands that night.

He was certainly being a great sport about all of this. Most shipwreck victims were inclined to be a little on the huffy side when they saw a mermaid, suspecting her role in their fates, but while he had declined to join Tulu before the ship actually sank, he had seemed glad to see her. Then he had handed her the gift, which at first she thought was another of their pieces of metallic garbage, but when she had heard the music form in her hand, she decided it was perhaps some sort of man-made nautilus horn. He had shown her how to use it and carefully instructed her in the taboos concerning it and then, most amazing, while his ship went down to the certain doom of himself and all of the others he seemed to care about, he told her to *keep* singing. Not to stop. Not to cease luring them to the bottom. He *wanted* her to sing.

She did, her voice rising for once over the roar of the waters and wind and all of the sounds of the seas. It was loud enough now, she knew, to be heard over the ship's engines, had they not stopped. Her voice soared to the heavens and probably clear back to the shores. "Jingle bells, jingle bells, jingle all the way—"

The ship shuddered and shifted and up above, a few passengers screamed as her friend tried to quiet them, hugging them and speaking to them. She sang up to him and he answered her, almost absentmindedly, in harmony, ". . . all the way."

*   *   *

The passengers filed up the stairs and onto the top deck shepherded by Win Jones, Randy, and the Armstrongs. "Randy, I can't find Mama," Rosalie wailed and Randy said, "We'll meet her upstairs at the lifeboat station near the theater. Come on, up you go, quick now."

At first there was some shouting, and someone fainted, but the voice of the mermaid singing below had an oddly calming effect on everyone—odd to them, if they'd thought about it, but not that odd to the mermaid, since using music to lull the seagoing into a false sense of security was something mermaids had been doing for a long time. But at this point, any sense of security was better than none.

The passengers looked blankly at the empty lifeboat berths, and tears streamed down Mrs. Matarelli's face. Rosalie found her parents, and hugged them as if she were a three-year-old, but then they, too, faced the empty bays and realized there was no way to go anywhere but down.

Rosalie put her knuckles in her mouth and bit, as if she were a baby, while the ship heaved again and "Jingle Bells," the song the mermaid knew best, stopped, along with her voice. The next song whirred on and Mr. Norwood, a veteran of World War II and all the movies associated with it, threw out his chest proudly in a "We who are about to die salute you" posture, and bravely began singing, or rather bellowing "Hark the Herald Angels Sing," and after the first time through, the mermaid joined him.

Win and the Armstrongs, after tentative glances at each other and Mr. Norwood and the railing over which the mermaid's voice soared, sang lustily along. They glanced at Randy, too, and he shrugged and also sang along, though a little more absentmindedly. They were the last of the crew and other than singing along to keep up morale there was little else they could do—especially while in the thrall of the mesmerizing voice of the siren below, a voice that captivated the attention of everyone despite the quite obvious and urgent competing distractions and the fact that the mermaid really didn't know the lyrics.

Randy sang encouragingly, but he was less enthralled than the rest of them. The mermaid's voice was beautiful, but he had heard her act before and her fumbling of the words bothered his professional ear more than it did those of the others. He alone tuned her out and concentrated on what he could do that would be of some practical use, some way to summon help. The ship-to-shore phones were two decks below, but the radio on the bridge should still be operational. There had to be some way of contacting help in case something catastrophic—like this, for instance—happened. The bridge was one flight up and Randy took it at a cautious gallop, hanging onto handrails all the way as the ship pitched and shook beneath him.

He had seen enough war movies and operated enough sound systems to figure this one out. At least he didn't have to try to land the damned thing with the help of the control tower—he just hoped he could reach the Coast Guard, another ship, some sort of assistance before they went down. The radio was on auxiliary—battery—power and still spitting static. He hoped they hadn't allowed the batteries to run down. Surely a ship this size had bigger batteries than that?

Below he heard the karaoke tape and the mermaid singing, quite plainly, though a stumbling beat behind Mr. Norwood, "Santa Claus is Coming to Town." She still sounded way better than he did, but that wasn't hard.

He picked up the microphone—there was the switch. "Uh, hi, is anybody there?" he asked.

Something crackled at him. "Mayday, mayday," he said. Under other circumstances he would have been pleased with the dramatic sound of it. "This is the Liberian liner *Idi Amin* and we're sinking. Over."

Crackle crackle. Hiss hiss hiss. Crackle.

"Your transmission's breaking up. Can you read me?" he asked, then thought he'd better not try to carry on a conversation and instead should keep talking until somebody was intelligible. "Repeat. This is the Liberian liner *Idi Amin* and we have a mayday here. We're sinking and the captain and crew have abandoned us, taking all of the lifeboats. I'm an entertainer. We've got some scared passengers here and I'm not doing real well myself. Please come after us! Send helicopters or the Coast Guard or somebody, *please*," he added with great feeling as, with another explosion, the ship lurched and threw him against the side of the cabin, then proceeded to dip to port. "Mayday, mayday."

"Pos—crackle crackle hiss," said the speaker.

"I got part of that!" he told the microphone, gripping it so hard he squeezed all the blood from his fingers. "Repeat please. Uh, like I said, this is a mayday from the *Idi Amin*."

"Pos—hiss crackle—'n."

"Position? Do you want our position? Oh, yeah, I guess you'd need that, wouldn't you? We uh—we left Sydney harbor last evening. How's that? I repeat, I'm a ship's entertainer, not a navigator. I can't pinpoint it more exactly. This is the *Idi Amin*, Randy Watson, ship's musician speaking. The captain and crew have taken the lifeboats and abandoned ship, deserting all of the passengers. Mayday. Mayday. Somebody please, for Christ's sake, help us."

There had been a momentary silencing of the singing when the ship lurched, but suddenly he heard the blurting of the karaoke tape and Mr. Norwood singing "Oh, Come All Ye Faithful," the mermaid right behind him.

*   *   *

This was the very most fun Tulu had ever had in her entire life! A sinking ship, a generous and talented singing partner who gave her nice gifts with which to make herself heard, and a captive audience who even taught her new songs and sang along with her. It was wonderful.

She sang so lustily that instead of calling *up* the storm, as her foremothers had done, she completely quelled it. As she launched into the fifth song, adding harmonies and the special harmonics only her species could sing to the words sung by the people above her, the seas began to calm, the waters to flatten, and the foam churned itself back into plain saltwater.

None of that affected her shipwreck, of course. The

ship was well and truly wrecked and sinking, but it was going down with such style!

The humans on this vessel were the best humans she had ever encountered, from her beautiful deep-voiced partner to the dear mature man who wasn't much of a singer but who was teaching her the words to these new, sea-soothing songs.

She sang with such clarity that her voice pierced the clouds, which broke and scattered with each new note and the stars came out to listen.

As she learned the words, her voice ornamenting them more gorgeously than ever a medieval illumina-tor's brush had ornamented bits of the same story in other guises, the message of joy, of love, of another kind of magic, calmed the raging seas.

To hear her new songs, even the wind hushed.

Her voice soared higher than the waves could splash and lower than the bottom of the sea, summoning all of the fishes and the whales and the dolphins and eels—all the jellyfish and sharks came too, but they behaved themselves in wonder at her songs. The whales began to sing along.

Overheard a particularly bright star shone in the clear sky on the calm waters silently filling with sea life.

Tulu saw that the promenade deck and the two decks above it were covered with water, that loose things from the ship were bobbing in the sea around her.

She could see also the faces of her fellow singers now, saw the old gentleman with his chest puffed out, the one who was belting the lyrics to lead her in the songs, and she heard her friend's voice saying, "May-day, mayday."

The ship gave another lurch and sank down so that her friends were getting their feet wet now. All of the passengers were holding onto each other, shivering and singing, clinging to the notes as if for warmth.

Tulu's voice gained ever more strength and power. She sang with such emotion and such volume, encouraged by her little microphone, the music, and the voices around hers, that she didn't hear the thwapping of helicopter blades overhead, took no heed of the rumbling of the engines of a large ship approaching behind her, and even less did she notice the silent return of a hundred and fifty orange life rafts filled with crew members, their faces fixed and their eyes staring, their mouths moving to the music as they paddled back toward the sound of her voice and their own sinking ship.

*   *   *

The music had stopped by the time the last passenger—Randy—was bundled aboard the rescue ship.

The helicopter had plucked him off the bridge just as the ship sank beneath the waters. Meanwhile, the Coast Guard ship had picked up the siren-stunned sailors and used the lifeboats to augment their own and rescue the rest of the passengers.

As the pretty Coast Guard sailor wrapped Randy in a blanket, dried his hair tenderly with a towel, and put a cup of hot coffee between his cold-numbed hands, the captain was congratulating him on his ingenuity.

"We'd never have been able to pinpoint you by your original transmission. Fortunately, the storm died down enough to delay the loss of the ship until we picked up that secondary sonic signal you sent out. How the hell did you do that anyway? High frequency boom box or what?"

The passengers knew a little more about it than

that, of course, but not much. Randy could hear them trying to figure out who the soloist was, the one who sang so beautifully behind Mr. Norwood. They had all been too busy being brave about getting ready to die to look for the mermaid, and she had dived beneath the waves as soon as she became aware of the vessels around her. If any of the sailors saw her, they said nothing, because anyone who admitted to seeing a mermaid was, of course, doomed. The *Idi*'s crew and captain were already about as doomed as they could be anyway, once the maritime courts finished with them.

Later, as he was leaving the ship, waiting his turn at the gangway behind the crowd of crew and the rescued passengers, many of whom were met in Sydney by family members who had flown over to be with them, Randy felt let down and lonesome again. No one was there to meet him and he'd have to check into a hotel and recuperate from the case of pneumonia the ship's physician had diagnosed. Then he'd probably have to sue the *Idi*'s owners for his paycheck. It was all just too much.

A miracle had saved him, but it had come and gone so quickly and in the midst of so much turmoil, he'd had no time to savor it. *His* had not been the voice that joined the mermaid's when she saved the ship. He sighed. Always the warmup act, never the featured performer.

He sighed again. He should be glad to be alive, glad he had been able to help save his passengers, and he was, he was, but he wished he could have had a few more of those private, magical duets. Seemed like his opportunities always slipped by.

He bumped up against one of the *Idi*'s lifeboats, stored aboard the Coast Guard ship, ready for offloading. A familiar-looking magenta nylon string dangled over the edge. He reached over and tugged, and out came the karaoke machine, still in its waterproof bag with the string drawn tight and the flap sealed. He opened the bag and pushed the button, but nothing happened. The batteries were dead, the life gone out of the machine.

It helped a little, when he got to the bottom of the gangway, to see a taxicab waiting, the driver refusing all other fares but waving to him. Good old Brian.

* * *

A month before, Tulu would have dismissed the sound as just another man-made noise, but now her keen ears picked it up across the waves from miles out to sea, where she was, with the help of the bottom dwellers, carefully burying the last of the remains of the *Idi Amin*.

"Dashing through the snow . . ." the vibrations seemed to say. She abandoned the job to the bottom dwellers and swam toward the sound, her own sonar zeroing in on the target. As she drew nearer, she surfaced and swam, as the humans did, letting her tail droop below the sea so she'd look like any other swimmer. Fortunately, the beach she was approaching was an isolated one. The waters were studded with projecting rocks. Only a single human being sat on the narrow sandy strand between the cliff and the sea, watching her approach.

She paid the tiny figure no heed at first, however, for she had located the thing she was seeking, the source of the "Jingle Bells." Her present—her lovely gift from her friend—beckoned merrily from one of the rocks, the magenta nylon bag wedged in a crack.

She sang back at it, heedless of the human, "Jin-gel bells, jin-gel alla way . . ." flapped her tail back and forth to give herself momentum, leaped up and snagged her gift.

"Oh, what fun it is to ride—" a familiarly deep mellow voice sang out to her from the shore. She jumped again and swam closer to hear him better. It was, it had to be, him! He had returned her gift to her, had caused it to make music again.

He was wading toward her now, saying something. "All it needed was new batteries."

She had the strongest urge to pull him down with her, to take him back to her home, but she knew that if she did, the music would go out of him the same way it had left his gift, and no one would be able to fix him as he had fixed her present. She pushed the button to save the music for later, and then, reluctantly, dived—to save him for later.

Farther out to sea, she surfaced, and could still see him watching, waiting, could still hear his voice singing after her. She sang back to him, "Jin-gel alla way," waved good-bye, and dived beneath the waves before he could try to follow her.

THE RAVEN TEACHES THE PROFESSOR A LESSON

by Jack C. Haldeman II

I didn't trust myself not to throw my cup of hot coffee in George's face, so I set it down on the lab bench next to my microscope.

"Five years' work," I snapped. "Gone! And all because of your careless stupidity."

"But, Dr. Peterson. . . . Dave, I—"

"Five freezing winters in this godforsaken Arctic wilderness, and all for nothing. You think grants like this grow on trees?"

"The sensors said everything was fine," whined George. "They've never been wrong before."

I mentally counted to ten before replying. Graduate students think they know everything. It's an arrogant attitude I work hard to eliminate.

Graduate students are the bane of my existence, but I'm forced by the terms of my contract with the University to bring a different one up here every winter. They are hopeless fools, trained to mediocre standards by a flawed educational system long before I get them. I try hard to make scientists out of them, but after the long winter months with just the two of us working and living in this small place, we invariably end up at each other's throats.

"But the sensor *was* wrong," I said in the calmest voice I could manage. "Am I correct?"

"Yes, but—"

"And the chamber *did* freeze when the heater failed? Correct? The plants all died. Correct?"

"It was only the one chamber," George said quickly. "That's bad enough, but there are eleven others. We can salvage the project."

"You cannot redesign an experiment halfway through and expect the results to reflect anything other than sloppy investigation."

"We have lots of good, solid data. I think—"

"You *think*! Since when have you taken up thinking?"

The silence that followed was as oppressive as the suddenly much smaller lab. I felt, not for the first time, hemmed in by the equipment-covered walls, the cluttered floor space and workbenches, the tiny cots set behind privacy screens at opposite ends of the building. I had to get out.

"I'm going for a walk," I said.

George just sat quietly as I pulled on my padded leggings, shoe-paks, and boots. My parka and gloves were hanging by the door. I put them on and left without another word.

For a moment I stood by the outer door, letting my eyes adjust to the darkness and listening to the familiar steady chug of the diesel generator that supplied our electricity.

After five years I was used to the months-long Arctic night. Not that I liked it all that much, but I was used to it. Our station was 250 miles north of the Arctic Circle, in the middle of the Mackenzie River Delta, where it flowed—when not frozen, as it was now—into the Arctic Ocean at the far northwestern corner of Canada. The nearest town, with a population of about 150 people, was a good 100 miles from where we had our research station. Civilization was light-years away.

My eyes adjusted quickly to the darkness, as I knew they would. The air was cold, and crystal-clear. I could see as well by the starlight reflected off the ice and snow as if I were standing under a street lamp back home.

To my left stood twelve plastic domes about 100 yards from the lab. Eleven of them glowed with a faint orange light as their heaters cycled on and off. Number 12, the point of conflict between George and myself, was dark and covered with ice.

Most of our research money came from NASA and the Engineering and Agronomy departments at the University. We were studying ways of maintaining plant growth in a hostile environment under a variety of conditions. Each chamber had a different atmosphere and temperature. Eleven data points were solid. The twelfth was a disaster.

I had thought about canceling this year's project, but George was right about the other data—though I wouldn't admit it to him. We might as well stick it out. Besides, it would be too expensive to have a small plane come out to pick us up. They wouldn't be able to do it for a couple of weeks, anyway. Everything shut down for the holiday season.

I started walking toward the dim, flickering light on the horizon. It was the winter camp of the Gordon family.

Although I had known Danny and Annie for five years, I really didn't know them at all. They were Inuit, Eskimo, whatever. During the summer Danny fished in the Arctic Ocean. In the winter they lived with several other people in a makeshift camp down the river, occasionally hunting.

It was a calm night, or maybe day, for all I knew.

I wouldn't see the sun for months. A light breeze was blowing. It was not too cold, maybe 15 or 20 below zero. The top layer of the snow crunched under my feet as I walked in the direction of their camp.

And no, I hadn't lost five years of work, only the one set of numbers from this year. But that was unforgivable. It was George's responsibility to monitor the chambers.

Of course, some might say it was my responsibility to monitor George, but that line of reasoning leads to everyone being responsible for everyone else's behavior. I do my job. I expect everyone else to do theirs, too.

Although the fieldwork of my project is held during the winter, I have been up here twice during the summer. To be truthful, as bad as it is now, I much prefer the winter.

During the short spring and summer, the place is crawling with mosquitoes and flies that bite and sting. There is no escape from them. You inhale them when you breathe and find their dead corpses floating in the bottom of your coffee cup.

The delta is unpredictable in the summer. Getting anywhere by boat is almost impossible, and it's easy to get lost. The river has dredged deep cutbanks down to the water's surface. Sometimes it's eight feet or more up to the tundra. The bottom of the channels shift from month to month and what was clear a week ago may now be a sandbar.

Even moving around on foot is difficult. Aside from the pines that skirt the delta, there are few plants here more than a foot high. The undergrowth is low and thick. It grabs at your boots as you walk. It's much easier when everything is covered with snow.

As I got closer, I could hear voices. Danny and Annie live with their extended family. They call everybody else brothers, uncles, sisters, cousins; but to tell you the truth, I don't know if they are really related or not.

The dogs started howling. I suppose I was their big excitement for the day. Nothing much happens out here, and mostly the dogs stay half-buried in snow, chained to stakes pounded into the ice, with just enough lead that they can't reach each other. Someone coming up on foot must be a big deal for them.

Danny came out and stood at the foot of his boat. In the winter he and Annie and whatever kids are around live inside his boat, which he hauls up to shore before things freeze up. It sits on a ramshackle frame of driftwood and is covered by snow most of the winter, which insulates it and helps keep it warm.

"Hey-yo!" cried Danny, whose voice carried clearly in the cold air. "Professor Dave!"

I waved back at him and made my way through some deep drifts past the dogs to the boat.

"Merry Christmas," he said, pounding my back.

"Is it Christmas?" I asked. "Already?" I lose track of dates. We don't use regular days in our records, only DOY, or Day Of Year. One day is pretty much like any other to me; all numbers.

"Almost. Hey, you should know Christmas," Danny said with a big grin. "After all, you folks gave us both Christmas and snowmobiles."

That was a joke. I knew that much, though sometimes it is hard to tell when these people are joking and when they are serious. Danny would sooner give up his arms than trade his dogsled in on a snowmobile.

Danny led me in, and I was immediately sorry I had walked this way. The air was thick with the smell of human sweat and other overpowering, more suspicious odors. Kerosene lanterns provided adequate, though flickering illumination.

We had to walk through the engine compartment first. Dinner was boiling in a large pot on a stove by the motor. I saw a duck head roll by in the water and something that looked like a bear paw. As Christmas dinner went, it left a lot to be desired, not that I cared one way or the other. I'd never touch it. Most of my dinners came out of cans.

Actually, the entire boat left a lot to be desired, though Danny seemed quite proud of it. It was relatively small and made of questionable wood. Myself, I would not dare take it out on Lake Placid on a calm day, much less the hazardous Arctic Ocean. Danny had been using it for twenty years.

It seemed that everyone in camp was crowded into the hold of the boat. The loud crush of laughing and dancing people in such a small place made me feel even more cramped than I'd been in the lab.

There weren't really all that many people, maybe fifteen adults and a whole bunch of kids, but they were all having a loud good time and the hold of Danny's boat was very small. It tapered toward the bow, with built-in bunks along both sides. The ceiling was low, and I had to duck as I followed Danny over to where Annie was sitting. She moved over to make room for me on the bunk and Danny sat on the floor next to her feet.

"Hello, Professor Dave," she said with a big smile as I squeezed in between her and a toothless old man who was keeping time with one of the dancers by beating on the neck of a beer bottle with a spoon. "It is good to have you visit. You should come more often."

"My work keeps me busy," I said. The mattress, which once might have been regular size, had been squashed down to less than an inch thick by years of sleeping bodies, which had also left their mark by a thick crust of sweat and dirt.

"Many experiments," laughed Annie. "As if there was much to know about plants. Better you should study seals. Seals are much more interesting, and far more useful."

"I prefer bears," said Danny, passing me a dented metal coffee cup. "Seals are playful, like children, but a bear's spirit is very strong."

The coffee cup was filled with a cloudy pink fluid. It was a sort of wine that Annie brewed each year from berries she picked on the tundra during the spring. It had a bitter taste. I rarely drink, but I took it out of politeness. I was aware that to turn it down would be insulting, no matter what the reason.

Likewise, out of enforced politeness I could not simply get up and leave right away, much as I would have preferred that option. The solitude of the snow-covered tundra seemed much more inviting than either the crowded party or the lab, where I could not get away from George.

So I remained, and drank the bitter wine and made uncomfortable conversation for what seemed to be an acceptable period of time.

It grew very hot in the hold of the boat, and I was starting to feel dizzy, perhaps from the wine, or maybe the heat. I started to rise in anticipation of leaving, but Danny put his hand on my shoulder.

"Watch," he said.

A man, perhaps thirty years old, perhaps fifty, was slowly dancing alone in the center of the boat. He was wearing jeans with a flannel shirt and his eyes were distant and unfocused. He was singing atonally—almost a moan—and held his right arm at an odd angle. Everyone was watching him. Even the children were still.

"Marcheck is my uncle," whispered Danny. "He brought the children up from the school in Aklavik by dogsled for the holiday. He is singing the Song of the Raven With a Broken Wing."

The song gradually increased in tempo. The man danced faster and faster, spinning around in the small, hot space, flapping his broken wing and for the briefest of moments it seemed to me he *was* a bird, a large bird with hard, black eyes. The moment passed as soon as it came and when I blinked, he was standing in front of me, sweating and chanting, foaming a little at the mouth with his eyes rolled back so only the white showed.

He was either in a trance or having a fit of some sort. I felt trapped and a little frightened. Suddenly his eyes snapped back and he stared at me.

"You have wandered too far from the path of the spirits," he said. "When they talk, you would do well to listen."

Then he collapsed to the floor. As if a spell had been broken, people started laughing and talking. Danny carried the man over to a bunk and stretched him out, while a small boy parodied the Raven dance with exaggerated movements to the delight of the other children.

"Is he a shaman?" I asked Danny when he returned.

"A holy man? Some think he is. Of course some people think he's a crazy man. Perhaps they are both right. To me, he is simply my uncle, nothing more. He has always been a little strange, especially after the summer he fell and cracked his head."

I quickly said my good-byes and left. The cold, crisp air cut through me like a knife and after the hot, stuffy boat, it felt wonderful. I started off toward the lab.

I never saw the storm coming.

One minute I was walking along, calculating CO_2

ratios in my head, and the next minute I was caught in a howling blizzard, surrounded by swirling snow. I stopped short. It was impossible to see more than a couple of feet in front of me. I didn't want to wander around and fall off a cutbank.

At first I tried to analyze my situation, as that is my nature. Even though I had been preoccupied, I should have noticed the approach of the blizzard. A storm of this magnitude was not likely to have come on so quickly, without warning. But that supposition did nothing to change the fact that I was in the middle of a serious snowstorm.

There would be no shelter here on the flat tundra. I was, I estimated, halfway between the camp and the lab, a considerable distance from either.

For a time I stood still, afraid to move. I tried shouting for help, but my words were swallowed up by the wind. It was getting very cold. I had to move to stay warm.

I walked in a small circle, watching my feet and trying to stay where I had already walked. I was getting dizzy. It was clear I should not have sampled Annie's wine.

My legs were very weak. I fell several times. Each time I fell it was harder to get up, and the last time I fell I simply could not rise.

They say that freezing to death is like falling asleep. There is probably much truth to that, for I no longer felt cold. My mind was drifting. I thought of people and events from my distant past, thoughts that had not crossed my mind in many years. It was not altogether an unpleasant experience.

I knew I was hallucinating when I saw the bear.

He was towering over me, a large brown mass of fur. Although the storm still raged, it did not touch us. We were in an island of calm with the driven snow

whipping around and over us. It was as if we were in
one of my plant chambers, protected from the blizzard. Out of the storm a fox padded into the circle
and curled up, covering his nose with his tail and
watching me with dark eyes. A large raven joined us,
shaking snow from its feathers and preening.

The bear settled down on its massive haunches and
faced me. His breath was sour.

"You can't be real," I said. "I'm dying and imagining you."

And then I *was* the bear. It was spring and I was
hungry. I lumbered across the delta to the fast-moving
stream. Wading out into the cold water, I stood mo-
tionless with one paw raised, waiting for a fish to
come.

*Patience. You must learn how to wait. You cannot
rush the fish. In time it will come.* I waited.

Biting flies circled me. They stung my nose and dug
into my fur to nip my flesh. I started to brush them
away.

*Tolerance. They are also living creatures, doing what
they will do. It is not worth the time and effort to be
so easily distracted by such minor things. Concentrate
on the moment.*

I waited. When the fish finally came, I flipped it up
onto the bank with one powerful swipe of my massive
paw. I thanked its spirit before I ate it.

It was delicious. Then suddenly I was back in the
calm area inside the storm. The bear was gone.

The fox rose to its feet and yawned, stretching its
legs. Its eyes were hard upon me.

And I *was* the fox.

There were ptarmigan in the clump of brush ahead.
I circled silently, aware of the shifting wind, being
careful to keep my scent from them.

Plan ahead. Think things through. Keep a watchful eye out.

I stayed low, ears pricked for the slightest sound, eyes keen for any sign of movement. I was almost on them when they flushed and took to the air with a ruffling flash of feathers. At that moment, a rabbit ran from a nearby hiding place, springing over the scrub willows. I started to give chase, but after a few feet I stopped. It was hopeless.

The fox, or maybe it was me, chuckled deep in its throat.

A backup plan is useful. Never lock yourself into a single course of action. Remain flexible.

Only the raven and I remained. I knew what would come next.

I flew with the flock, coasting the thermals above the delta. We cawed at each other for the sheer joy of it, the reaffirmation that others of our kind were near. Below us, the tundra stretched to the sea. It was a good life.

Live the fullness of the moment. Existence is fleeting and life is too short to . . .

A muffled, distant boom. An instant later the buckshot tore into my right wing. As I spiraled to the ground, I closed my eyes.

And when I opened them, I was standing outside the lab. The sky was perfectly clear. I barely glanced at the frozen chamber in my rush to get inside.

"I was worried about you, Dave," said George. "You were gone a long time."

"I got caught in the storm," I said, hanging my parka on the hook. My right shoulder ached.

"What storm?" asked George. "The nearest bad weather is south of Reindeer Station."

I looked at him.

"I went over the numbers," he said quickly. "If we

shift the CO_2 level on chamber 5 to 660 ppm, I think we can salvage most of the data."

No storm? I leaned against the table.

"I'm sure you're right," I said. "I spoke in haste. I'm sorry."

George blushed. He handed me a package wrapped in blue foil.

"What's this?" I asked.

"It's Christmas," he said. "I hope it's okay."

Inside was a box of chocolate covered cherries, my big weakness. I usually bring some along, but this year the airplane had crushed my supply on the way up.

I set the box down on the table and turned around so he wouldn't see my tears of shame and embarrassment. I shoved my hands in my pockets.

"I'm afraid I . . ."

There was something in my pocket. I pulled it out.

It was a raven's feather. Attached to the shaft of the feather was a small gold nugget in a leather thong. I held it out to George.

"A raven's feather at this time of year?" he asked. "It's beautiful. Where did you get it?"

"It's a long story," I said, opening the box of chocolates and offering it to George. "Merry Christmas."

"Merry Christmas to you, too."

THE ROCKING HORSE CHRISTMAS

by Barb Jernigan

"Two days before Christmas!" read the great calendar above the door to Santa's workshop. Of course, no one had time to look at it—not that anyone needed reminding, anyway. "At least the last of the 'Dear Santa' letters have been processed," said the chief elf with a sigh. "Not counting the final-final Christmas Eve post—" He took a deep breath and slowly counted to ten. The staff doctor had warned him about his blood pressure. "I only hope we can fill them all in time. You there—!"

Except for the staff doctor, no one worried much about his grumping; they heard the same thing every year. Besides, nobody had time to worry—each and every single creature in the workshop, toys included, had too many things to do.

The rocking horse was in the thick of the action. "Lightning-Bolt," one of the wrapping elves named him (after very nearly being trampled). The white horse merely tossed his mane and swished his tail— both of real hair—and dashed off on another errand.

Now you may wonder how a rocking horse is able to dash about, tied down with his rockers and all. The answer is very simple: the rockers are the very last parts to be put on, just before the horses are loaded

onto the sleigh late on Christmas Eve. Until then,
rocking horses are just like real horses.

"Hey, Lightning!" an elf called. "We need more
gift boxes! Take Teddy and the porcelain doll to the
storehouse with you. They'll help you load."

"Come on, friends!" called the rocking horse.

The teddy bear and doll leapt onto his back and
they raced away, nearly upsetting an umbrella stand
full of stick horses. "Stick horses!" The rocking horse
snorted to himself. "How can they even call themselves 'horses' without a body and legs?"

"Whoa, Lightning!" Teddy and the doll grabbed his
mane as the rocking horse reared and pawed the air.
"Warn us before you do that!"

"Sorry, friends! But it's so good to be alive! And
it's Christmas!"

The storehouse was a dark, dusty place, full of old
Christmas decorations, Santa's files, and, off in the
back corner, a rickety pile of boxes that towered almost all the way to the roof.

"Some new recruit must have stacked that one,"
said the bear.

The rocking horse and doll nodded their agreement.

"Well, let's get started." Teddy took charge. "I'll
climb on top and throw the boxes down to you."

"Do you think it's safe?" asked the doll, eyeing the
box mountain.

"Of course. We bears are excellent climbers."
Teddy scurried up the pile, only dislodging two or
three boxes on the way.

"Watch out up there!" shouted the horse, stepping
between the porcelain doll and the falling boxes.
"Dolly is fragile!"

"Sorry!" By now Teddy was on top, puffing only a
little from the climb. "I'll just start tossing boxes
down. Look out below!" He reached for the first box.

"What's this? It's not empty! Neither is this one! Hmmm." Teddy cracked open a third box. "What do you know? All those decorations we couldn't find. They must have gotten mixed in with the empties in the rush to clean up last year." He tsked-tsked and shook his head. "I wonder how many—" The box mountain swayed dangerously as Teddy reached for another box.

"Be careful!" called the doll, peering from behind the rocking horse's legs.

"Don't worry!" retorted the bear. The boxes settled back against the wall. "See? No problem!"

Just then a young mouse decided to make some fun. "Boo!" He jumped from his rafter perch onto the box Teddy was holding.

"Yeow!" Teddy dropped the box and stumbled backward. The box mountain leaned outward with him. "Yeow!" he cried again, as boxes began to tumble and slide.

"Run!" shouted the rocking horse to the doll as he leapt forward, throwing his weight against the teetering pile to push it back toward the wall. This worked for a moment, but as Teddy scrambled for footing, it tilted forward again.

The mouse was barely able to jump onto a rafter as the mountain, teddy bear and all, tumbled over.

Teddy managed to stay on top, riding the box-avalanche down. The porcelain doll raced to safety. But the rocking horse had nowhere to run.

Boxes and boxes covered him. The weight became unbearable! Something had to give!

Something did give. With a loud "SNAP!" the rocking horse's front leg and shoulder shattered and he fell, buried under the mountain of boxes.

The doll and a shaken Teddy rushed to uncover him. Even the mouse scrambled down to lend a paw.

Several elves, attracted by the noise, arrived, and in no time they uncovered the battered rocking horse.

"Are you all right?" Teddy asked.

"I–I think so."

Made of wood, the rocking horse hadn't felt his leg break. He struggled to stand up, but when he tried to put his weight on the missing leg, he fell again.

"Oh, no," he moaned.

"Go get Santa," someone whispered. An elf ran from the storehouse.

"I'm sorry," said the mouse, wringing his tail. "I didn't mean for— I didn't think— I only wanted to have a little fun."

"There, there. We know it was an accident," said Teddy.

The rocking horse merely stared at his shattered leg.

Santa arrived. "What's happened?"

"It's all my fault, Santa!" cried the mouse. "I thought I'd have a laugh and give the bear a fright. I didn't know the whole pile of boxes would fall. I'm sorry!" He began to sob anew.

"Well, I hope you've learned your lesson," Santa said sternly.

"Oh I have, Santa, I have!"

Santa examined the rocking horse.

"It's my leg."

"Yes," Santa replied softly. He frowned. "Joachim, take a look."

One of Santa's master craftsmen knelt beside him. He picked up the leg, then thumped the rocking horse's splintered shoulder. "Maybe, maybe," he muttered. "Bad splitting up here. Have to replace the entire joint. Patch job at best. Yes—hmm—long shot for sure. Take time, too." The elf straightened. "More time than we've got this Christmas."

"I was afraid of that," Santa whispered.

The rocking horse groaned.

"There, there, Lightning-Bolt, don't you worry." Santa patted his neck. "We'll have you shipshape before next Christmas."

The rocking horse nodded, trying to blink back his tears.

"We have one extra rocker," the supply master elf said.

"It will have to do." Santa patted the rocking horse's neck again. "Well, let's get this mess cleaned up and back to work. And you," he turned to the guilty mouse, "after you're done helping here, you report to Evelyn in the Painting Department. Idle paws make trouble."

"Yes, Santa."

"Penelope, make certain he does."

"Yes, sir!" The elf gave the mouse a hard look.

"What a thing to happen only two days before Christmas," Santa muttered. "Albert! Take a memo."

"Sir!" His secretary snapped open his notebook.

"Regarding the imperativeness of safe box stacking." He paused at the door to take a last look at the mess. "This will *not* happen again!"

"Yes, sir!"

*   *   *

Teddy and the porcelain doll spent as much time as they could with the rocking horse. Everyone was very kind. But Christmas Eve was upon them quick as reindeer on rooftops.

"Take care of yourself, Rocker," Teddy said. (Since the accident, no one called him "Lightning-Bolt" out of kindness.)

"I hope your child is gentle." The rocking horse tried to ignore the lump in his throat.

The porcelain doll hugged him. "Good-bye." She tried to say more, but a sob blocked her words. Instead she kissed him, then rushed away.

The rocking horse watched the sleigh being loaded. A bold black stallion had taken his place.

"You know, old chap," the black said, "I feel ruddy awful about this. It's just not cricket."

"It's not your fault," mumbled the rocking horse, staring at the floor.

The black turned away.

"Black—"

"Yes?"

"Make the child," the rocking horse choked on the word, "happy."

"I'll do that. Take care, old chap." The black raced to take his place with the other rocking horses.

I was faster, thought the rocking horse. *And will be again.* He looked at his shattered shoulder. *Yeah, right.*

The sleigh was finally loaded with its noisy, excited cargo.

Santa, dressed in his Christmas best, took his seat. "Ho, ho, ho! Are we ready?"

"Yes!" shouted everyone together.

"Ho, ho, ho! Away we go!"

The reindeer strained against the load, then, with a lurch, the sleigh was moving. With a jangle of bells and a scattering of shimmering Christmas snow, it lifted into the air.

The rocking horse watched until the sleigh was lost among the cold winter stars, and even the harness bells' jingling had faded. Then he hobbled off to an abandoned corner of the darkest storehouse and cried for a long, long time.

*   *   *

Many Christmases passed.

An apprentice woodcarver made the first attempt at repairing the rocking horse. But the severity of the break and the elf's inexperience left Rocker worse off than before—and still without a leg. Each year a new experiment was tried, but all failed in the end. At last the chief woodcarver just shook her head. "I'm sorry, old friend. Everything we've tried has just made this worse. I'm afraid the only fix now is to completely rebuild you."

Rocker looked at her. "Okay."

The elf sighed. "If we did that, 'you' wouldn't be you any more. Besides—"

"—Besides, you'd make a better rocking horse starting completely from scratch. And this is Santa's shop. Only the best. I understand."

Believe me, my friend, if there were any way—"

"I know. I know. Thank you for trying." The rocking horse hobbled away. His own sadness blinded him to the elf's genuine sorrow.

To forget a little, the rocking horse kept busy: advising on Christmas decorations, singing carols, keeping Mrs. Claus company, and telling Christmas stories to the elf children and smallest toys. Every year (though he promised himself he wouldn't) he watched the ritual of the sleigh loading, just a three-legged bystander. But he couldn't turn away until the last jingle of harness bells was lost among the cold Christmas stars. And every year the stars seemed colder, like icy knives piercing his heart.

*   *   *

This year was no different. Christmas Eve was upon them again, reminding him of everything he would never have. He inspected his chipped paint and sighed. And his tail, his beautiful tail, was now only a few scraggly hairs, the rest gone for generations of mouse nests.

The rocking horse shook his head at his self-pity. He had given the hairs willingly, baby mice needed to keep warm.

In fact, some of those very mice were now using him as a step-stool for hanging their Christmas stockings. And the rocking horse would be sure that some of that big Christmas cheese from the larder would fill the tiny socks.

An elf rushed in. "Where's Santa?"

"Here!" Santa came out of his office, followed by Mrs. Claus. "What's the problem?"

A messenger pigeon reeled in behind the elf. "Sorry, sir," he gasped. "Ran into some rough weather. Here's the last of the mail." The bird collapsed, exhausted.

Santa gently took the mail pouch. A single letter floated out. "It's from Carole," he said, opening it.

"Dear Santa." Each letter was carefully drawn. "I'm sorry this is so late, but Momma has been very sick and I have been helping her. She is getting better now, though."

Santa paused. The workshop was very quiet.

"I only want one thing for Christmas. I know I can't have a real pony, so may I have a stick horse, please? Thank you very much. I love you, Santa. Sincerely, Carole."

Santa carefully refolded the letter.

"Er, Santa," the supply master elf said, "this has been a big year for stick horses. There aren't any left."

Every one in the workshop looked at the big clock on the wall. No time to make one, either.

"What shall we do?" asked Santa. "I hate to disappoint Carole."

The rocking horse stared at the stick horses and remembered when he snorted and kicked his heels at them. All head with only a broomstick for a body! No bright saddle. No feathery tail. They had to be propped up in umbrella stands! Stick horses couldn't run errands, or tie bows, or even hang tinsel on the Christmas tree.

But they could sing. The workshop resounded to their caroling, with the toy instruments playing along joyously.

"They have no body," the rocking horse thought. He looked down. "Are three legs so much better than none?" He pictured a little girl on Christmas morning, running to the tree to hug a lively stick horse, only to find a doll or a drum or a—

The rocking horse stared again at the stick horses. "They really aren't so bad. Quite a happy lot, actually." And, when he thought about it, a rocking horse once stabled in the nursery, could never leave it. A stick horse, on the other hand, could go anywhere. The rocking horse imagined a child's hugs around his neck, loving kisses on his nose.

He took a big breath. "Santa Claus, sir?"

"Yes, my friend?"

"Well, I know there isn't time to make a stick horse from scratch. But maybe if—uh—I mean—"

"What would you suggest?"

"Well, sir, you could make me into a stick horse and it wouldn't take much time at all."

Every one stared at him in stunned silence.

"Heck," he hurriedly continued, "I'm just in the way around here anyway. A three legged stool, now that's useful. But a three legged rocking horse?" He looked at Santa. "And it would mean so much to that little girl. We can't disappoint her on Christmas!"

"Are you sure that's what you want?" asked Santa, his voice very quiet.

"Yes, sir," the rocking horse said firmly, "it is."

The stick horses let loose a chorus of cheers.

"Right on, Rocker!" cried the black with yellow spots.

"Yahoo, Buckaroo!" the pinto whinnied.

"Brave chap!" a chestnut thoroughbred shouted.

"Noble, too," said the big white stallion in King Arthur armor.

"Hooray! Hooray!" everyone in the workshop yelled together.

Even the pigeon managed a weak "Whoopee!"

Santa laughed. "Ho, ho, ho! Let's get to work! Only a few hours left! Ho, ho, ho!"

Mrs. Claus scooped up the exhausted pigeon. "What you need, you poor dear," she told it, "is some hot sunflower seed mush!"

"That sounds wonderful, Mrs. C. That headwind almost killed me!"

The rocking horse was now the center of a lot of attention. One elf fitted him for a new body while another stripped away the old paint. On with a coat of white, then a spattering of red and green dapples. "You're a Christmas miracle," his painter said, wiping her brush. "And now red with just a touch of gold for your bridle."

His scruffy mane was soon replaced with a new fluffy one. (Rocker made them promise to give the old mane to the calico cat. Her kittens were due any moment.) And his marble eyes shone with Christmas fire as the mice lovingly tied a radiant green ribbon about his new neck.

Mrs. Claus added the final touches. Tenderly she

tied two golden jingle bells to his bridle. "You're the handsomest of them all," she said. Then, smiling despite a sudden tear, she stroked his neck. "We'll miss you, old friend, but I'm very, very happy for you. Merry Christmas!" She kissed his nose, not minding the slightly wet paint a bit.

Rocking horse no longer, the stick horse was placed among the others. They sang as if they would never stop: "Deck the hall with boughs of holly! Fa la la la la, la la LA LA!"

As usual, it took forever to load the sleigh, but finally they were all in. The storm had cleared, and the moon turned the fresh snow to sparkling silver. The reindeer stamped impatiently as Santa climbed into the driver's seat and shouted the long awaited words, "Ho, ho, ho! Are we ready?"

"Yes!" everyone answered.

"Ho, ho, ho! Then away we go!"

With a jingle of bells, the reindeer leapt forward.

The wooden horse took a final, loving look at the workshop. Then he stared forward at the Christmas stars. The warm, friendly Christmas stars guiding him home.

THE ABOMINABLE SNOWMAN

by Laura Resnick

To be abominable is easy. To be a snowman, however, is not. In fact, in Yeti's case, it was his status
as a snowman that accounted for any abominable behavior on his part. For Yeti, you see, simply *hated*
cold weather. He loathed the crisp, fresh whiteness of
the fluffy snow which covered the North Pole from
year to year. He detested the long, crystalline icicles
that glinted beneath the midnight sun all summer long.
He utterly despised the feeling of old Jack Frost nip-
ping at his nose.

Yeti was an ungainly ice skater, a hopeless skier,
and a hapless hiker. He was therefore unable to participate in any of the typical, vigorous, outdoor activi-
ties of the North Pole which kept Santa's elves fit and
trim despite the long hours they spent sitting around
making toys or reminiscing about the Good Old Days
(that long-ago time, now only a dim memory, when
there were no such things as computer games, which
are abominably hard for elves to make by hand).

It was probably as a direct result of Yeti's self-
imposed isolation that he developed his reputation in
the first place (since nobody likes a loner) and became
the most feared and awesome creature at the North

Pole. Unfortunately, however, as is so often the case, his reputation exceeded him.

For one thing, Yeti was an old-style Buddhist and a strict vegetarian. Despite the rumors that erupted after Jimmy Hoffa's disappearance, Yeti had never eaten a person. In fact, he hadn't even touched animal flesh since sharing a little campfire feast with a sweet American lady named Amelia, who had flown off course and never did manage to find her way back home. The North Pole was full of people like that, which was why everyone assumed that Yeti knew what had happened to Jimmy Hoffa and why Elvis could still give an occasional concert there without causing too much of a stir.

The point is, Yeti really had no interest in eating elves or reindeer. And to give him credit, it wasn't always easy to be a vegetarian in a frozen tundra.

Moreover, Yeti was a pacifist, which was apparently one of the reasons he'd had to leave China so quickly after the Mongol invasions. He was always a little secretive about his past, and no one really knew much about what he'd done in Siberia and the Gobi Desert before turning up in Santa's Village. He was, however, usually the first one to welcome a newcomer to the North Pole—though perhaps that's because his cave was invariably the first place wanderers and wayfarers stumbled across after getting lost.

So, you're probably wondering how a vegetable-eating, xenophilous pacifist got a reputation like Yeti's. Well, to be honest, his appearance had a lot to do with it. He stood about nine feet tall and was covered with thick, shaggy, white fur from head to toe. His hands and feet were tipped with great, gleaming, razor-sharp, silver claws, and the many white fangs in his mouth made anyone who didn't know him very well feel quite skeptical about his professed vegetarianism. His massive torso contained four stomachs, all of which growled loudly and incessantly; no amount of herbal tea could silence them, and a course of pre-scribed antacids had only made the whole situation worse. Finally, his icy, glowing eyes had an unnerving habit of rotating independently, giving him a half-mad look just when he was trying to put someone at ease. All in all, one could forgive elves, who are small, timorous creatures, for being terrified of Yeti.

Now Yeti didn't really mind the isolation all that much. After all, the hothouse garden he kept deep in the recesses of his cave took a great deal of his time and attention; he was attempting to grow his own bok choy, bean sprouts, and snow peas, and the project was extremely demanding. He was also a great reader and was, at the time of the events about to be related, halfway through the Russian romantics. All of them.

It was a typical day, then, which found Yeti testing soil temperatures in his artificially lighted greenhouse and pondering the problems of Anna Karenina, when Santa came to call.

"Good morning, Yeti!" Kris Kringle cried merrily, his jowls shaking with good-natured mirth, his chins quivering, his cheerful blue eyes very nearly concealed by his layers of fat.

"Morning, Kris," Yeti said gloomily. "You've put on a little weight, haven't you?"

"Ho, ho, ho!" Kris patted his vast belly and beamed with pride. "Got to keep warm, you know!"

"I know." Yeti sniffed.

"Is that bronchitis of yours still hanging on?" Kris asked with concern.

Yeti nodded. "I hate this weather," he said morosely.

"You must get some real *food* into you, son! Mrs. Kringle sent me to invite you for Christmas dinner."

"Oh, thanks, Kris, but I don't think—"

"Oh, pish!" cried Kris, which was strong language for him. "You've made excuses for the past three years, Yeti. It's time you got out of this cave, socialized, and ate a hearty meal."

"Kris, no offense intended, but one of Mrs. Kringle's Christmas meals could raise my cholesterol count to disastrous levels. Breaded veal with cream sauce, croissants, cheesecake, egg nog . . ." Yeti shuddered feelingly.

"Well, I think it would do you some good. You can't keep living on foreign-type vegetables. Look how pale you've become!"

"I'm *supposed* to be pale. I'm a snowman, for God's sake. It's protective coloring to help me hide from my natural enemies."

Kris looked stunned. "Enemies? What enemies, Yeti?"

"Oh, you know, I.R.S. auditors, door-to-door religious fanatics, bigger snowmen . . ."

"*Are* there bigger snowmen?" Kris asked in awe.

"Steroids," Yeti explained dismissively. "Anyhow, Kris, I appreciate the invitation, but I just don't feel up to walking all that way in this awful weather."

"But it's barely half a mile!" Kris protested. "And we're having fine weather this Christmas season! It's supposed to get all the way up to eighty-seven-below today!"

Yeti shivered, causing his stomachs to growl ferociously. "Oh, blast it! I hate winter!"

"I thought it was *summer* that you hated."

"Kris, in this part of the world, I hate *every* season."

"But Yeti—"

"It's always cold, snowy, icy, frigid, leafless, bleak, barren, arctic . . ." The adjectives went on for quite some time; Yeti was very well read. When Kris remarked on this, Yeti blustered, "Well, of *course* I'm well read! What else can I do but read and tend the greenhouse in this hideous climate?" He grimaced fearsomely and said, "I want to go south, Kris. I want to go somewhere warm, where the sun can thaw my bones, clear my lungs, and ease my sorrows."

Kris gave a heavy sigh, or sighed heavily, and plumped himself down on a rock. "We've been over this before, Yeti."

"I know, I know."

"You're an Abominable Snowman."

"I *feel* abominable," Yeti said disagreeably.

"Abominable Snowmen just don't go wandering around Hawaii, California, or Tahiti. How many times have I explained this? Believe me, Yeti, I've traveled, I *know*. People just don't understand. I mean, do you have any idea how difficult it is for me to get around on Christmas Eve these days? And I'm Santa Claus, for God's sake! People are *expecting* me, and it's *still* hell on wheels! I was nearly shot down by NASA last year."

"I remember. Rudolph's got to do something about that nose."

"So imagine how people would behave if you wandered down to Cancun and started sunning yourself on a beach there! Trust me, Yeti, it wouldn't work out."

Yeti's enormous shoulders slumped. "Not even for Christmas, Kris? The whole world goes on vacation at Christmas, except for me. I still have to hang out in this freezing cold cave, being abominable. It's just so depressing!"

"Remember what it was like in Siberia? And in the Gobi Desert?" Kris was the only person who knew some of the details of the persecution Yeti had suffered in the old country. "You've read the papers.

You know about the nonsense that goes on in Saskatchewan." Yeti nodded and Kris persisted, "You don't want to go through something like that again, now do you?"

Yeti shook his head, but he moped and grunted unresponsively when Kris again invited him to Christmas dinner and tried to encourage him to participate in all those gay Christmas festivities that any informed person automatically associates with the North Pole. It was clearly hopeless, however, and with a sigh that shook his piles, Kris finally left Yeti alone.

No one bothered Yeti much during the next few days, since that fourth week in December is always such a busy time in Santa's Village. The company controller discovered a shortage in Lettuce Patch Dolls due to an error in paperwork, and the elves really had to put their shoulders to the wheel, so to speak, during those last few crucial days. Then on Christmas Eve, there was, as usual, a big send-off for Kris, Dasher, Dancer, Prancer, Vixen, Comet, Cupid, Donner, Blitzen, and Rudolph. The event was sort of a combination food fest, parade, and cleanup party (because all that frenetic activity of the pre-Christmas week always left Santa's Village looking like there'd been a rock concert there).

Yeti, as Kris had feared, didn't attend the send-off. Standing around in the snow made his feet go numb and his nose run, and he had never really enjoyed the hot buttered rum and steamed cider that Mrs. Kringle pressed on him—particularly not with all those elves quivering every time his stomachs growled.

So Yeti stayed home in his cave on Christmas Eve, dreaming of the things he really wanted to do. He longed to lie in a softly rocking hammock strung between two banyan trees and sip strawberry daquiris— or maybe margaritas—while fanning himself lazily and listening to the chirping of tropical birds in some steamy southern clime.

The howling of the north wind, however, broke in upon his thoughts, reminding him that, as Kris had pointed out at least a dozen times, Abominable Snowmen lived in the snow, not in steamy jungles or seaside resorts. With a great, sad sound, Yeti took himself off to bed.

His ruminations on Tolstoy were disturbed the next day when he heard the cry of a loud male voice, a voice characterized by the somewhat jarring nasality most commonly associated with an English public school education.

"I say! Is anybody there? Hullo!"

Wrapping several warm blankets around himself, since it was a bone-chilling ninety-eight-below today, Yeti left his cave and went in search of the owner of that voice. He had long since stopped being amazed at how many people lost their way at the North Pole and stumbled upon his cave, but he honestly hadn't expected to find a stranger wandering around on Christmas Day. Most folks, even mad dogs and Englishmen, could be counted on to stay where they belonged on December 25th. But not, Yeti was about to learn, an intrepid explorer like Sir Hilary Winston Gladstone Edmundson-Smythe III.

"Speak English, do you? Jolly good show!" cried Sir Hilary when Yeti introduced himself. "Bit lost, y'know. Devil of a time! Sherpas deserted eight days ago. Rotten luck, what?"

"Uh, yes," Yeti said carefully. Sir Hilary was either snowblind or terribly jaded, since he was acting as if it were an everyday thing to encounter an Abominable Snowman.

"Yeti . . ." Sir Hilary said musingly. "Tibetan

word, eh? May apply to a real but unknown Himalayan creature, or to a mountain spirit or demon."

"That's . . . quite impressive, Sir Hilary. Not many people know the origin of my name."

"Nothing to it. Something of a linguist, y'know," said Sir Hilary modestly. His long nose had grown quite red in the cold, and some ice was crusted on his enormous blond mustache. He was dressed in sensible, warm, Arctic gear and was carrying a big knapsack on his back.

"Would you like me to carry your camping supplies?" Yeti asked politely. Lost explorers were usually pretty tired by the time they got this far off the beaten path.

"Not camping supplies," Sir Hilary said. "Had to leave them behind when the last sled dog died. Roughing it now."

"How dreadful for you!"

"Oh, piffle! Nothing to it. Enjoy a bit of a challenge, y'know."

"I see. Then what's in the backpack?"

"Scientific equipment, of course! Mustn't leave that behind. Mustn't let my end down just because of a few mishaps. One has one's duty to fulfill, and all that."

"Yes, of course. What are you looking for?"

"Why, the North Pole, man!"

"Really?"

"Any idea whereabouts I might find it?"

"Well . . . This is it, actually." Yeti was basically a goodhearted fellow, and he hoped the anticlimax wouldn't be too much of a blow to Sir Hilary.

"Marvelous!" cried Sir Hilary, rallying to the occasion. "Simply marvelous!"

Yeti smiled, causing even an intrepid fellow like Sir

Hilary to fall back a step or two. "I say! Are you some relation to *Gigantopithecus*?"

"I don't know. I'm afraid my Latin's not very good."

"Ah, educated at Harrow, eh? Damned misfortune. Nothing like a good grasp of Latin to give one the basics of a sound classical education. Went to Eton, m'self," he added, as if Yeti hadn't already guessed. He stepped closer and studied Yeti with interest. "I must say, if you don't mind my saying so, you're a fascinating looking chap." After another moment of professional evaluation, he said, "An Abominable Snowman, aren't you?"

"Yes," Yeti admitted.

"Yes, yes, thought so. The auxiliary maxillae and prehensile vertebrae are a dead giveaway," Sir Hilary muttered almost to himself. "Should have noticed right away, but feeling a trifle fatigued, y'know."

"You don't mind?" Yeti asked, surprised. Most people were very nervous about the idea of socializing with an Abominable Snowman, even in a tolerant place like the North Pole.

"Of course not! You seem a decent sort of a chap." He peered at Yeti and asked abruptly, "Not a socialist, are you?"

"No. I'm fairly apolitical," Yeti assured him.

"Well, then, jolly good, we'll rub along tolerably well together, I should think. Now, to business."

"What business?" Yeti asked curiously.

"Must stake my claim, mark my discovery, that sort of thing. Honor of Queen and country, y'know." He pulled a British flag out of his backpack, planted it firmly in the ice outside Yeti's cave, and sang "God Save the Queen." Then, brushing off some of the snow which had accumulated on his person during his chat with Yeti, he said, "Right, ho! That's done."

"Congratulations," Yeti said, rather hoping that Sir Hilary, who seemed like a nice guy, wouldn't notice any of the fifty-odd other flags planted in the general vicinity.

"D'you think there's any place hereabouts where a chap could get a bit of grub? Dreadfully hungry, y'know. Haven't eaten since I killed a yak with my bare hands four days ago."

"Well, Mrs. Kringle is making a huge Christmas feast. I said I wouldn't be attending, but seeing as you're here now . . ."

"Good Lord, is it Christmas already? Where does a year go? I'm supposed to be in South America by New Year's Eve."

"I'd say they're just about ready to sit down at the Kringles'. We can make it if we hurry," Yeti urged.

"Afraid I'm not exactly dressed for dinner, dear chap. Hope it's not formal."

"Oh, no, don't worry," Yeti assured him. "Elves and reindeer aren't really great ones for dressing up."

"Good show!"

Mrs. Kringle was, of course, delighted to have two more guests at Christmas dinner. Besides being a naturally generous person, she loved to watch folks eat—which was what initially attracted her to Kris. Not only did she find it a special treat to have Yeti at Christmas dinner, but she was thrilled to face the challenge of fattening up the skinny Englishman he had brought with him.

"Sir Hilary, have some more plum pudding and brandy sauce! Have some blintzes! Have some rumaki!" she insisted, piling carcinogens on his plate before he could object.

As Sir Hilary waxed poetic about his arduous journey through frozen wastelands and his triumphant discovery of the North Pole, everyone listened politely.

Folks at the North Pole were too inherently courteous to point out to the intrepid explorer that someone had been there before him, or that there were easier ways to get there these days.

"Now that you've found the North Pole, Sir Hilary . . ." Kris winked a piggy eye as he said this, but you had to know him well to really notice. "What's next?"

"Off to Brazil. Looking for the source of the Amazon, y'know."

"Really? That sounds interesting," said Mrs. Kringle. "Have some cheese souffle! Have some Yorkshire pudding!"

"Thanks awfully," said Sir Hilary. "Yes, it should be interesting. Very isolated, y'know. Rather like this place. Full of strange and wondrous things, weird creatures, and missing people."

"Really?" asked Kris with interest. "But it's hot there?"

"Oh, yes. Frightfully so."

"It sounds wonderful," said Yeti dreamily. "Like paradise."

"There aren't, however, as far as I'm aware, any red-nosed reindeer in the Amazon," said Sir Hilary, staring at Rudolph with interest.

"Well, you can't have everything," said Kris philosophically. "Will you have to leave right away?"

"Afraid so. Dreadful problem, though. A proper expedition needs a good secretary. Someone to keep records, take notes, bribe border officials, that sort of thing."

"And you don't have a secretary?" Yeti asked.

"I *did*. Fell off Mount Everest three weeks ago, though, when we took a wrong turning. Probably should go back to England and find someone new to fill the position. Damned nuisance, all in all."

Kris, who hadn't built an empire like Santa's Village

on sheer dumb luck, said, "You know, Sir Hilary, I think we may have someone here who's admirably qualified for the post."

"Indeed? Who?"

"Yeti."

"What? This fellow here?" Sir Hilary took a hard, appraising look at Yeti.

"He's well read, has beautiful penmanship, speaks eight languages (including two dead ones), has cast iron stomachs, amazing endurance, and has always longed to travel to the tropics. Your description of the Amazon jungle makes it sound as if a fellow of Yeti's, uh, unique appearance would get along all right there. And speaking as the president of Santa's Village Incorporated, I can assure you he'll be a first-rate asset to your expedition."

"Hmmm. Well, what do you say, old chap?" Sir Hilary finally said to Yeti. "Interested in signing on?"

Before Yeti could spoil his bargaining position by appearing too eager, Kris added, "Of course, there's the matter of salary to be discussed. And we'll want to know what sort of benefit package you're offering. I couldn't, in good conscience, turn Yeti over to an employer whose health insurance program didn't cover all four of his stomachs."

The two men haggled for a while, finally agreeing that Yeti would work during Christmas and Hanukkah when necessary, but never on Yom Kippur or the Chinese New Year. They were still working out the final details when Yeti went back to his cave to pack a few of his belongings. The next morning, he set out on his journey with Sir Hilary to realize, at long last, his dream of living somewhere warm and green.

About a year and a half later, during the slow season, Kris was relaxing outdoors on a beautiful day (twenty-seven-below) when one of the elves, who had

just received a long letter from a distant relative working in Florida, told him the news. Several sightings of
a strange creature deep in the Amazon rain forest had
led people to believe that some prehistoric creature
had survived the eons and was still living in Brazil.
Noted explorer Sir Hilary Winston Gladstone
Edmundson-Smythe III, who was still looking for the
source of the Amazon, refused to confirm rumors that
he'd been seen playing cards with the creature.

Kris smiled and went in search of a pre-dinner
snack.

A BIRD OF A DIFFERENT COLOR

by Blake Cahoon

The winter wind whipped down the snow-covered sidewalk of west Manhattan. Kate Muldoon braved the icy winds on her way to the shelter. But even with her head bent low, she saw those poor souls who lingered in doorways, rags for clothes, threadbare blankets wrapped around starving bodies. Her heart went out to them, and despite the scolding she knew she'd receive from her fiancé, Raoul, she stopped and told them where they could find food and a warm place for the night.

"It's on the corner of second and Madison. There's food—and shelter," she said, and handed them a card with the name of the mission on it. Some would smile and nod, others would just stare at her blankly. She moved on quickly. She knew that some would not come. Instead, the authorities would find a frozen corpse, her card still in a stiff hand. It had happened before.

Now she moved away from one of these, her heart heavy. She tried to think of all that needed to be accomplished today at the shelter. Christmas was almost here, and so much still had to be done. It was usually the busiest day of the year, and she still had several more restaurants to visit and ask for donations.

Hopefully, *Angelo's* would come through and then there was—

Her thoughts were interrupted as she slammed into somebody. She looked up quickly but found no one there. "What the—?" she started and looked around. But the street was empty. Instinctively, she glanced down and found at her feet a feather.

It was not a standard feather though. This was almost a plume with brightly colored hues of purple, red, and orange. It was a beautiful feather and Kate picked it up. Glancing around once more, she stuck the feather in her lapel. Hurrying off to the shelter once more, she was puzzled yet felt a sense of hopefulness that hadn't been there moments ago.

"Good news, Kate!" Madge, her assistant, greeted her when she reached the shelter.

"What? Did Raoul finally get a job?" she said, taking off her wet coat and draping it over a chair. The shelter was already busy serving up lunch, and several regulars smiled and nodded at her. She waved back, looking around for Raoul, who, since he'd been laid off from his drafting job, often spent time helping down at the shelter.

"No, sorry, I haven't seen him today. But *Angelo's* called, and you should see the list of things he's going to donate," Madge told her in her soft, southern-accented voice. "Lordy, child, he's really outdone himself this year. Said he had a dream about the Holy Mother visiting him and telling him that he needed to contribute more this year. And you know how Catholic the man is!"

Kate raised an eyebrow, "Which isn't a bad thing," she said, taking the list. "Wow—this is great. I think we're going to make our food goal this year. Now if we can get the Regency Hotel to donate a few of their worn blankets—" she started when the phone rang.

"I'll get it," Madge said. "Maybe that's them now." She hurried off as Kate turned to get her coat and hang it up, before checking out the serving line. There was an old woman standing there, admiring the feather she had found.

"Such a beautiful creature this must have come from. Such unusual colors!" the woman said. She was a small woman, with flyaway gray hair and several teeth missing. Her dark coat was threadbare, she had sneakers on her feet, and dark leggings that had a hole in them. But her eyes were the prettiest shade of pale blue and her face was warm and kind.

"It is pretty, isn't it?" Kate agreed. "I found it on the street on my way in." She studied the woman, who continued to inspect the feather. "You can keep it if you'd like."

"Oh, may I? I don't own much these days—but this would be most special. Thank you, my child." She stroked the feather ever so lightly, a smile on her thin lips. There was a light of merriment in her eyes, Kate thought.

"You're welcome. I don't believe I've seen you here before. Have you had a chance to—" she started.

"Sadie." the woman suddenly said.

"What?"

"Sadie—that is what you may call me."

Kate nodded, with a smile. "Okay, Sadie. I had a great-grandmother whose name was—"

"Yes. I know . . . Kate. Or as Raoul calls you sometimes, Katie. Which you really can't stand, can you? But you don't want to hurt his feelings, because you two do love each other, don't you?" Sadie told her with a wicked grin.

Kate blinked. "I . . . why, yes . . . but—"

"Katie!" As if on cue, her name was called out from

behind, and she turned to see Raoul standing in the door, a large smile on his face.

She waved at him, noting how handsome he looked today with a suit on—black, of course, always black. She gave him a smile and then turned back to Sadie, but the woman was gone. She glanced around, worried for a moment, then saw the old woman with one of the children. She smiled and hurried over to her fiancé.

"Hey, you look . . . very handsome," she said, with a glint in her blue eyes.

"Gracias," he told her and gave her a large hug. "Guess what happened to me today?"

"You found a job!" Kate said, as he nodded. "Oh, that's fantastic!" she said and gave him a hug and a long kiss.

When he had been laid off, they had put off the wedding, which had originally been scheduled to take place in October. Kate hadn't seen a problem, but Raoul insisted that he be properly employed before getting married. Male Spanish pride won over female Scots-Irish temperament and the wedding had been indefinitely postponed. "It's with a construction company. I'll be doing CAD layouts and stuff for them."

Madge had wandered up to the couple and she cocked her dark head. "CAD?"

"Computer-assisted design," Kate said. "Raoul's very good with computers."

Raoul just smiled at the compliment as Madge raised an eyebrow, "Well, Mr. Martinez, congratulations. Now, you two might just be able to get married—finally." She turned to Kate. "Well, I'm glad you two got some good news—'cause I don't. That was Mr. Malcolm Bartlett on the phone. He wants to come down and see you—in person this time."

"Oh, no—in person? Didn't his two henchmen get the message already? I'm not selling."

"I don't think Mr. Bartlett cares. He's determined to get this building one way or another."

"This building has been in my family for over a hundred years. I'm not selling. I've got this shelter downstairs and Raoul and I plan to live upstairs."

"Kate, what are you talking about?" Raoul asked.

"Malcolm Bartlett is a developer. Wants to buy the entire block and put up another goddamn office and apartment building, along with a mall. He first approached me last week with some solicitor. Then, a lawyer called and two days ago a couple of goons came by with idle threats."

"Idle threats? Why didn't you tell me about this?"

"I didn't want to worry you. You've been busy pounding the pavement. You don't need to worry about—"

"Well, damn it, I do! Katie, when Bartlett comes, let me talk to him, okay? I'll settle this." Raoul said.

"Raoul, there isn't anything to settle. I'm not selling. I know the neighborhood isn't what it was, but this is my home."

"I'm not arguing with you, hon. But let me talk to Bartlett, okay?"

Kate sighed. The only problem with Raoul was that she had to deal with his headstrong temperament and felt obligated to give in to it. "Fine. But I'm not selling."

"Fine. You're not selling," he echoed and went to help out in the serving line until Bartlett arrived.

"He means well, dear."

Kate looked behind her to see Sadie. "I know. And I love him for it. But—"

"Remember, this is his home too. Your family was crowded out by his people and his people were crowded out by others. He has an investment here, too," Sadie told her. She looked around the shelter, which once upon a time was the kitchen and living room of a grand townhouse. "This place has seen its ups and downs. Such a wonderful place it once was."

"Did you live here? In this neighborhood?" Kate asked.

Sadie looked up with those pale blue eyes of hers and a special light danced there. It was of older days and wiser times. Of parties and merriment, of youthful days of love and romance, of an era washed away with the tide of time. "A long time ago, indeed. A long time ago," she said with that faraway look in her eyes.

The sharp cry of a baby pierced the air and both women turned, as a young mother hurried in from the cold, an infant in hand. There was a nasty bruise forming on the mother's cheek and she looked lost and very alone as she stood there. Both Kate and Sadie rushed to help.

When the shelter door opened again, it brought with it a blast of cold air. They had just gotten the child to sleep and the mother's bruises taken care of. Kate looked up to see a tall man, dressed elegantly in an expensive suit, standing in the door, a rather expensive parrot perched on his shoulder. Another man, a bodyguard, no doubt from his muscle-bound physique, stood just behind him with an unpleasant look on his frozen face.

The tall man, whose hair had a touch of gray at the temples and who could pose as a power executive in a cologne ad, looked uncomfortable standing there as patrons came up to feel his clothes and inspect the bird. Kate could swear that the bodyguard growled at them, as they scattered back to their corners like scared mice. Bartlett, who carried a cane, raised it to threaten the others. Even from here she saw that the top of the cane was a gold falcon's head.

Already she didn't like Malcolm Bartlett, for there was no doubt that was who this man was. She started toward him, her lips pressed tight together, fists at her side. Out of the corner of her eye, she saw Raoul start toward him too, shirt sleeves rolled up and tie loose at his neck. He was trying to beat her to Bartlett; he knew her temper only too well. He threw her a look that said, Stay out of this, I'll handle it but she was already getting up a full head of steam.

"Mr. Malcolm Bartlett, I presume," she reached him first, staying calm but coldly professional as she extended a hand. "I'm Kate Muldoon, owner of this building. And as I told your people earlier, I have no intention of—"

"Mr. Bartlett," Raoul came up in front of her, extending his hand. "I'm Raoul Martinez, Miss Muldoon's fiancé. I've been looking forward to meeting you." Raoul was almost a head taller than she, but Bartlett towered over him. The developer glanced down at both of them and then shook Raoul's hand, choosing to ignore the uncooperative Miss Muldoon.

"Martinez, eh? Your name is familiar to me, sir. Wasn't I looking over your resume just this morning?" Bartlett asked in a cultured accent straight from Yale Business School.

"Yes, sir. I start next Monday as one of your CAD draftsmen," Raoul told him.

Kate's mouth dropped open. This bit of news came as a complete shock to her. Her fiancé working for the enemy? "Raoul?" she managed.

Raoul glanced over at her, a light of discomfort playing in his brown eyes, even as he tried to maintain a professional demeanor with Bartlett. "Kate has told me about your offer concerning this building."

"It is quite generous. All her neighbors thought so. But your fiancée doesn't seem to want to listen. I know that under the current circumstances, you'll be able to understand my position."

"Of course, and I'm sure we can—" Raoul started.

"I don't believe this!" Kate interrupted. "Don't you dare offer this man—"

"Kate—let me handle this," Raoul's tone was firm.

"Handle this? You go and get a job with this— this—man and now you think because we're about to get married, you'll be able to—"

"Kate, I didn't even know that Mr. Bartlett was—"

"The hell you didn't! What is this, some sort of conspiracy?"

"Kate, you know better than that," Raoul's anger was beginning to surface. "Now, if you would leave and let me—"

Kate was about to tell him what she thought of that idea, when Sadie cried out in pain. She looked over to see Bartlett's bodyguard grabbing the old woman by the coat collar. "Hey, you let her go!" she shouted and rushed the huge man as he let Sadie fall to the floor. He immediately defended himself against Kate's attack by knocking her to the floor, too.

"Hey!" Raoul's voice was sharp and angry. Several patrons hurried to help Kate and Sadie, despite the attack stance of the bodyguard. On Bartlett's shoulder, the parrot gave out a nasty shriek. "I think you'd better leave, Mr. Bartlett, and take your goon with you."

Bartlett's pleasant manner disappeared. "Martinez, I strongly suggest that you convince your girlfriend to sell."

"Or what?"

"Or for a start, you won't be coming to work for me Monday," he replied.

Raoul glanced back at Kate, and saw she was okay.
"Let me walk you out, Mr. Bartlett," he said, and
together the two men walked out of the shelter,
henchman in tow.

"Kate, are you all right?" It was Madge. "Ma'am,
how about you?" she asked Sadie.

"I'm fine, dear. But that young man could stand to
learn some manners."

"I can't believe this. I think Raoul is going to try
and work a deal with that—monster."

"Raoul loves you. He's not going to do anything
that would jeopardize—" Madge started.

"You heard him. He's working for Bartlett!"

"But he didn't know about Bartlett's offer. I'm sure
that if he knew—"

"Well, I'm not," Kate said. She turned to Sadie.
"Are you—oh, my gosh, you're bleeding!"

Sadie touched her forehead, where there was a
nasty gash. "Oh my, so I am."

"Come on, let me take you upstairs and get you
patched up," Kate told her. She glanced over at
Madge. "Can you handle things here for a while?"

"Sure, child. Go on up. If Raoul comes back in—"

Kate shook her head, and nodded toward the front
window. "I don't think so," she said. Madge looked to
see that Raoul was climbing into Bartlett's limousine.
"It's still my property. He can't do anything about that.
We're not married yet. And now, we may never . . ."

Madge watched and saw Bartlett and Raoul drive
away, then turned, but Kate and Sadie were gone.

Upstairs, Kate tended Sadie's wound and tried to
make her lie down. But the old woman wouldn't hear
of it.

"If I need to lie down, then I'll lie down on one of
the cots downstairs, like the rest. You didn't need to
bring me up here, Katie."

"I thought it might be better up here. Cleaner . . . quieter," Kate replied. It was true, she wanted to do more for this old woman. There was something about her, an underlying strength and determination that she needed right now.

"That's thoughtful of you. But you're a giver, aren't you? If you weren't, you wouldn't fight so hard for those people down there."

"I try to do what I can. I feel so sorry for them. They have nothing and some of them have tried so hard to escape the streets. But the streets just keep them prisoner."

"Like a bird in a cage," Sadie said, as she wandered the apartment and noted an empty bird cage in a corner. There was still seed on the cage floor. "Where is the bird?"

Kate's face clouded. "I brought the cage up from downstairs." She crossed over to Sadie and fingered the golden bars of the empty cage. "I had two lovebirds in it. Raoul gave them to me. I named them Tony and Maria—after the characters in *West Side Story*. And up till two days ago they kept the children happy with their songs."

"Did they escape?"

"No. I had their wings clipped so they couldn't fly away. No, they didn't escape. They died."

Sadie put a hand on the girl's shoulder. "Bartlett's men?"

Kate nodded, biting down on her lip, holding back the tears. "I don't have any proof. But that's what I suspect."

"And you didn't tell Raoul?"

"No. He knows that they're . . . gone. I told him there was an accident. He said he was going to replace them for me. A Christmas gift. But—"

"You told him not to. Because Bartlett might poison them again," Sadie said, not with a question, but as if she knew. She nodded. "Bartlett will try something more desperate this time."

"You act as if you know that to be true," Kate said.

"There will always be men like Bartlett. Greedy men who will take advantage of the poor and innocent."

"I can't believe Raoul went with him."

"Do not underestimate your fiancé, dear. He is an intelligent young man with your best interests at heart. He will not fail you."

"How can you be so sure?"

"Do you not love him?"

"Yes. Of course, but—"

"And do you not trust him?"

"Yes. I trust him," Kate said, feeling just a tad guilty. "I love him and I trust him."

"Then he will not fail you. Remember, 'tis the season. Keep your faith and all will be as it should." She gave Kate a gentle pat on the shoulder. "Now come, we must go downstairs. It is almost supper time."

Kate almost believed things might turn around. During supper, Mr. Pickens, the corner grocer, came in, dragging a huge evergreen. Both the children and adults were delighted.

"It's beginning to look like Christmas around here, after all," Old Henry said.

"I think we have decorations in the back," Madge said.

"See, things are looking up," Sadie told Kate.

"But Raoul isn't back yet," she said, checking her watch. She looked up to see one of the small children needing help and she had no more time to dwell on Raoul, as her patrons needed attention first. Raoul would have to take care of himself.

Raoul only wished he could. He was nursing a bro-

ken lip and a sprained arm in the hospital. He had
gone with Bartlett to try and reason with the man.
See the potential of redeveloping the area, instead of
tearing it down. He even showed him how it could be
done, cheaply and efficiently. How the structures were
still sound in the area and how they could be developed into townhouses that the yuppies would kill for.
But Bartlett had his own ideas and when Raoul had
left his office, his henchmen reaffirmed those ideas,
putting the pressure on for Kate to sell.

Except he knew Kate wouldn't. He didn't want her
to either. That neighborhood was part of his past, too.
Both he and Kate had grown up there; the first time
he had laid eyes on Kate, he knew she was going to
be his wife one day. That together they would help
the neighborhood come back to life. That was why he
had gone to architectural school. Only the money had
run out and he had to settle for being a draftsman.

Of course, if Kate did sell, he could go back to
school and . . . but no. Kate wouldn't sell, and they'd
have to get by. Helping others from being homeless,
when they were nearly homeless themselves. Maybe
he could talk to Kate. Make her see the benefits of
. . . no, she'd never see.

Damn it, anyway, he thought. So close and yet so
far. He argued with himself while the hospital patched
him back together. He was still arguing about it, trying
to come up with a sound, logical solution to the whole
situation as he headed back to the neighborhood,
where somehow he was going to have to make up with
Kate. Of course, his arm in a sling might soften her
attitude toward him some. He could only hope.

"It's beautiful," Maria said. In the glow of the
Christmas lights, the bruise on her cheek was barely
noticeable. In her arms, she held up her son to see as

she cooed something to him. The child reached out toward the pretty tree and smiled.

"Yes, it is," Kate agreed. She glanced at her watch again. Almost eight-thirty. She glanced around the shelter, where people were putting the children to bed.

She watched as Sadie helped a young father put his three children to bed on the cots and couldn't help but smile.

"Tomorrow is Christmas Eve," Maria said. "The first one away from my family. I wanted it to be happy."

"Your family is where?"

"Florida. It is too cold up here. That is where I met my husband. He brought me up here. I didn't know him for long before we got married. I didn't know what kind of man he was."

"Well, you can stay here as long as you need to, Maria."

"Thank you, Miss Muldoon. You are very kind," she said. "I'd better put Matthew to bed," she said.

Kate nodded and watched her go. Then she glanced at her watch again.

It was almost nine and Mulligan's Pet Store was just closing. But Pete Mulligan opened the door when he saw Raoul.

"What happened to you?" Old Man Mulligan asked. "Your street fighting days should be long gone, boy," he scolded.

"They are," Raoul reassured him. "Listen, did those love-birds come in?"

"I thought you were going to pick them up tomorrow."

"I was, but I know you'll be closing early and, well, I was going to go back to the shelter tonight, but . . ."

"But Kate would want to know who you were fighting with?"

"Something like that." He had decided not to go back tonight. Instead he would call her. Maybe she wouldn't hang up on him.

"Well, actually, they haven't come yet. I was expecting them in the morning."

"Oh, I see." Now, he'd have to make another trip. "Oh, well, then—," he started, but something took his eye. It was a bird on a perch, but it was like no other bird he had ever seen. "Wow! Will you look at this—it's beautiful." He walked over to the large plumed bird. It look like a cross between a falcon and a peacock with long feathers of purple, red and orange. "What kind of bird is this?"

"Isn't is just?" Pete agreed. "Very rare. It was just delivered about half an hour ago. It's a special delivery for a client who's a big bird collector."

"A bird collector?"

"Yeah. He owns this big aviary. Owns all sort of exotic and rare birds."

Raoul began thinking about Bartlett and the bird motifs he had seen in his office. "This client wouldn't be Malcolm Bartlett, would it?"

"Yeah, that's him. Do you know him?"

"Yeah, I know him." He stared at the bird. "And this creature is too beautiful for the likes of him."

"Maybe so," Mulligan said. "But he's the type that can afford such beauty."

"Where's Sadie?" Kate asked Madge as the last of the children were put to bed.

Madge glanced around but didn't see the old woman. "She's not back yet? Said she had to do some errands. Left before nine."

"She shouldn't be out alone in the cold," Kate said.

She crossed to the front window and peeked out from behind the shade. A light snow was falling. There was a draft by the window, and she huddled her arms together for warmth. She looked at her watch. Nearly ten.

The phone rang and Madge answered it. A moment later she called out to Kate. "It's Raoul."

Kate couldn't help but hurry to the phone. "Where are you?"

"Home. Listen, I'm sorry about this afternoon. I went with Bartlett to try and reason with him."

"There is no reasoning with that man."

"Yeah. I know that now."

Kate knew something was up by the tone in his voice. "Raoul, what is it?"

"Nothing. Look, I've got some chores to do in the morning, then I'll be by, okay?"

"Are you okay?"

"I'm fine. Get some rest. See you in the morning, okay? Love ya," he told her and rang off before she could say anything further.

She knew him; something was going on. But despite her anxiety, she found herself suppressing a yawn.

"Go to bed, honey. It's late," Madge told her. "I'm going to shut off the lights and head home myself."

Kate didn't argue with her. She just hoped that Sadie would be okay out in the cold.

But she worried for nothing, for the next morning when she came downstairs, Sadie had returned and was helping serve breakfast to the children. One child held the bright feather Kate had found the day before and she smiled at the delight the child saw in it. She greeted the old woman with a smile, then fell to work. Much still needed to done, for it was now the day before Christmas. Angelo's food promised to fill many a Christmas stomach, but she still had to visit the Regency Hotel for those blankets.

It was after the noon hour by the time she returned, and she had not only blankets but toys as well. She and several of the regulars began a gift wrapping spree for the children.

"Where's Sadie? And has anyone seen Raoul this morning?" she asked, wrapping a stuffed teddy bear that would be perfect for Maria's son, Matthew.

"Sadie was here this morning. She left just before ten—more errands. And I haven't seen Raoul," Madge said.

Old Henry looked up; his worn face wore a smile. "Raoul stopped by around ten-thirty, asked for you, then left again. Think he went upstairs for a while, though."

Kate nodded. "Let me know if anyone sees him. I need to talk to him."

"What have you gotten him for Christmas, Kate?"

Kate stopped her wrapping, her mouth opened. "Oh, oh."

"Oh, girl," Madge said. "Now, don't tell me that you forgot to buy something for the boy?"

"I—oops," her face grew red with embarrassment. "I meant to—but I've been so busy here and . . ." She looked up at Madge. "Madge, can you handle things here? I think I have to go shopping."

Madge just shook her head and watched Kate hurry out. "Sometimes I don't know about that girl. She'd forget her head if it weren't screwed on real tight."

"And who said it is?" Old Henry said with a laugh.

Kate took a cab down to 34th Street and hurried into Macy's. The crowds were thick, but then what did she expect the day before Christmas? She checked out the men's department and found a tie for Raoul, then went over to the music department and found him a compact disc of a jazz group he liked.

Great, a tie and a CD. Some gifts. She had to find him something special. Maybe some drafting supplies or art supplies. Something for his new job—oop. His new job with Bartlett. Did he still have a new job? Had he really sold her out? Maybe a tie and a CD were too much for the creep.

She fought the crowd and she fought with herself, going back and forth—forgiving him one moment and wanting to kill him the next. But what had Sadie told her—to have faith?

Kate made her way out of the store finally and moved along the row of gaily decorated windows dressed in holiday style. There were moving figures in an old-fashioned home, celebrating an old-fashioned Christmas. Beneath the tree was the manger with baby Jesus, Mary, and Joseph standing with the wise men. Sheep, cows, and chickens were nearby and overhead was an angel looking down.

Tonight would be Christmas Mass, where traditional songs of the season would be sung. She and Raoul would go, as they had last year. Perhaps she would invite Sadie to join them this year.

She looked down at the tiny scene with a smile, and then something gold caught her eye. She squinted, for the small figurine was toward the back. She angled herself to see it better and caught more colors—purple, red, and orange.

Yes, she thought so. The figure was a bird of some sort. It was large, looking like a cross between a peacock and . . . an eagle. "What an unusual creature," she muttered. "And so beautiful."

"It is, isn't it?" A voice said at her shoulder.

Kate looked up and found Pete Mulligan, one of the shop owners from the neighborhood standing by her side. One of the neighbors who had already sold out to Mr. Bartlett. "Mr. Mulligan, what are you doing down here?"

"Shopping, what else? So, you find everything you need for young what's-his-name?"

"Raoul," she told him with a frown. "As if you don't know." Raoul had worked for Old Man Mulligan while in his teens. The old man had a pet store and it was where Raoul had bought Tony and Maria for her.

"Grown up to be a good lad. Wasn't so sure there for awhile," Pete told her with a smile. Then nodded at the window. "You two going to Mass tonight?"

"Of course. You'll be there?"

He nodded. "Pretty little bird, don't you think?"

"Yes. Beautiful. You know it looks kind of familiar though. Those colors, purple, red—hey, wait—the feather!"

"Feather?"

"I found a feather yesterday. It might have come from that bird," Kate said.

Pete shook his head. "That bird is very rare. Not from around these parts."

"You know about that bird?" She pointed to the window.

"I know what that bird is supposed to represent. It's a Phoenix. Legend has it that there was a Phoenix present at the birth of baby Jesus. It was there as protection and to serve as a symbol for the new cycle of things to come. Stands for rebirth, good luck. Stuff like that."

Kate looked at the tiny figurine. "A Phoenix, eh? But they aren't for real?"

"Supposed to be mythological creatures. But you never know." Pete glanced up as it began to snow.

"Well, I better get going. It'll be dark soon." He patted Kate on the shoulder. "Merry Christmas, Katie."

Kate smiled, "Merry Christmas, Mr. Mulligan." She watched as he disappeared into the crowd, then turned back to the manger scene and to the tiny figurine of the Phoenix. "Good luck, eh? Or maybe rebirth? Maybe that's why I found that feather. Maybe you're trying to tell me that it is time to sell. I could get some big bucks for the place." She shook her head and moved on, down the street. There was an art supply store nearby, if she remembered correctly.

She did and she hurried inside to the smell of paints, erasers, new canvas, and varnish. She looked around the shelves of paint and artist's supplies, then moved to where there were drafting tables and artist's easels.

"Can I help you find something?" a young female clerk asked with a smile.

"My fiancé is a draftsman. I thought maybe a new drafting table . . . ?" she felt unsure of the whole thing, glancing around. She picked up a green piece of plastic with cutouts for trees and houses.

"Well, we have drafting supplies over there. That's more for an architect."

"Raoul was going to be an architect," Kate said. "He couldn't finish—he ran out of money."

"I'm sorry," the girl said. "Well, if you need any more help . . ." she started, but it was clear that Kate was no longer with her. She left her with her own thoughts.

Kate's thoughts were of Raoul and his lack of money. "If I sold the shelter, Raoul could go back to school easily. But Old Henry, Maria and Matthew, and Sadie . . . where would they go?" she said out loud to no one in particular. She looked down at the architect's tool, feeling at a loss.

"Miss, we'll be closing soon, so . . ." the clerk had come back up.

Kate turned, "What? Oh, I'm sorry. It's Christmas Eve, isn't it? Of course."

"Are you going to get anything?"

Kate looked around. "Ah, no. Not today. Thank you," she said and hurried out. It was time to go home.

Raoul glanced at his watch and noted it was getting late. "Kate, should be getting home by now." He glanced out the shelter's front window once more.

"She'll be here. It's bound to be murder out there with the traffic and all," Madge said.

"Here, have some eggnog," Sadie came up and handed him a glass.

"What?" He turned, to see the small woman. "Thanks," he gave her a smile and noted the feather she wore in her hair. "Hey, you haven't been upstairs, have you?"

"Me? No, why?"

He reached out and gently touched the feather. "I have a surprise for Kate up there. And this feather—" he started, but a blast of cold air hit him as the door opened and Kate walked in. "Katie! Where have you been?" he scolded and went to her.

"Shopping," she answered, hiding her packages from him. "And I could ask the same of—what happened to your arm?" she said, seeing the sling. "Raoul!" she started, as Sadie came up and took her packages.

"I'll take these and take care of them," the old woman said with a smile, but Kate's attention was on Raoul's injuries.

Madge came up as Sadie passed her. "Those two," she commented, shaking her head. "Did you see that creature he bought for her? It's upstairs. Do you know who that bird was supposed to go to?"

"Malcolm Bartlett," Sadie said.

"That's right. Pete Mulligan said it cost him a fortune."

"Raoul's getting even with Bartlett."

"Nothing but trouble there," Madge said. She glanced up as she saw one of the children playing with the Christmas tree lights. "Oh, oh, speaking of trouble. . . . " and she hurried over as Sadie headed upstairs with Kate's presents.

The evening commenced with dinner, carols and then at Kate's invitation, she, Raoul, and Sadie went to midnight Mass, leaving Madge and Old Henry in charge of the shelter, while nearly forty adults and twenty children slept, waiting for Christmas morning.

"That was quite beautiful. Thank you for inviting me," Sadie told Kate and Raoul as they walked back home.

"You're quite welcome," Kate replied.

"You know, Miss Sadie, you reminded me of someone. A picture of someone—I just can't place it," Raoul said.

Sadie laughed, "I'm always being told that—someone's grandmother, usually."

"Hey, that's it," Raoul said, snapping his fingers. "Kate, do you remember that photo of your—" he started, but the wail of a fire engine fast approaching drowned him out. Two more engines quickly followed. Raoul looked to see where they were heading and saw a reddish glow in the night sky. "Hey, that looks like some fire."

"And it looks like it's coming from our neighborhood," Kate said, suddenly worried. "Come on!" she told them and hurried ahead while Raoul helped Sadie along.

Kate was right; it was coming from their neighborhood—worse, it was coming from her building. Flames shot out of the roof and from the third and second floor windows. "My home!" She looked down to see where the shelter people were still streaming out of the building. "The shelter!" She started forward, but a fireman stopped her.

"You can't go in there, miss. The whole building's going to go anytime now," he told her.

Madge's voice cried out to her and Kate hurried over to her. "Most everyone is out. Several firemen are in there now, getting out the rest."

"But how did it happen?"

"I don't know. It started on the roof though," Madge told her. Both turned as Old Henry came out with several others, coughing and hacking. Quickly, they went to help.

"Oh, my God!" Raoul said, rounding a corner. He looked up to see Kate's home being destroyed. "This has got to be Bartlett's doing," he said, his fist clenched. He looked around for Kate. Then he glanced down at Sadie. "Stay here. You'll be safe." She nodded, her eye wide, staring at the flames as he hurried off.

Halfway across the street, Raoul remembered his present to Kate. He had hidden it in a third floor room, so Kate wouldn't find it. Now he looked up there and saw only flames. "Oh, no . . ." It wasn't even the money, but the terrible destruction of such a creature. He had no more time to think about it though for people needed his help. He fell to work, alongside Kate, Madge, Old Henry, and the others.

"Is there anyone left?" a fireman shouted, while Madge was counting heads.

"I don't know," Kate said, looking around. Then she heard it, the wail of a baby. She looked around and found Maria, who was being fed oxygen. "Matthew! Where's Matthew?" she cried out, but it was too obvious where the baby was. Still inside.

Raoul, covered with soot, started to turn to head back inside. "I'll get him!" he said, but there was a sudden explosion from above and fire, brick, and glass rained on them. "Get back!" he shouted, pushing Kate and the others farther away from the building. Several firemen tried to lead them away; Kate protested, still hearing the baby, and then Maria's anguished cries concerning her child. She looked over to see Maria trying to fight the fireman who held on to her, dragging her off, shaking his head.

"Matthew's still alive!" she cried out to Raoul.

Raoul looked back at the building, unsure. Was he going to be a hero or a dead fool? He glanced up at the building as the roof started to cave in. Then down at Kate. "I think it's too—" he started, when something caught his eye. "Sadie!"

Kate looked and saw what he saw. It was Sadie, running toward the shelter. "Sadie! No!"

The old woman paused for just a split second to look their way and smiled. Then she disappeared into the flames.

Kate started toward the building, but Raoul held her back, "It's too late!" he shouted and he was right, for there was another explosion and the roof caved in. A moment later the building was totally destroyed as it collapsed on itself in a mighty roar of rubble and flame.

The sun was rising by the time the last of the flames were put out. Dawn's early light washed the snow with shades of red, orange, and purple. The fire trucks were leaving. Kate and Raoul had spent the night shepherding the shelter's patrons to the local churches for the night. They were both exhausted and down-trodden when they came back to the remains of what was to be their home.

"It's gone. And Matthew and Sadie are dead," Kate said. She couldn't even cry, it was just beyond her.

"I went to Bartlett to see if he'd redevelop this area. Not tear it down," Raoul explained, his good arm around her. He looked around. Several other build-ings had been destroyed as well, their remains like blackened skeletons, still and cold. "This area had so much potential. I drew out the plans myself, but he wanted his grandeur. His name on a building."

"I should have sold. Then this wouldn't have hap-pened. I would have had enough money to send you back to school. And Matthew—and Sadie . . . oh, God, why did this have to happen? Why didn't I just sell when I had the chance?" She could feel the tears beginning to build as Raoul held her tighter.

"You still own the land," another voice said. "And now have no excuse not to sell."

Kate turned to see Malcolm Bartlett standing there. "You! You did this! You bastard!" She tried going for him, but Raoul held her back.

"Whoa, Kate!" He looked over at Bartlett. "Come to gloat, Bartlett?"

"I always get what I want," he said, looking around, with a smile. Then his face darkened. "Except for a certain rare bird that I was very much looking forward to owning."

"Rare bird?" Kate asked.

"Mr. Bartlett's quite the bird collector," Raoul said with a smug smile. "Mr. Mulligan had a bird in his store on special order for Mr. Bartlett. But I saw it, found out who it was for, and convinced Mr. Mulligan to sell it to me instead. It was going to be your Christ-mas present." The smug smile disappeared as he glanced over at the building. "But it was destroyed in the fire. I left it upstairs." He glanced at Bartlett. "Guess, you don't always get what you want, Bartlett."

Malcolm Bartlett's look of self-satisfaction disappeared as he, too, looked at the burned-out remains. "That bird was worth a fortune!" he muttered.

"What kind of bird was it?" Kate asked, but before either man could answer she heard the distinct sound of a cry. A baby's cry. It was coming from the burned-out remains of the building. "What the—?" she said and then hurried toward the ruins.

Raoul was quick to follow. "Careful, Katie."

Kate was careful, as she stepped over the blackened lumber and scorched rubble. Then she saw the baby. It lay among the ashes, in a nest of evergreen, wrapped in a clean white blanket, and totally unharmed. "Oh, my gosh—Matthew!" Carefully, she picked up the crying baby. "Raoul—look, it's Matthew!"

"That's impossible," he said, joining her. But he couldn't deny that the baby was alive and unharmed. "But how?" he said. Then he heard another sound, the flapping of wings. He looked up and saw the bird of beauty that was to be Kate's present. It perched on a blackened timber above them and let out a small song.

Kate looked up to see the large bird of red, purple, and orange, which gleamed like gold in this early light. "That's a Phoenix!"

"That's a Pyravis Athansia!" Malcolm Bartlett said. "And it's supposed to be mine!"

"That's the bird I bought for you, Kate. But how did it . . . ?" Raoul asked, then looked up at the bird and crossed himself, muttering a prayer.

"It's Christmas," Kate said. "Time of miracles, love, and magic. And that is a Phoenix. Old Man

Mulligan told me so. Said that according to legends, a Phoenix was present at Jesus' birth. A Phoenix can rise from the ashes, can't it? This one saved Matthew's life."

"But not Sadie's," Raoul pointed out. He glanced over at Bartlett. Then at Kate. "Katie, I've got an idea," he said, then looked up at the Phoenix. "I'd hate to see you own such a thing of beauty, Mr. Bartlett, but seeing how bent you are on having that bird— maybe you'd like to reconsider your offer."

Bartlett raised an eyebrow, immediately seeing where Martinez was leading. "Maybe so. But first you have to catch the damn thing!" he said.

Raoul smiled, and the huge bird promptly landed on Bartlett's shoulder. "Okay, Bartlett, let's talk."

"It's beautiful, isn't it?" Kate said with a smile.

"Over a hundred and fifty rooms and a cafeteria big enough to feed over two hundred a day," Madge said, as they stood outside the new homeless complex. Above them were two new hotels and four new restaurants, all willing to donate items to the huge complex. "Raoul did a real nice design job."

"He sure did, didn't he?" Kate said. "And I like the name—the Phoenix Plaza. Has a nice ring to it." She glanced down at her own wedding ring. "I wish Sadie could see it though."

"And what makes you think she can't?"

Kate turned and blinked. "Sadie?" She stared down at the woman whose face was familiar but whose appearance was not. "But how—"

Sadie smiled up at her with mischievous blue eyes. Instead of rags she wore a beautiful suit of red, with yellow and purple accents. Cleaned up, she looked years younger. She grabbed hold of Kate's hand. "See, I told you to keep the faith."

"I don't understand. I saw you—"

"What you saw—does it matter? You're happy, Maria is happy, Raoul is happy, and even Malcolm Bartlett is happy. He has his precious plaza, you have your shelter and a new home. Right?"

"But—?" Kate started once again.

"Well, I must fly. My work here is finished. Good luck to you both. And remember—miracles, love, and magic—they work wonders," Sadie told her and gave her hand a squeeze.

Kate started to say something more, but she heard Raoul call out her name. She turned as he came running up.

"Guess what happened today," he said with a smile.

"Raoul—look at who—" Kate said and turned, but Sadie was gone. She looked around, listening to Raoul as he continued.

"Bartlett's precious bird—guess what? It flew away today. And I'm glad—that was always the part of the bargain I hated. Giving him the bird for everything we wanted. Katie? Are you listening to me?" Raoul asked.

Kate was listening, as she continued to look and see where Sadie could have disappeared to so fast. Then she felt something in her closed hand. She opened her hand. And smiled, understanding.

It was a feather—a beautiful, familiar feather—of red, yellow, purple, and gold.

CHRISTMAS SEAL

by Jane Lindskold

Regina waddled when she walked—a short, broad-assed woman with wiry, graying black hair. Had she not been so obviously poor, the shiny brown coat she wore might have been mistaken for genuine sealskin.

"Merry Christmas!" said the guard at the Southern Boulevard entrance to the Bronx Zoo, as he helped her get her wire grocery cart through the baby carriage gate.

"Merry Christmas to you," she answered, tilting the cart onto its two wheels, "Working on Christmas?"

"No matter to me," he grinned, "I'm Jewish. Are you doing anything for the holiday?"

"Going to visit some relatives."

When the guard headed back to his sheltered booth, she set off along the downsloping asphalt path, the cart rattling behind her. Humming "Jingle Bells," she passed the snack bar, gift stand, and Children's Zoo, all closed for the season. On her right the refurbished Elephant House, now the Orientation Center, was also quiet. It was too early for most winter patrons and on Christmas Day the Zoo was open with only a skeleton staff.

Regina had counted on this as she shopped yesterday at both of the fish markets on Arthur Avenue. They'd been packed with people shopping for the traditional Italian Christmas Eve dinner. Despite crowd-

123

ing so thick that just getting a place on the narrow sidewalk was an achievement, the mood had been festive. Overhead, electric lights shone from tinsel stars and bells that arched between streetlights. Tinny Christmas carols in both Italian and English played from several shops. She would have liked to do her shopping today, but the good Catholic merchants were closed and Arthur Avenue, when she had trundled by it on her way to the Zoo, was a holiday desert.

The outdoor cages of the former Lion House were empty as she rattled past. Only the stone wild cats on the high relief frieze watched her go by. The Zoo was so silent that Regina could almost believe that the sculptured animals that crouched and prowled on the older buildings were the only tenants. That is, until there was a sharp bark from the Sea Lion pool.

The single bark became a loud chorus. Water sprayed up when the lookout, a svelte female, exuberantly dove into the Pool. Regina hustled as fast as she could, hauling the cart behind her.

"Hush! Hush!" she chided, "Do you want to bring the keepers?"

The bull heard her and silenced his harem with a basso profundo bellow that was (she knew) audible for blocks outside of the Zoo. The others instantly became silent. The water was alive with swirling brown-black bodies.

Glancing behind her to make certain that no one was watching, Regina extracted an assortment of plastic bags from beneath the cart's covering. As she shook a mess of silvery smelts into the Pool, the dank smell of raw fish made her stomach rumble. A few of the smaller pups broke and dove after the fish, but the rest of the herd waited, swimming in easy, graceful circles.

Next, Regina slid heavier paper-wrapped bundles

from their plastic coverings. The red snapper had set her back a bit, but she felt well repaid as she hung over the rail and one by one the herd members snatched their Christmas gifts from her fingers. For the bull she had a bluefish large enough to feed a small family. Lastly, Regina heaved an entire mesh rucksack of mussels from the cart. Scattered over the bottom of the Pool, they'd give the sea lions something to dive after.

Little bits of pale pink fish standing out against his black bewhiskered nose, the bull snorted his thanks. A few of the pups, forgetting the mandate about staying quiet, yapped excitedly until their mothers dunked them. Enjoying the suspense, Regina folded the cart flat and tucked it under the thorny Japanese quince hedge that bordered the Pool. Stooping awkwardly, she stepped between the iron pipe railings and onto the narrow Pool wall.

Glancing back and suspecting that she saw motion near the Orientation Center, she hurriedly buttoned up her coat, attaching the gloves to the sleeves with toggles at the wrists. Then she unrolled the hood from beneath the collar, positioning it so that it covered her head.

Just as she was getting the eyeholes centered over her eyes, she heard a man's shout from behind her. Fortunately, the water looked awfully inviting: clear, cold, and black, festooned with shreds of fish and the occasional silvery smelt. So, taking a deep breath, she leapt into the Pool.

Her change was complete before she resurfaced, barking playfully at the astonished keeper and luxuriating in the tingle of the cool water against her hide.

"Dive and swim, folks," ordered Bull. "You know he's a new one and doesn't know us all yet. He'll get cold and go inside in a minute."

Taking his own advice, he dove and surfaced near her, the water skating off of his scarred, blubbery hide.

"Merry Christmas, Bull," she said, splashing his wake back at him.

"Merry Christmas, Selkie," he replied, "So nice of you to drop by—and in!"

Rubbing his head and muttering about too much Christmas cheer, the bemused keeper had vanished inside when two of the girls pushed a long herring over to Regina.

"Merry Christmas, Selkie," they chorused, "from all of us. We're so pleased that you came."

Politely, she ate her gift in two bites, "Merry Christmas! You know I wouldn't have missed this for anything. There's nothing like sharing the holidays with family."

"The keeper!" yapped one of the pups from his vantage on Diving Rock, "and he has a bucket!"

Regina looked up to where the young man stood at the railing, getting ready to dive deep if he was going to drag the Pool. But all he did was stand for a moment as if still trying to count the herd. Then, with a shout of "Merry Christmas!" he skimmed the bucketful of herring across the water. Regina swam after one, then surfaced, watching as the keeper gave a cheerful shrug and went shuffling inside. She knew what he must be feeling.

But on Christmas, even in the Bronx, one can believe in miracles.

IN THIS SEASON

by Harry Turtledove

Sunset came early to the little Polish town of Puck as winter began. The Baltic slapped in growing darkness against the shelving, muddy beach. The Poles grubbed clams and cockles and whelks from the mud and fried them or ate them in soups. For Puck's three families of Jews, shellfish were, of course, forbidden food.

The hunger that gnawed Berel Friedman's belly made him wonder with increasingly urgent curiosity what fried clams tasted like. In the three months since the Germans overran Poland, Puck's Poles had come to know hunger and want. As for the town's Jews—well, falling under Hitler's yoke made Friedman long to be ruled by Poles again, and what comparison could be worse than that? None he could think of.

A soft knock on the door distracted him from his gloomy reflections. His wife Emma said, "That will be the Korczaks. We're all here now."

"Yes." He opened the door, nodded to Jacob and Yetta Korczak, chucked their two little boys under their chins. "Welcome, all," he said. "*Gut yontif*—happy holiday."

"*Gut yontif.*" Deep lines of worry lost themselves in Jacob Korczak's graying beard. He laughed bitterly. "As if there are any happy holidays any more."

"We go on day by day, as best we can," Friedman said. "What else can we do?" Behind him, Isaac

Geller nodded, not so much from conviction (for his nature was less sunny than Friedman's) as from despair at finding any better course.

Friedman made sure the curtains were tightly shut before he took down the silver menorah and set it on the mantel. For the Poles to see him lighting Hanukkah candles would be bad enough. For the Germans to see him would be catastrophic.

He set a slim orange candle in the leftmost space in the menorah, then took another from the box and laid it on the mantel for a moment. He got out a match, scraped it against the sole of his boot. The match caught. Coughing a little at the sulfurous smoke, he picked up the candle from the mantel, lighted it, and used it to kindle the one already in the menorah. Then he put the *shamas* candle in the menorah's centermost place, which was higher than the four to either side of it.

That done, he chanted in Hebrew the blessings over the candles, than translated them into Yiddish for the women and children: "Blessed art thou, O Lord our God, king of the universe, who hast sanctified us with thy commandments and commanded us to light the lights of dedication." ("Which is what 'Hanukkah' means, after all," he added in an aside.) . . . "Blessed art thou, O Lord our God, king of the universe, who wrought miracles for our fathers in those days and in this season . . . Blessed art thou, O Lord our God, king of the universe, who hath preserved us alive and brought us to enjoy this season."

Though Friedman was in most circumstances a man far from imaginative, the irony of the Hanukkah blessing struck him with almost physical force. God might have helped the Jews against Antiochus long ago, but what was He doing about Hitler, whose venom was enough for twenty Antiochuses? Nothing anyone could see.

Shaking his head, Friedman read and then translated the explanatory passage that followed the blessings in the prayer book: "These lights we light to praise thee for the miracles, wonders, salvations, and victories which thou didst perform for our fathers in those days and in this season, by the hands of thy holy priests. Therefore, by command, these lights are holy all the eight days of Hanukkah; neither are we permitted to make any other use of them save to view them, that we may return thanks to thy name for thy miracles, wonderful works, and salvation."

All the adults in the crowded little living room exchanged troubled glances above the heads of their children. Where were the victories? The wonderful works? As for salvation, who under the Nazis had even the hope to pray for it?

If there were miracles, they lay in the hearts of the children. As soon as Friedman stepped away from the menorah, his daughter Rachel and his son Aaron, the two Korczak boys, and the Gellers' son and daughter all squealed, "It's Hanukkah!" so loud that their parents looked alarmed. Children didn't worry about hard times, but they made the most of celebrations. In a moment, four dreidels, some of wood, others baked from clay, were spinning on the floor and on the low, battered table in front of the fireplace.

"Here, here," Jacob Korczack said gruffly. "If you're going to play with dreidels, you need some Hanukkah *gelt*, don't you?" He dug in his trouser pocket, took out a handful of mixed German and Polish small change, and passed the little coins to all the children. Friedman and Geller did the same.

The letters on the four sides of the dreidels began

the Hebrew words that meant "a great miracle happened here." The sounds of joy from the children as
they played, the delight when the person who spun
won the pot on a *gimel,* the moan when *shin* landed
face up and the spinner had to add to the pile, made
the house sound like all the Hanukkahs Friedman remembered. In these times, that was not the smallest
of miracles itself.

It even began to smell like Hanukkah. The rich
odors of hot grease and onions flooded in from the
kitchen as Emma fried potato *latkes:* a man could still
come by potatoes. But the *latkes* would be the entire
Hanukkah feast. No fat goose, no brisket marinated
in wine, not this year. Friedman could count on the
fingers of his hands the times he'd tasted meat since
the swastika flag replaced Poland's red and white banner over the town hall.

"We'll just stuff ourselves the fuller with *latkes,*
then," he declared. Jacob Korczak glared at him. He
just smiled in return. If your children were happy,
could you stay grim for long?

Someone knocked on the door.

In an instant, the house was silent. The children
looked frightened. The adults looked terrified. All the
Jews in Puck were gathered together here. Whoever
stood outside had to be a *goy,* then: maybe a Pole;
maybe, worse, a German. The Germans were de-
porting Jews from this part of Poland now that they'd
annexed it to their country. Ice in his veins, Friedman
waited for the harsh cry, *"Juden, heraus!"*

The knock came again. But for that, silence.

Emma poked her head out of the kitchen. "What
shall I do?" Friedman mouthed in her direction.
Opening the door and not opening it were equally
appalling choices.

"Open it," she said without hesitation. "It's Hanukkah, after all. Feeding the stranger is a *mitzvah*."

If the stranger outside was a cruelly grinning SS man in a coalskuttle helmet, Friedman did not think even God would reckon feeding him a blessing. Of course, if it was an SS man outside, he had better things to eat than the poor fare a handful of Jews could offer him.

Whoever it was knocked for a third time, not loudly but with persistence. The slow, steady raps helped hearten Friedman. Surely an SS man would not politely knock three times; an SS man would hammer down the door with a rifle butt.

Friedman raised the bar, threw the door wide. Outside stood the tallest, widest man he'd ever set eyes on, dressed in rags far too small for him. Friedman had never seen him, or anyone like him, before. He looked as though he could have ripped the door off its hinges with his little finger.

The big man did nothing of the sort. He just stood quietly, looking down at Friedman even though the living room floor was a tall step above the street. His eyes reflected the flickering glow of the Hanukkah candles like a cat's.

Seeing those candles, even if at second hand, reminded Friedman why he'd opened the door. He forced his voice not to wobble as he said, "Will you come in, friend, and take supper with us? We have an abundance of good *latkes,* so help yourself to all you can eat." He knew he'd lied—no one but Germans had an abundance of anything in Poland these days—but it was not the sort of lie God recorded in his book of judgments.

The stranger looked at him a moment more. He did not answer, not with words. All at once, though, he nodded. He had to go sideways through Friedman's door, and duck his head to get under the lintel. When he straightened up inside the house, the hairless crown of his head just missed scraping the ceiling.

Rachel Friedman was only four years old, too little to be perfectly polite. She stared up and up and up at the stranger, then started to cry. Through her tears, she wailed, "If he eats all he can eat, the rest of us won't have any!" That set a couple of the other children crying, too. They'd all been hungry too often of late to think of losing a promised feast.

As host, Berel Friedman did what he could to repair the damage. He knew a certain somber pride that his chuckle sounded natural. "Don't worry about the children, my friend. What do children know? As I said, we have plenty. And Emma," he raised his voice, "bring out the plum brandy for our guest, will you?"

The big man still did not speak. David Korczak, Jacob's older boy, was twelve. His *bar mitzvah* would have come next summer, had the Germans not come first. Now he nudged his father and said, "Why does the stranger—"

"The guest," his father hissed, also mindful of the proprieties.

"The guest, I mean." David corrected himself, then went on, not quite quietly enough, "Why does the guest have *emes* written across his forehead?"

"What nonsense are you bleating?" Jacob Korczak made as if to cuff his son. But he was just as well as stern, and looked before he struck. Friedman looked, too. He'd taken the brown patches above the stranger's eyes for a birthmark, about which any comment or even apparent notice would have been rude. Now, though, he saw David was right. The marks did spell out the Hebrew word for truth.

For a moment, he accepted that as a freak of nature. Then he remembered the Talmudic teaching that the word *emes* was the Seal of God, which had also adorned Adam's forehead when he and the world were newly created things.

Since Adam, no man had borne that sign. It was instead the mark of a thing newly created, though not by God: the mark, in short, of the *golem*. Fear all but froze Friedman's heart. There were other terrors than Germans loose in the world—and he had just invited one of them into his house!

A low choking noise from Jacob Korczak said he'd come to the same dreadful realization. Isaac Geller hadn't, but Isaac Geller, while a good man and a good Jew, was not overly burdened with brains.

What to do? What to do? Friedman didn't dare even moan, for fear of angering the undead creature. He wanted to command it to leave, but feared its wrath since he knew he had no authority over it. Besides, having accepted it as a guest, he could not turn it out when it had done no wrong without incurring sin himself.

That left him no choice but to treat the thing as if it were a man like any other. He waved it to the table. When it sat, he said, "Will you honor us by leading prayers this evening?"

The *golem* shook its head, pointed to its throat with a massive index finger, shook its head again. *Of course,* Friedman thought: *it can't speak—only true divine creations can do that.* He racked his fear-frozen wits for other bits of lore, but it was as if he was trying to get money from a bank that had failed.

As if with a magic of her own, Emma had set an extra place for the *golem,* shifted her husband's chair to it, and found him an old splintery stool, all without being noticed. Now, red-faced and beaming, she placed a big tray of *latkes* on the table. With her spatula, she filled the *golem*'s plate. Berel poured *slivovitz* into its glass.

Since the *golem* had declined, Isaac Geller led the prayers. After the final *omayn,* he lifted his snifter of brandy and made the usual toast: "*L'chayim*—to life!"

Friedman was more convinced than ever that his friend had rocks in his head. Of all the things that might enrage a *golem,* he couldn't think of one more likely to infuriate than praise for something it would never have.

But the *golem* only raised its glass along with the rest of the adults. It let the potent plum brandy moisten its lips, but whatever passed them did not lower the level of the *slivovitz* by a hair's breadth. It used its fork to cut a tiny crumb from one *latke,* then put the rest of that potato pancake and all the others back on the platter.

That was too much for Emma. She could extend hospitality to a *golem* with aplomb, but to see the hospitality refused roused her ire. "You're not eating," she said sharply, as if in the one accusation she condemned the creature for crimes uncounted.

The *golem* obediently dipped its head to her, then lifted the scrap of fried potato to its mouth. It chewed but, Friedman saw, did not swallow. *What need has a thing of clay for nourishment?* he asked himself, and found no answer. Politely nodding once more to Emma, the *golem* put both hands on its belly, as if to show it was stuffed to overflowing. She let out a loud, unimpressed sniff but otherwise held her peace.

With the *golem* so abstemious, the *latkes* were enough to feed everyone. Friedman had trouble remembering the last time he'd been so pleasantly full— not since the Germans came, that was certain. He sipped his brandy, savored the heat spreading from his middle. Even that heat, though, was not enough to keep him from wondering when he'd enjoy a full belly again.

After the last pancake had vanished, Emma started carrying dishes back into the kitchen. She let Yetta Korczak and Bertha Geller help, but when the *golem* started to do likewise, she stopped in her tracks and looked so scandalized that even the undead creature got the message. It sat back down; Berel's chair creaked under its weight.

He didn't let that worry him. He'd had food and drink; now he lit his pipe and blew a happy cloud toward the ceiling. Then, emboldened and perhaps a trifle *shikker* from the *slivovitz*, he turned to the *golem* and said expansively, "What shall we call you, my friend?"

The moment the words were out of his mouth, he felt a fool for forgetting the thing of clay was mute. But it answered him even so: it pointed with one forefinger to the letter written on its forehead.

"Emes?" Friedman said. The *golem* nodded. Friedman raised his own forefinger, something he did only when he'd had a bit to drink. "All right then, Emes, show us some of the truth you are."

"Berel—" Jacob Korczak began. He stopped there, but Friedman could fill in what he'd meant: *Berel, shut up, you damned fool, before you ruin us all.* It was good advice; he wished he could have taken it.

Too late for that—the *golem* was nodding again. Friedman's vision suddenly blurred, or rather doubled strangely. He could still see the room in which he sat, the *golem* next to him, Korczak and Geller across the table, the children back to playing with dreidels.

But set side by side with the familiar, homely scene, he also saw other things, the *golem*'s truth he had so rashly requested. He saw Jews jammed insanely tight into a tiny corner of a great city he somehow knew to be Warsaw. He saw Germans smirking as they clipped Jews' beards, more Germans holding their sides and howling with laughter as they dipped other beards into oil and set them ablaze. He saw twelve-year-old girls selling their bodies for half a crust of bread. He saw the starved corpses of others who perhaps had not sold themselves enough, leaning dismally against battered buildings. He saw Jews walk by the corpses without even glancing at them, as though they'd grown numb even to death.

As if at the cinema, the scene shifted. He saw a big pit gouged out of the ground. Under German guns, a line of naked people walked up to the edge of the pit. All the men and boys among them were circumcised. The Germans shot them from behind. They tumbled into their ready-made mass grave. The Germans led up another line.

The scene shifted again. He saw a wrought-iron gate, and above it, in letters of iron, the words AR-BEIT MACHT FREI. He saw more naked people, these mostly women and children, slowly walking toward a low, squat building. Signs in Yiddish, Polish, and German said TO THE SHOWERS. He saw end-less piles of bodies fed into what looked like enormous bake ovens. He saw black, greasy smoke rise from the stacks above those ovens.

Slowly, slowly, the other seeing faded. He was alto-gether back in his own warm room in his own little house. But a chill remained, a chill in his heart no fireplace could touch. He looked across the table to his friends. Both men were pale and stunned and look-ing at him. They'd shared the vision, then.

He looked at the *golem,* hating it. If it had given him the truth, how much more comforting a lie, any lie, would have been! He'd looked into the open grave of his people. What man could do that and then go on as if he'd seen nothing? He hated himself, too, for asking the undead creature into his home.

While he berated himself, simple, practical Isaac Geller said, "If that's how it's going to be, what do we do about it?" Having less imagination than either Friedman or Korczak, he yielded less readily to horror.

"Dear God, what can we do?" Korczak said. But Geller had not asked him; he'd spoken to the *golem*.

That second sight returned, this time blurrily, as if the thing of clay presented not truth but only possibility. In fragmented visions, Friedman saw the Jews of Puck walking down the main street of town, saw them approaching a fishing boat, saw them in the boat with sea all around. The compass showed they were sailing northwest.

Again he was back only at his own table. "That's *meshuggeh!*" he cried. "The Germans would shoot us for breaking curfew. Nobody among us knows how to run a fishing boat, and the boats have almost no fuel anyhow. The fishermen spend more time complaining than they do fishing."

As usual, though, Isaac Geller looked at things differently. He asked the *golem*, "What happens if we don't try, Emes?"

Friedman saw that wrought-iron gate again. He shuddered, though the vision lasted but a split second. Set against what lay beyond that gate, any risk at all seemed worth trying. He found his own question for the *golem*: "You'll help us?"

The undead creature nodded. That was enough to satisfy Friedman. He twisted in his chair, called into the kitchen. "Emma!"

"What is it?" She stood in the doorway, the sleeves of her dress rolled up past her elbows, soapy water dripping from her fingers onto the floor. "What is it that won't wait till I finish washing?"

Our lives, he thought. But that would have taken explanation and argument. He just said, "Get coats for the children and for yourself, too. We're going out."

"What?" Her eyes went wide. "The curfew, the Nazis—"

"I don't care," he said, and her eyes went wider still. He turned to the *golem.* "Show her too, Emes. She needs to see."

He never figured out precisely what the thing of clay showed his wife, but she gasped and put a hand to her mouth. Without a word, she walked over to the closet and pulled out coats. "Come here this instant, Rachel, Aaron! This instant, do you hear me? We need to dress warmly."

Yetta Korczak and Bertha Geller came out of the kitchen to find out what was going on. Like Emma, they started to protest when they learned they'd be out and about in the night. Then the *golem* looked at each of them in turn, mud-colored eyes somber in his great ugly face. Argument was cut off as abruptly as a chicken's head when the *shochet* wielded his cleaver. Friedman wondered if he could learn that trick himself. But no, it was probably supernatural.

A few minutes later, he stood outside his home. Even wrapped in his coat, he was cold. The *golem* started down the street, toward the docks. The three families of Jews followed. Friedman looked back at the house where he'd lived his whole life. To abandon it suddenly seemed insane. But even more insane were the visions Emes had granted him. Life away from everything he'd known would be strange and hard, but it would be life, for him and his children. Even without the *golem*'s power, he saw again in his mind's eye naked Jews standing at the mouth of their ready-dug grave.

The main street was almost eerily quiet. Nothing moved—no cars, no bicycles, no people on foot. The town of Puck might have been cast headlong into the strange space from which the *golem* drew its visions. Berel Friedman shook his head. The Germans had powers of their own, chief among them fear.

Every step he took seemed to echo from the houses, from the solid stone front of the Catholic church that was much the biggest building in town. Every time one of the children coughed or stumbled or complained, he expected a division of panzer troops to burst from an alley, engines bellowing, cannon and machine guns all pointed straight at him and his. But the silence held.

Puck was anything but a big city; even the main street, the one straight street it boasted, was only a couple of hundred meters long. Soon most of the houses were behind the Jews, the dockside fish market straight ahead. Hope rose in Friedman. The *golem*, after all, was a creature of might. No doubt its spell lay on the Germans, lulling them into taking no notice of the families it was spiriting away.

He had no doubt—until the German patrol came out of the market, heading back toward town. Then fear flooded into him, all the more fiercely for having been held at bay. His legs turned to jelly, his bowels to water. He started to gasp out the *Shma yisroayl* so he would not die with the prayer unsaid: "Hear, O Israel, the Lord our God, the Lord is one!"

Even as the harsh cry of *"Halt!"* rang in the air, the *golem* ran straight for the Germans. They were not first-quality troops: who would waste such on a fleabag town like Puck? They were not expecting trouble, so their reactions were slower than they might have been. But they were soldiers, and they did carry guns. Before the *golem* reached them, a couple flung Mausers to their shoulders and started shooting.

Amidst screams from the women and children, Friedman's head filled with a sudden urgent vision: the *Pilsudski*, Tadeusz Czuma's fishing boat. As usual, it was the one moored farthest north in the little harbor. "This way!" he shouted, and the rest of the Jews followed—incidentally, he thought some time later, taking themselves out of the line of fire.

Muzzle flashes from the Germans' rifles gave them flickering light, like small lightning bolts, as they ran. Bullets slapped into the *golem*, one, two, three. The impacts were shockingly loud. A man would have been down and dead, maybe cut in two, with such wounds in him. But the thing of clay had never been alive, so how could rifle fire kill it?

All the Germans were shouting, in terror now, as their prey refused to fall. Then the *golem* was among them. It might not have been alive, but it was immensely strong. Its great fists smashed ribs, caved in steel helmets and the skulls beneath them. The Germans' shouts turned to screams that shut off one by one.

Friedman leapt from the pier down into the *Pilsudski*, then whirled to catch his wife and children as they sprang after him. Korczak and Geller were doing the same for their families. Faster than he could have imagined, everyone was on board. Only then did he remember he hadn't the faintest idea how to sail the fishing boat.

Isaac Geller was already in the cabin. "Cast off the lines, you two," he called to Friedman and Korczak. Friedman dashed to the bow, Korczak to the stern. By the time they'd obeyed, Geller had the noisy old engine going.

Booted footsteps pounded toward the fishing boat—the last German soldier, running for his life. Behind him came the *golem*, gaining with every enormous stride. The German whirled round in desperation, dropped to one knee, and fired at point-blank range straight into the *golem*'s face.

Maybe he'd intended to hit it between the eyes. Friedman knew even less about matters military than he did about sailing, but he had a vague idea that was what you were supposed to do. If it *was* what the German had in mind, he didn't quite succeed. The muzzle flash showed that his bullet smashed into the *golem*'s forehead just above its left eye.

In so doing, it destroyed the letter *aleph*, the first letter of the word *emes*. *Mes* was also a word in Hebrew; it meant *death*. Just as a man would have, the *golem* ceased when that bullet struck it. But its heavy body smashed into the kneeling German just the same. Friedman heard bones snap; the soldier's last cry abruptly cut off. Two corpses lay unmoving a few meters from the *Pilsudski*.

The racket from the fishing boat's engine got louder. The boat pulled away from the dock. Friedman had hardly ever been on the water despite a lifetime by the sea, and wondered if he'd be seasick. For now, he didn't think so. The motion wasn't that unpleasant; it reminded him of bouncing up and down on the back of a mule.

He went into the cabin to see if he could do anything to help Isaac Geller. Geller didn't seem to need help. Despite long black coat and big black hat, he looked surprisingly nautical. Maybe it was the cigar he'd stuck in the corner of his mouth.

"I didn't know you could handle a boat," Friedman said.

The cigar twitched. Geller grunted. "I may not be

much for *pilpul* about the Talmud, Berel my friend, but give me something with a motor in it and I will make it work."

"This is also a *mitzvah*," Friedman said, adding, "especially now." He looked around the cabin. Once he'd seen it, he couldn't imagine what sort of help he'd thought to give Geller. For all he could make of the instruments, they might have been printed in Chinese. The only thing he recognized was the compass. He studied that for a while, then said hesitantly, "Excuse me, Isaac, but are we not sailing south and east?"

"Yes," Geller said. *"Nu?"*

"In the vision Emes granted us, were we not supposed to go northwest?"

Geller laughed so hard, the cigar jerked up and down in his mouth. "Berel, not even the help of a *golem* will make this boat sail across the dry land of the Hela Peninsula."

"Oh," Friedman said in a very small voice.

"Let me get around the peninsula before I make for Sweden," Geller went on, "not that we have much real chance of getting there."

"What? Why not?"

Geller poked a finger at one of the incomprehensible gauges. "You see how much fuel we have there. It isn't enough. It isn't nearly enough. God only knows what will happen when it's gone. I'm sure of only one thing: whatever it is, it will be better than what the *golem* showed us."

"Yes," Friedman said. "Oh, yes."

He went out on deck. Emma came rushing up to him. "Will it be all right, Berel?" she demanded fiercely. "Will the children get away from—that?"

He still didn't know what the *golem* had showed her. He didn't want to know; Emes had shown him too much for him to want to find out more. He shook his head, blew out a long sigh. "I just don't know, Emma," he answered, thinking first of the fuel gauge Geller had shown him and then of what his friend had just said. "But whatever we find on the sea, how can it be worse?"

His wife nodded. "This is true enough."

Friedman walked over to Jacob Korczak, who was watching the low, flat coast of the Hela Peninsula flow by. Every few kilometers, lights defined the land: though there was a war on, no British or French planes could reach Poland, and as for Russia—Russia had helped Hitler carve up his neighbor. So the lights kept burning.

Korczak might have been reading Friedman's mind: "With the kind of pilot Isaac is liable to be, he'll need all the help he can get."

"He's better than either of us," Friedman answered, to which Korczak replied with a cough. After a moment, Berel went on, "I had thought—I had hoped—the *golem* might save more of our people before it met its fate. For a moment, I had even hoped it might save all our people. For what other purpose could it have been made?"

"I asked myself this very question." By his slightly smug tone, Korczak had come up with an answer, too. "My thinking is this: the *golem* is a power in the world, not so?"

"Indeed," Friedman said, nodding vigorously. "A very great power. This is why I hoped it might accomplish more than freeing us alone—not that I am not grateful to the Lord for preserving us, but what are we among so many?" He had another queasy flash of memory from the *golem*'s vision. That camp with ARBEIT MACHT FREI on the gate had been *huge*— and were there more like it?

"The *golem* is a power," Korczak repeated. "But— the Germans, are they not also a power? Ten years ago, who had heard of that *mamzer* Hitler? And when power meets power, who that is not a power can say which of them will break?"

Friedman thought it over. "Whether this is *the* answer, Jacob, I cannot say: *I* am no power, as we both know. But *an* answer you definitely have, one good enough for mortal men. I will say *kaddish* for Emes on his *yortzeit* each year."

"And I," Korczak agreed. He returned to more immediate matters. "Does Isaac truly know enough to keep from drowning us?"

"I think he may." Friedman hesitated, then told his friend what he had not mentioned to his wife: "He says we are low on fuel."

"*Oy.*"

Since that one word summed things up as well as anything Friedman could say, he kept quiet. The *Pilsudski* passed another light. Emma found some grimy wool blankets. She and the other mothers wrapped the children in them. Before long, in spite of the terrifying excitement of the day—maybe even because of it— the youngsters fell asleep.

Another light, this one higher and brighter than any of the rest. In its blue-white glare, Friedman saw that the long spit of the Hela Peninsula had ceased. Isaac Geller saw that, too. The fishing boat heeled in the water as it changed course. *Northwest now*, Friedman thought, and remembered what the *golem* had revealed to him.

Northwest now, but for how long? He had to know. He went into the cabin, waited for Geller to notice him—who could say how complicated steering a boat was? After a while, Geller turned his head. Feeling as if he were asking a rabbi to explicate a thorny passage of the Talmud, Friedman said, "How do we stand for fuel?"

Geller scowled. "Not very well. I think the gauge is broken. It's scarcely changed from when we set out."

"That may be good news," Friedman said. He was looking for good news. "Maybe it lies when it says we have only a little. Maybe we have a great deal."

"We don't," Geller said flatly. "When I saw the gauge seemed stuck, I put a stick down into the tank to find out how much it held. What the stick says comes near enough to agreeing with what the gauge says."

"Then—" Friedman quavered.

"Yes, then," Geller agreed. "Then we will run out of fuel and the boat will stop. If God is kind, a Swedish ship or a Danish one or even a Russian one will find us and pick us up. If God is less kind, no one will pick us up and we will die. If God is most unkind, a German ship will find us."

"A German ship." Friedman hadn't thought of that. Geller was right—it would be most dreadful to come so close to freedom only to have it snatched away by a ship flying the swastika banner. "Surely God would not permit it."

"After what the *golem* showed us, Berel, who are we to say what God would and would not permit?"

"How can I answer that? How can anyone answer that?" Friedman left the cabin; between them, the rolling of the boat in the open sea and the stink of Geller's cigar were making his stomach churn. So was worry. Back in Puck, running had seemed the only possible thing to do. Now when it was too late, he wondered whether running had been wise.

The last lighthouse faded astern. Friedman cast himself into the hands of God—not that he hadn't been in them all along, but now he abandoned the usual human feeling that he had some control over his own fate. Whatever would happen would happen, and there was nothing he could do about it.

The fishing boat chugged along. After a while, a thick, clammy bank of fog rolled over it. It left damp droplets in the tendrils of Friedman's beard. When he held his hand out at arm's length, he could not see it. Maybe God was stretching His hand over the *Pilsudski*. No German ship would ever find them in this soup. Of course, no Swedish or Danish or Russian ship would, either.

Of course, likeliest of all was that no ship of any nation would come anywhere near. The Baltic Sea all around had seemed incomprehensibly vast, as if the fishing boat were traveling the darks of space between the stars. Somehow the fog intensified the effect rather than diminishing it.

And then, from out of nowhere, felt and heard rather than seen through the mist, a huge shape, vaster than the great fish that had swallowed Jonah, flowed blindly past the bow of the boat. From the cabin came Isaac Geller's startled exclamation: *"Gevalt!"* Friedman had not even the wit for that. He waited, heart in his throat, for the brusque hail that might mean rescue or disaster. No hail came. The big ship sailed away, intent solely on it own concerns.

Friedman said, "That was close."

From out of the fog somewhere close by Jacob Korczak answered, "That was very close." He called to Geller, "How are we doing for fuel?"

"I'll check," Geller said from out of the pale, milky smudge that marked the cabin's place. After a pause, he went on, "We still have—about what we set out with." He sounded surprised, but far from displeased.

"How could we?" Korczak demanded. "We set out quite a while ago, so surely we've burned some."

"You'd think so, wouldn't you?" Geller said. "I'd think so, too. But the gauge doesn't think so, and the stick doesn't think so, either. The gauge may be mistaken. How the stick could be mistaken, I tell you I do not see."

"It makes no sense," Korczak complained. "Fuel burns, it burns just so fast. When so much time is gone, so is the fuel."

"Tell it to my stick," Geller said. Korczak subsided with a wounded sniff.

Northwest, northwest, northwest . . . Friedman hoped it was northwest, hoped Geller was minding the compass. For all he could tell, the *Pilsudski* might have been sailing in circles. He recognized Emma's footsteps on the deck before she came close enough to be seen. "Berel, are you here?" she called. "Oh, you are here. Good. Look—I found more blankets."

"Thank you." He took one and draped it over his shoulders like a huge prayer shawl. It smelled of wool and stale tobacco and even staler sweat; Friedman's opinion of Tadeusz Czuma's cleanliness, already low, fell another notch. Emma was already swaddled against the chill and fog. He turned to her. "You ought to sleep if you can."

"So should you," she retorted. He nodded; he knew she was right. Neither of them lay down. She moved a step closer to him, lowered her voice. "Berel . . . is it going to be all right? Why is Geller going on about how much fuel we have?" He heard the undercurrent of reproach in her voice: *Why didn't you tell me about this?*

He answered the undercurrent, not the question: "I didn't want to worry you."

She amazed him by starting to laugh. "I had a *golem* come into my living room, I ran from the house where I lived since I was married to you and the town where

I lived all my life, German soldiers shot at me and I watched them die, and you didn't want to worry me about *fuel?*"

"All right, all right." He started laughing, too; looked at from that direction, it was funny. But his self-conscious chuckles quickly faded. "The trouble with the fuel is, we don't have much."

"We've come this far," Emma said.

"Already it's farther than Geller thought we could."

"If it's already farther, then what does Geller know?" she said, and nodded decisively, as if she'd just won a subtle point of logic. "We'll sail as far as we'll sail, and, please God, it will be far enough."

"All right, Emma," Friedman repeated. Oddly, her reasoning reassured him. If he was in God's hands, then God would take care of things. And if God would take care of things, then Berel Friedman didn't need to stay awake to watch. He redraped the blanket so it covered all of him. "Maybe I will try and rest."

"This is sensible," Emma agreed. They stretched out side by side on the hard planks of the deck. He took off his hat and gave it to her for a pillow. She shook her head. "I'll ruin it."

"If everything turns out all right, I can get another hat. And if everything does not turn out all right, what difference will a ruined hat make?"

She put it under her head. "Sleep well, Berel."

"And you."

He didn't think he would sleep at all, let alone well. But when his eyes opened, the black mist surrounding the *Pilsudski* had turned gray. His neck, his back, his legs were stiff; everything crackled like breaking ice as he painfully got to his feet.

The children were already awake. They'd adapted to life on the fishing boat faster than their parents; they sat in a circle round a spinning dreidel one of them must have stuffed into a pocket when they fled the house. *"Gimel!"* Friedman's daughter Rachel shouted. She couldn't read, but she knew her Yiddish letters, and they sprang from the Hebrew ones. She knew something else, too: "I win!"

Smiling, Friedman stepped around the game. In the cabin, Isaac Geller still stood at the wheel. His face was as gray as the fog all round him, gray with fatigue. The cigar in his mouth had gone out; Friedman didn't think he'd noticed. But he steered on.

Friedman said, "The fuel hasn't run out, I see."

Geller jerked violently; he'd forgotten everything but the wheel, the compass, and the window that barely showed him the boat's bow. "Oh, it's you, Berel," he said, as if reminding himself. "No, the fuel hasn't run out. As God knows why; I've given up trying to figure it out." He sounded indignant; maybe he held Friedman responsible for the engine's still chugging along, or maybe his friend just made an easier target than the Lord.

Outside in the mist, Rachel Friedman squealed, "Another *gimel*! I win again!"

"If she keeps on like that, she'll end up owning this boat," Friedman said, hoping the feeble joke would help keep Geller alert and ease his burden. He went on, "The little one, she's always been lucky with a dreidel. I remember once when she—"

He stopped. Thinking about dreidels made him think about the letters on them, about what those letters stood for, and about the nature of the miracle they commemorated.

"You remember when she what?" Geller snapped. "Don't just stand there like a cow, with your mouth hanging open. Say something if you're going to talk. Otherwise, go away."

"Isaac, last night was the first night of Hanukkah," Friedman said softly.

"Nu?" Geller said: "So what? I take it back. You shouldn't talk if you're going to wander all over creation and confuse me."

"I'm sorry," Friedman said, bowing his head. "I just thought to wonder whether God, who made one day's worth of pure oil burn for eight days in the Temple, might not let a tiny bit of fuel take a few of His people farther than anyone would guess? You said to ask God why it hadn't run out. I think I just have. On that night, with what happened that night . . . what do you think, Isaac my friend?"

Geller slowly turned his head. Now his mouth fell open. The dead cigar fell out. He nodded, once, twice, his eyes wide. Then he gave his attention back to the *Pilsudski.*

Less than a minute later, the fishing boat came out of the fog bank. All at once, the winter sun sparkled off the ocean, cold and bright and clear. Ahead—not far—lay the Swedish coast. The engine kept running.

A WEB FOR CHRISTMAS

by Karen Haber

The striped brown spiders that lived in the Ayalas' blue-walled adobe house in the village of Itagua were fat-bellied, fond of gossip, and very, very smug.

And why not? They had a good life, spinning their webs in the corners of rooms and windows, feasting upon plump flies and other insects that buzzed in the kitchen and throughout the house. Rosa, the wife, rarely disturbed them, and for this they were grateful, taking special care to protect Rosa's children, Pilar and Ignacio, from marauding mosquitoes that whined above their coverlets, above tender exposed ankles and wrists, in the night.

In truth, Rosa's sewing business kept her so busy that she had little time for housekeeping. The children were too young to help much, and Rosa's husband Antonio worked the fields for the rich landowner Jose Rodriguez Flores. At the end of the day, Antonio was exhausted and often fell asleep without bothering to remove his boots. Rosa would unlace them when she came to bed, many hours later.

So the spiders flourished through benign neglect rather than any sort of deliberate altruism on Rosa's part. The spiders didn't know the reason for their cozy existence. They were merely appreciative.

They kept Rosa company, although she rarely acknowledged them, as she sat up late into the night making her neat stitches, sealing seams, shortening skirts, mending holes in the knees of pants. They listened to Rosa's sighs, to her prayers, and, occasionally, to her sobs.

"Pobrecita," said Carmen, the oldest and largest of the spiders. "She works hard, so very hard. And everything for the children."

"What else? Of course, everything for the children," said Juana tartly. "We are the same, are we not?"

"How many children have you, Carmen?" asked the second-oldest spider, Angelita.

"By now? Counting all the daughters of my daughters? Over a thousand. Who can say? They come, they go. That is the way of it."

If Rosa had overheard the spiders' conversation, it would have sounded to her like twigs rubbing one against the other in a high wind. But the voices of spiders are very high and very faint, and scarcely any adults are able to hear them, much less understand what they are saying.

Occasionally the children in their play heard the sounds the spiders made. But they never understood the meaning of them. And Antonio rarely noticed anything except whether or not his dinner was ready.

It would be Christmas in another month. Soon they would be hanging the bright red blossoms of the flame tree on the doors; soon they would be stringing the colorful cut-paper garlands and wreaths of aromatic cassia blooms above the hearths; soon the pan dulce and corn bread would be bubbling in the ovens, scenting the air with holiday aromas. The nights would be punctuated by the pop of firecrackers, the hiss of sparklers.

And in her tiny cottage Rosa Ayala was constantly busy sewing Christmas finery for her neighbors, working well past midnight, bent over the sewing table as she stitched lace to the hem of a fine linen christening gown, fixing pleats and darts in a silky taffeta blouse. Her fingers, red and callused from the needles, flew over the fabric. To protect her skin from the fine lines around the eyes that came with squinting in the lantern's light she rubbed butter over the lids until Antonio began to complain that she smelled like a dairy. Then she stopped applying the butter at night, using it only in the morning, after he had left for work. Rosa had sent the children to stay with their Barraca cousins on the other side of town so that her every hour could be spent at the sewing table. With the money she made she would be able to buy Ignacio the hard laced leather ball he had been begging for, a pair of good shoes for Pilar, a sweater for Antonio, and perhaps even a little something to put in the stewpot. It would be a fine Christmas, indeed.

The spring storms of November set a steady rhythm against the tile roof as Rosa stitched and cut and stitched: plink plink plonk, plink plink plonk. She was huddled over a complicated bundle of red silk ruffles and purple velvet. Now and then she would glance up at the clock, purse her lips, look down again. And in their corner, snug in their intricate webs, the spiders watched Rosa's fingers dance over her work. Outside the wind howled, rattling the roof tiles.

"Where is Antonio?" asked Carmen the spider. "He is usually home by now."

"And to labor on such a dreadful wet day." Angelita made a tch of sympathy. "What can that Rodriguez Flores want him to do in the rain?"

"They need the money," Juana reminded her. "Always, always the guaranis. Really, it is a shame they are not spiders. Then all they would need to worry about would be catching enough food."

Carmen was about to make a wise observation concerning the unfortunate clumsiness of humans when there came a frantic pounding on the front door.

"Antonio?" Rosa called.

"Silly," Angelita said in her high spider voice. "Why would he bother to knock?"

The door burst open, and two burly men in dripping clothing backed into the room. Between them was a sodden sack, quite peculiar, for it was wearing the leather jacket that belonged to Antonio.

"Mother of God!" Rosa cried. "Antonio! What has happened to my husband?"

The men set the sack down on the table with such force that the floorboards creaked. The spiders rocked back and forth in their webs. And now they could see that it was not a sack at all that was lying on the table. It was Antonio: He was dripping wet, his eyes were closed, and there was a livid bruise on his throat.

"Senora Ayala?" said the shorter man. "I am so sorry." He shrugged helplessly. "Senora, we did not know where to bring him and Carlos here said we would do best to take him home."

Rosa's face was white as milk and her eyes burned darkly in their sockets. She gripped a piece of purple velvet, twisting and tearing the cloth as she stared at Antonio.

"How did it happen?"

"A storm surge," said the one named Carlos. "The Paraguay swarmed over its banks, picked up a Lapacho tree, and threw it right at Antonio. He became tangled by the roots and the water covered him. We tried to pull him free, but we were too late."

"No," Rosa said. Tears glimmered in her eyes, overflowed, and swept down her cheeks. "Oh, no, Antonio. No. No. No." She fell, weeping, upon her husband's chest.

"We have asked Father Ramon to come," said the one whose name was not Carlos. "He will be here soon."

"A terrible accident," Carlos said apologetically, as he and his friend backed slowly out the door. "Terrible. A great misfortune."

The priest came, dressed in black. He put down his black umbrella and sat beside Rosa, wringing his hands.

"A tragedy," Father Ramon said. "An utter tragedy. God must have work for him to do. God always has his reasons."

"That is fine for God, but what am I going to do?" Rosa said, sobbing. "And the children? How will we survive without Antonio? Without his income?"

"God will provide," the priest intoned in his Sunday voice. "He always does."

After Father Ramon had prayed a bit, he left and Rosa's neighbors came, shyly, silently, by twos and by threes, to help her prepare the body. Itagua was a tiny place, and all news, bad or good, was quick to pass through it.

Soon Antonio was clean, dry, and dressed in his best suit, the gray one with the fewest patches. The next door family offered to stay, but Rosa said no, she would see them tomorrow night, at the wake, and they seemed relieved to leave.

When she was alone, Rosa wept again. "Thank God the children will not see him until tomorrow," she whispered. "Somehow I must ease the terrible shock of it for them. Somehow, at the wake." And, still weeping, she slowly made her way to bed and cried herself to sleep.

"Oh, pobrecita. Pobrecita Rosa," Carmen whispered.

"Could they be wrong?" Juana asked. "He just looks asleep to me."

"Well, he looks dead to me," Angelita said. "You can always tell with humans."

"That's not true," Juana said hotly. "Remember the time the etranjera with the hair orange-like-a-mango sat down outside in the sun and fell asleep? Well, I thought she was dead and I wanted to get around her to the other side of the wall where a juicy grub was waiting. Since she was dead anyway I thought it would be all right to crawl over her face. Dios mio! She let out a shriek and began slapping—thank the Goddess these humans are so clumsy or I might not be here now to tell you this. I almost missed that grub."

"Nevertheless," Carmen said. "Antonio is definitely dead. And we must do something for poor, dear Rosa."

"What do you suggest?" Angelita said. "If we were poisonous, at least we could sting Rosa and send her to join her loved one in the afterworld."

Carmen flexed a red, multifaceted eye at her. "A good thing we can't, too. If we dispatched Rosa out of sympathy, who would take care of the children?"

"Well, we could sting them, too."

Carmen looked as disgusted as it was possible for a spider to look "No, no, no! That is not a solution. That is absolutely not a solution."

"Well, it makes no difference," Juana said. "As Angelita has pointed out, we are not poisonous."

"Hush," said Carmen. "Let me think. I have an idea. Yes. I know what to do. I will pray to the Goddess for guidance."

"The Goddess?" Angelita said. "Invoking the spirit of the sacred Arachne for a human?"

"Be silent unless you want to help me."

Angelita grumbled for moment. Finally, she fell silent in her web.

Carmen raised her two front legs, waving them gently before her. "Arachne," she chanted. "Oh, mother of us all, great weaver, come to us. Come! Come!

"Your daughters beseech you, wise one, old one, wisest of all spiders, cunning huntress, come to us now. Come! Come to us and help us."

There was the sound of logs popping on a hearth. A small flame sprang to life in midair, glowing red and yellow, blue and green. It was a slender flame that gave no heat but grew and grew until it had engulfed the very room. And at its center the elongated shape of an extraordinary spider could be seen glowing white and gold. It was a spider with long, graceful legs, a shapely rounded body, and her eight amber, multifaceted eyes gleamed with the wisdom of the ages. Carmen and the others had never seen such a beautiful spider.

"Why have you summoned me, daughters?" Her voice was low, thrilling.

"Great one, we would ease a human's pain," Carmen said.

"A human?" Arachne laughed. "But why trouble yourself with their problems? Certainly they have never had a care for any of ours."

"Goddess, this one has been good to us," Carmen replied. "We have flourished in her benevolence. Now her husband has been killed. She sorrows greatly. What can we do for her?"

Arachne was silent for a moment. Then she rubbed two of her feet together thoughtfully. "You insist on helping her?"

"Please, yes."

"You are absolutely certain?"

All three spiders nodded.

"Then listen carefully, my daughters, and I will tell you how to do the very thing that will help to ease the sorrow of this human of yours."

And the spiders gathered close around their goddess and she told them what needed to be done. When she had gone, Carmen and Juana and Angelita summoned their daughters and their daughters' daughters to them by a secret spider signal, and told them all what the Goddess had said. And then they set to work.

They worked all through that long night and well into the dawn.

"Hurry," Carmen whispered. "Rosa will awaken soon."

"I'm so tired," said Maria, Juana's daughter, a white-bodied spider with slender brown legs. "Mother, can't I rest for just a moment?"

"Lazy one," Juana snapped. "Stay awake a little longer and finish what you have started. Your webs were always half-done."

"Hsst!" Angelita cried. "Be quick. I hear her stirring."

Footfalls shook the floorboards as Rosa got out of bed. The spiders scattered to the four corners of the room, out of sight, safely hidden.

Rosa crept into the room, her head bowed with grief. With heavy hands she pushed the wooden shutters open, and a bright flood of sunlight streamed in, spread across the room, and caught the figure of Antonio lying on the table. He seemed to be covered in shimmering liquid silver.

"What?" Rosa whispered. "What is that?"

From head to toe Antonio was covered in a mantle of finest spiderweb which seemed to glow with hidden lights. Delicate whorls and lines billowed into the air, caught the sun's light, and radiated it along thousands of silken strands.

Rosa burst into tears at the sight of it. "Oh," she said. "It's so beautiful. So very beautiful. A sign from God. Everyone must see it. Everyone! But how? If I move my Antonio even an inch the web will rip and be gone." She pondered the problem for a moment. "No, I will copy it in the best silk thread and he will be buried in spiderweb lace. In God's grace."

She leaned close over the webbing, studying the pattern of whorls, tracing it with her fingers in the air, learning its complex connections, its deft trickery, all its secrets. She stepped back, squinted, nodded.

Like a woman possessed by the very spirit of the Goddess Arachne herself, Rosa grabbed up her thinnest needles, her finest threads, and began to follow the delicate tracery of the spiders' work. All morning she worked. At midday, there was a knock at the door. Rosa ignored the sound and continued to toil at her careful stitching. By dusk, the work was finished. She stood back to admire it and nodded. Then she hurried into the bedroom to wash and change for the wake.

"Oh, mucho gusto," Juana said.

"I can't imagine a human doing better work," Angelita added.

"She's pleased, so pleased," Carmen said. "Well done, sisters, and thank the Goddess. We have made Rosa happy."

First to arrive for the wake was the priest, Father Ramon. He gasped as he saw the beautiful shroud Rosa had fashioned. "Bonita," he whispered, and tears came to his eyes as he listened to Rosa's tale. "Truly you have made a masterpiece, Rosa. I would wear such lace as my vestments."

"Then, Father, I shall make you some for Antonio's funeral," Rosa replied proudly.

Her children came next, shepherded by anxious cousins. "Papa," Pilar cried. Ignacio said nothing but stood beside his sister, lip trembling.

"Is this not beautiful, children?" the priest said.

"Your mother has done tribute to your father, and to God. Never have I seen such beauty come from needle and thread. Truly blessed is her skill."

Now the children moved closer to the table, their dark eyes shining, and exclaimed in wonder over the delicate shroud. "Mama, you made this? Mama, how pretty. Did you spin it?" They were laughing and crying, all at the same time. Rosa put her arms around them, pulled their dark heads against her breast, and kissed each of them on the forehead.

And quickly the house filled with friends and neighbors bringing roasted meats, boiled mandioca root, empanadas, sweet cheese, honey cakes, and egg custard. Together they sang and laughed and cried long into the night. And before the wake was over, Rosa had taken seventy orders for her spiderweb lace. She did not know how she would finish everything by Christmas. But somehow, she did. By the time the clay crèche had been set in the window and the onions for the sopa paraguaya had been fried in lard, Rosa had finished all her work for the year. Ignacio received his baseball, Pilar got her black leather shoes, and Rosa had bought herself a new coat. The rest went into the stewpot, with a little left over.

* * *

Christmas was over, New Year's Day had come and gone, and even the chickens for the feast of the Three Kings had been cooked, eaten, and the bones swept away. But the demand for Rosa's spiderweb lace continued unabated. She taught Pilar and even Ignacio how to do the delicate stitchwork and they sat beside her, toiling away. Eventually that was not enough and Rosa hired two giggly young women who were friends of Pilar's and, despite their giddiness, good with a needle and thread. Soon every available space, every tabletop, dresser, and bed, was overflowing with lace.

When, in February, Hugo Romero died and his wife, Estrellita, closed their butcher shop, Rosa rented it, spent a week scouring and sweeping, and hired Estrellita to work there selling lace. Noisy buses filled with tourists and belching diesel fumes began to lumber down the dusty clay road from Asuncion, to stop, brakes wheezing, outside Rosa's shop. The tourists with their sunglasses and cameras and handbags were like locusts. They would buy and buy and buy, emptying the shelves. Soon Rosa bought the shop, stopped paying rent, and hired Estrellita's daughters, Josefina and Maria, as well.

Rosa's hallmark was a small graceful spider sitting, hidden, in a corner of her designs. It became a local tradition to try and find the spider in the lace, but this was not always easy, especially as Rosa developed new patterns, incorporating the life-giving sun, the abundant corn, the cascading coco bloom, and the four-petaled guyaba flower into her work. Very quickly the term nanduti—spiderweb—lace became synonymous with Itagua, and Rosa Ayala.

At the end of March, as Autumn winds blew and the Itaguans prepared for the procession of the Virgin de la Candelaria, Rosa packed up her needles, her threads, her pots and her patterns, and moved across town. Her lacework had earned her a large house where there was plenty of room to work, and a walled garden in which her children could play. Rosa even hired a maid. But she never allowed her, or anyone else, to disturb a spider's web or to hurt any spider, anywhere.

Carmen, Angelita, and Juana missed Rosa and her children. They were growing old now, and feeble. But they still met daily to reminisce.

"Humans are fickle," Juana said.

"They come and go," said Angelita.

Carmen nodded. "That is the way of it. And why not? We are much alike, humans and spiders." And she settled down to dine upon a fat mosquito which she had saved from yesterday for her procession day feast. Mosquitoes were always better the next day.

BABE AND THE CHRISTMAS TREE

by Lawrence Schimel

This is a story Lars Larsen's grandson told me about Paul Bunyan's great blue ox, Babe. It took place five or six years after the Winter of Blue Snow when they were camped up in Maine, and the weather turned so cold that the Great Lakes froze up solid through, and Paul could just pick them up and move them around. But the worst of it that winter was the snow, the unending snow, and all of it as blue as indigo.

Now Babe was also this color blue, but he was an extraordinary ox and the loggermen all loved him, for he was powerfully strong and worked hard, performing feats that a thousand oxen couldn't have done. But the blue snow, the unending blue snow, really got their spirits down, and Paul decided he would go and find the men some white snow to cheer them up. So he set out, and a few strides brought him to the Mississippi River, where he had hoped the snow on the other side would be white. But it was just as blue as it was on his side, blue like a summer sky, or one of Babe's big round eyes. So Paul kept going West, and a few more strides brought him to the Pacific, but nowhere could he find anything but blue snow. He had to go all the way to China to find some white snow (for only white snow has ever fallen in

China) and he brought back a great armful of it to the camp and gave a white snowball to each of the men for Christmas.

This story that Lars Larsen's grandson told me also happened around Christmastime, but it took place a few years after the Winter of the Blue Snow, when they had their logging camp set up in Michigan. Lars Larsen was the foreman of the camp at the time, and one day Paul came up to him asking if he'd seen Babe anywhere abouts. Thinking about it for a moment, Lars realized that he hadn't, and began asking around the camp if anyone had. Babe was known for his enormous appetite, but it seemed from what the cook said that he hadn't shown up at breakfast, even though the cook had made fifty stacks of flapjacks special for the great blue ox. No one had seen him since last night, and nowhere could he be found around the camp.

Now in case you don't know, I'll tell you a bit more about Babe. There are some who say Babe was twenty-four ax handles and a plug of chewing tobacco between the horns, others who say it was forty-two ax handles (and a plug of chewing tobacco). Either way, Babe was so long that an ordinary man standing on his head needed a spy-glass to see what the hind legs were doing. So if he were around, someone would be sure to see him.

Paul thought Babe might be playing a game with him again, wanting Paul to go out and find him. Paul Bunyan was a brilliant tracker, being able to follow any tracks no matter how faint or how old. It's said that one day he came across the carcass of a bull moose, and having an hour or two to kill he followed its tracks back to the place it was born. He was the only man who could follow Babe's tracks, which were so far apart that an ordinary man couldn't see from one to the next to follow them.

So Paul went to Babe's barn and found the tracks right off, headed North. In two strides Paul was in Canada, where the tracks continued to point straight north. Paul climbed all the way to the top of the world, where he stood on top of the North Pole and looked around. The tracks were all scuffed up there, as if Babe had run around and around, and the earth was torn up where a giant tree had been torn out of the ground. Looking up, Paul noticed there were no stars left in this part of the sky. Paul was real curious now.

He followed Babe's tracks, which led back South (it's the only direction you can go from the North Pole!) into Canada again but taking a different route than the one Paul had followed there. The tracks led back in the direction of camp, and as Paul got nearer (just before he stepped over the Canadian border) he saw the biggest fir tree he had ever known in his life sticking up from where camp was, all decorated with thousands of shining white lights. Paul Bunyan broke into a smile as two quick strides brought him back into camp. Babe had gone out and brought back the greatest Christmas tree in the world! It was so big that it had tangled up all the stars when Babe took it down.

When Paul gave Babe a big hug for the best Christmas present he'd ever had, Babe licked him on the back of his neck (which was the only place Paul Bunyan was ticklish) and gave a great "moo" as Paul began to laugh.

OF DUST AND FIRE
AND THE NIGHT

by Barry N. Malzberg

Once again, the high star appears in the East. Sometimes there is anticipation, most of the time there is only the familiar, dull sense of obligation. Nights come and in the passage of time we perform our slow gathering, hoping that this time the plumage of the great bird will be seen. Nothing yet but then again, steadfastness and the maintenance of belief are our mission. We wait as upon a watch to morning and so forth.

So from the usual places we gather spices, herbs, fine jewels, strange and wonderful carvings, the riches of the old regime and the new; we find heirlooms of the most priceless sort to cast before the Risen One. Almost certainly it will come again to nothing, but it is our responsibility to try. Rise to fall to rise again. The others await me in the usual gathering place, my fellow regents Frankincense and Myrrh are already there and as we see one another in the darkness, we exchange greetings. "I have brought horses this time," Myrrh says. Of we three, he is the most practical, also the most gullible, which is perhaps the same thing. "No need to walk and we will get there more quickly this way." He fixes me with a steady and level gaze. "Do you think that *this* is the time?" he says. "The conditions are favorable and I have never seen the star so bright nor so perfectly formed. Perhaps our time has truly come around again."

"What is there to say?" I answer and then, because this is true, add nothing at all, make a gently dismissive gesture. Frankincense, the most cynical of us, far more despairing but less serious about the situation than I, gives me a wink from his position of concealment behind Myrrh, and in that gesture of complicity I realize truly and as if for the first time that there is no escaping this, that our mission lies again before us. "Let's get to the horses," I say. "We can worry about omens later." In the shadows behind Frank, from their places roped to the trees, the beasts whicker. "Come," I say, struggling with the bags of gifts, noting that my companions, as has been our custom, are more lightly laden, the burden of transport falling upon Myrrh, of hopelessness upon Frank, of gifts to me. "We must be on our way at once." Indeed, the star already seems to be retreating, scuttling backward in the sky. A familiar illusion of transcendence which we have noted before—an illusion of rustling, wings, of dust and fire—passes over. Groaning, I stumble with the bags, Frank and Myrrh supporting some of their weight as we stagger toward the horses.

I should note that their names are not "Frankincense" or "Myrrh" any more than the preposterous name they have for me is mine. These tags were placed upon us early in these dry adventures by Joseph, who, attendant upon Mary and the humiliations which had brought them to this circumstance, became impatient when we would not tell our true names and said, "Well, then, I'll call you *this*." And so it has gone from that point onward. Our names, as befit our rank and station in life and also the miraculous dreams which have brought us to this circumstance (the bird plunging, the feathers shriveling, the worm emerging, and then the fire, that rising fire), are secret. So are our places of origin. Be it known that the kingdoms we command are small but thrive, that the environs in which we sleep are indeed royal . . . but in these difficult and increasingly egalitarian times, we have been forced from our moats not only by dreams but by simple need. If we do not dwell incognito among the people, we might be in the castle when serious uprisings begin, or so at least Frank has explained. Less despairing than he, I suspect that our rule will continue through our lives, that it will be our sons and youngest counselors who will have to deal with the consequences, but that as so much else is beside the point.

Everything is beside the point except for the miraculous assumption which has yet to occur, but we remain as hopeful as we can, considering how many times we have lived through this. The star rises, it twinkles and beckons, in our dreaming spaces the bird of fire repents and occludes only to emerge again; our horses and gifts are later assembled. In the glade, wearing false robes and beards to conceal our controversial identity, Frank, Myrrh, and I assemble and go on our way, seeking signs and wonders. *And suddenly there was an angel*— The credulous Myrrh, the suspicious Frank, the weary but efficient scribe wearing these very robes . . . we three are compelled or so the writings would have it, to do what we can. We all have our roles even if up to this point there has been no sign, no wonder, no fiery bird, no hint of portent other than that mocking and translucent star.

And so we wander across the desert, our horses sliding in the occasional treacheries of sand, pulling at the reins, making as good a pace as they can. The camels we once used were better, but we were instructed after a recent expedition more frustrating than most that they were no longer acceptable, that they added a grotesqueness to an event which was meant to be solemn. I did not understand this, but Frank said that he did at once. "It was not so much transcendence as a good appearance which was being sought," he said. Less important than the visitation was the way that the preparations would be reported to the provinces. "Kings must be kingly, even as they simulate humility," Frank had said. "Camels must be put away. If true ships of the desert with sails and gallery sculls were possible, they would give us that." Which, however, they did not. It was Myrrh's decision the last times and this, then, to take horses and who would dispute him?

It is not Frank who speaks this time as we follow the star toward its declining point of origin. Rumors of unrest in his kingdom have come to me during this most recent interval. He seems preoccupied. It is Myrrh who is talkative, who seeks to fill the primal night with the sounds of commitment. "Don't you think he'll come this time?" Myrrh says. "I have a strong feeling that he will come. Last night, or maybe it was the night before, in the dream, I saw not only the bird but He. He was astride the bird, cresting on the path of fire. When I awoke, I had the feeling that I had seen the truth, the final vision. What do you think? Don't you think that this time he will truly be there?"

To such questions there are really no answers. Myrrh's simple credulity, his honesty, his willingness to expose himself as not only a king but a fool are the most affecting part of him and suggest that he will probably be the longest to rule, that he will outlast Frank and the rest of us who not only have internal rivals but a real weariness, a stinking, impure sense that we are after all in the service of a lie and hysterical dreams.

"If he comes, he comes," I say, "and there's nothing that we can do about this." I point to the star, now sinking in the near distance, guiding us toward the assemblage of tents and oases which merge in the sudden light, indicating that once again we have reached our point of destination. "All that we can do is bear witness."

"Oh, I don't think so," Myrrh says. "I think it's more than that. Don't you think so, Frank?"

Sensing the proximity of destination, the horses are cantering sidewise, neighing at the newly resplendent star which sinks ever more rapidly. Now there is the sound of babble from the tents, high excitement in the air. All seems distant, yet palpable. "After all," Myrrh adds, "this can't go on happening again and again in the same way. It's a preparation, a great preparation, I think. A waiting for some splendid outcome. I can feel it, I tell you, I can feel it!"

"He feels everything," Frank whispers. He brings his horse against mine, nudges the shoulders of my animal with his hand. "When was the last time that you and I could feel anything? A simple dolt, but perhaps he has secrets which will never, never be ours."

Of course, I have heard this, too. So many times we have approached this place, so many times we seem to have had this exchange. Nothing changes and yet everything does, in staticness itself is a kind of shift or at least one could argue that this is so. We come to the outskirts of the cluster of tents and crevices, stabling areas and a small pool which has been placed in the center, and we dismount, struggling with our limbs after such a long time in saddle, then tether the horses. Servants, recognizing us from the many times before and knowing our exalted position, spring forward to struggle with the bags. Myrrh waves them off. "No," he says, "we will take no help this time. We will bring them ourselves. He is risen."

"No, it isn't," Frank murmurs. "It's not our duty at all. Why does he have to be so enthusiastic, so believing? Why can't he just accept the hopelessness of it all as do we? It would be easier for all of us, then."

There is no answer for this either. I take one bag, Myrrh another, Frank, grunting, helps us along. Escorted by servants and witnesses we follow a narrow lane, move toward the stable, peer into the small, hot, bright spot at the center where the dreaming place awaits. The place seems empty although in this trickery of light it is difficult to tell.

"Here," Myrrh says, "Here we are. Make way for us. Make way for the Magi." He giggles, a high excited giggle sounding like the horses.

"Oh, the poor fool," Frank says to me, "Over and over toward the same end. Will he never learn. Will *we?* You and I, we know so little, but at least we can learn. But he, he that lamentable king—"

But he is cut off, hands are upon us, guiding us toward the light. We enter the stable and see the tableau.

And here they are, the donkeys and oxen, the tails of the oxen shifting, the attentive dumb faces of the asses fixed upon emptiness. It is as before and Frank sighs, lets that sigh fill the air, but then it is *not* as before. Something is different. In the distance a cock crows and the animals seem to gather even more tightly around that spot, a bestiary of loving attention. And then, as if from the highest place, thunders and falls the bird of fire.

Its plumage is cold with the light of stars, its beak

is shaped toward apostolic fury and it plunges toward the floor of the stable, then—as in dreams, as in all of the portents we have known—it becomes ash, a fine, glowing scattering of embers across the floor in the faces of the animals and then the fire comes high again and the ashes seem to tumble toward the resolution once again of the bird. We see, transfixed in the gaze of the dumb animals then, we see the bird of fire.

"The Magi are here," voices say. "They're here, they're here now, we're all here," and sighing, Myrrh falls to the earthen base of the stable, his arms extended. The bird sheers from the fire, soars lifelike in the air, reassembles, and sounds with the voices of angels. Frank and I do as did our companion, plunging down, sighing and adjusting ourselves, then letting the bags spill open, the gifts tumbling on the earth, the lovely and miraculous spices which we have brought like prayer to this place of the sinking star.

And the phoenix is everywhere. It is everywhere within and without us as the bestiary nods and bleats and moos, the faces of the witnesses ranged across the wall tightening in the sound of trumpets. And then, as the bird rises and falls, the fire freeing the roof and letting in the cold, lively light of the star, we clutch one another in that spilled and affectionate light. The barn brightens again, then shifts toward a dampness as if filled with a rush of tears and in the dense center of that most perfect attention, the phoenix shouting, the animals crying for deliverance, Mary and Joseph and He appear. They are grouped on and around one another, their faces torches of light in the cast fire of the Phoenix. The star did not betray us at last nor the dreams. The star is not the star of betrayal. It is the star of Ascension, of Assumption, of miracles and incense, of the prayers of children. As old Herodotus knew all those centuries before. Warm in the protecting shadow of the Phoenix, arching toward deliverance, we attend and await our transmogrification.

I'LL BE HOME FOR CHRISTMAS

by Tanya Huff

". . . yes, you'll be dressed in holiday style if you come down to Big Bob's pre-Christmas clothing sale. All the fashions, all the frills, all major credit cards accepted . . ."

"Are we there yet?"

"Soon, honey."

"How soon?"

"Soon."

"I'm gonna be sick."

Elaine Montgomery took her eyes off the road just long enough to shoot a panicked glance at her daughter's flushed face. "We're almost there, Katie. Can't you hold on just a little bit longer?"

"No!" The last letter stretched and lengthened into a wail that completely drowned out the tinny sound of the car radio and threatened to shatter glass.

As Elaine swerved the car toward the shoulder, an echoing wail rose up from the depths of the beige plastic cat carrier securely strapped down in the back seat. The last time she'd assumed Katie could hold on for the two kilometers to the next rest stop, it had taken her over an hour to clean the car—which had allowed the cat's tranquilizers to wear off long before they arrived at their destination.

Neither Katie nor the cat were very good travelers. "Mommy!"

Wet gravel spun under the tires as she fought the car and trailer to a standstill. "Just another second, honey. Grit your teeth." *How many times can you throw up one lousy cheese sandwich?* she wondered unbuckling her seatbelt and reaching for her daughter's. *Thank God she's not still in the kiddie car seat.* It had taken a good twenty minutes and an advanced engineering degree to get Katie in and out of the safety seat and all signs indicated she had closer to twenty seconds.

"It's all right, baby. Mommy's got you." She slid them both out the passenger door and went to her knees in a puddle to better steady the four-year-old's shaking body. December rain drove icy fingers down the back of her neck and, not for the first time since leaving Toronto that morning, Elaine wondered what the hell she was doing heading into the middle of nowhere with a four-year-old, a very pissed off cat, and all her worldly goods, two weeks before Christmas.

Trying to survive, came the answer.

I knew that. She sighed and kissed Katie's wet curls.

"Ms. Montgomery?" Upon receiving an affirmative answer, the woman who'd come out of the house as the car pulled up popped open an umbrella and hurried forward. "I'm Catherine Henderson. Your late aunt's lawyer? So nice to finally meet you at last. I was afraid you weren't going to make it before I had to leave. Here, let me take the cat. . . ."

Elaine willingly surrendered the cat carrier, tucked Katie up under one arm, and grabbed for their bag of essentials with the other. The two-story brick farmhouse loomed up out of the darkness like the haven she hoped it was and, feeling more than just a little numb, she followed the steady stream of chatter up onto the porch and into the kitchen.

"No need to lock the car, you're miles away from anyone who might want to steal it out here. I hope you don't mind going around to the back, I can't remember the last time the front door was opened. Careful on that step, there's a crack in the cement. The porch was a later addition to the original farmhouse which was built by your late aunt's father in the twenties. You'll have to excuse the smell; your aunt got a bit, well, eccentric later in life and kept a pair of pigs in here over last winter. I had the place scoured and disinfected after we spoke on the phone, but I'm afraid the smell is going to be with you for a while." She dropped the umbrella into a pail by the door and heaved the carrier up onto the kitchen table. "Good heaven's, he's a big one, isn't he? Did he wail like that all the way from Toronto?"

"No." Elaine put Katie down and brushed wet hair back off her face. "Only for the last one hundred kilometers or so."

"I'll let him out, Mommy." Small fingers struggled with the latch for a second, and then a gray and white blur leapt from the table and disappeared under the tattered lounge by the window.

"Leave him be, Katie." A quick grab kept her daughter from burrowing beneath the furniture with the cat. "He needs to be alone for a while."

"Okay." Katie turned, looked speculatively up at the lawyer, and announced, "I puked all over the car."

"I'm sorry to hear that." Catherine took the pronouncement in stride. "If you're feeling sick again," she crossed the kitchen and opened one of four identical doors, "the bathroom is through here." Reaching for the next door over, she continued. "This is the bedroom your aunt used—I suggest you use it as well as it's the only room in the house that's insulated. This is the hall, leading to the front door and the stairs— another four bedrooms up there, but as I said, uninsulated. And this is the cellar."

Elaine took an almost involuntary step forward. "What was that?"

"What was what?" the other woman asked carefully, closing the cellar door.

"The music. I heard music . . . just for a second. It sounded like, like . . ." Obviously, the lawyer hadn't heard it, so Elaine let the explanation trail off.

"Yes, well, these old houses make a lot of strange noises. There's an oil furnace down there, but it must be close to twenty-five years old so I wouldn't count on it too much. I think your aunt depended on the wood stove. You *do* know how to use a wood stove, don't you?"

"I think I can figure it out." The question had hovered just on the edge of patronizing and Elaine decided not to admit her total lack of experience. *You burn wood; how hard can it be? Whole forests burn down on their own every year.*

"Good. I've left a casserole and a liter of milk in the fridge, I don't imagine you'll want to cook after that long drive. You've got my number, if you need anything don't hesitate to call."

"Thank you." As Catherine retrieved her umbrella, Elaine held open the porch door and wrinkled her nose. "Um, I was wondering, what happened to the pigs when my aunt died?"

"Worried about wild boars tearing up the property? You needn't; the pigs shuffled off this mortal coil months before your aunt did. There might still be packages marked Porky or Petunia in the freezer out in the woodshed."

Elaine closed the door on Catherine's laugh and leaned for a moment against the peeling paint. *Porky and Petunia. Right.* It had been a very long day. She started as skinny arms wrapped around her leg.

"Mommy? I'm hungry."

"I'm not surprised." She took a deep breath, turned and scooped her daughter up onto her hip. "But first we're both putting on some dry clothes. How does that sound?"

Katie shrugged. "Sounds okay."

On the way to the bedroom, Elaine dropped the overnight case and pulled the cellar door open a crack, just to check. There was a faint, liquid trill of sound and then the only thing she could hear was water running into the cistern.

"Mommy?"

"Did you hear the music, Katie?"

Katie listened with all the intensity only a small child could muster. "No," she said at last. "No music. What did it sound like?"

"Nothing, honey. Mommy must have been imagining it." It had sounded like an invitation, but not the kind that could be discussed with a four-year-old. It probably should have been frightening, but it wasn't. Each note had sent shivers of anticipation dancing over her skin. Elaine was willing to bet the farm— well maybe not that, as this rundown old place was the only refuge they had—that she hadn't been imagining anything.

The forest was the most alive place she'd ever been; lush and tangled, with bushes reaching up and trees reaching down and wild flowers and ferns tucked in every possible nook and cranny. She danced through it to the wild call of the music and when she realized she was naked, it didn't seem to matter. Nothing scratched, nothing prickled, and the ground under her bare feet had the resilience of a good foam mattress.

Oh, yes! the music agreed.

The path the music led her down had been danced on before and her steps followed the imprint of a pair of cloven hooves.

She could see a clearing up ahead, a figure outlined in the brilliant sunlight, panpipes raised to lips, an unmistakable silhouette, intentions obvious. She felt her cheeks grow hot.

What am I thinking of? Her feet lost a step in the dance. *I'm responsible for a four-year-old child I can't just go running off to . . . to . . . well, I can't just go running off.*

Why not? the music asked indignantly.

"Because I can't! Yi!" She teetered, nearly fell, and made a sudden grab for the door frame. The cellar stairs fell away dark and steep and from somewhere down below the music made one final plea. It wailed its disappointment as she slammed the cellar door closed.

A little dreaming, a little sleepwalking, a little . . . Well, never mind. Elaine shoved a chair up under the doorknob and tried not to run back to the bedroom she was sharing with Katie. *I'm just reacting to the first night in a new house. Nothing strange about that . . . And old furnaces make a lot of . . . noises.*

Of course, she had to admit as she scrambled under the covers and snuggled up against the warmth of her sleeping daughter, old furnaces don't usually make lecherous suggestions. . . .

"How much!?"

The oilman wiped his hands on a none-too-clean rag. "You got a two hundred gallon tank there Ms. Montgomery. Oil's thirty-six point two cents a liter, there's about four and a half liters a gallon, that's, uh . . ." His brow furrowed as he worked out the math. "Three hundred and twenty-five dollars and eighty cents, plus G.S.T."

Elaine set the grubby piece of paper down on the kitchen table and murmured, "Just like it says on the bill."

He beamed. "That's right."

She had just over five hundred dollars in the account she'd transferred to the local bank. Enough, she'd thought, given that they no longer needed to pay rent, to give her and Katie a couple of months to get settled before she had to find work. Apparently, she'd thought wrong. "I'll get my checkbook." If her aunt kept the house warm with the wood stove she must've been relighting the fire every half an hour. Which was about as long as Elaine had been able to get it to burn.

The oilman watched as she wrote out his check then scrawled "paid in full" across the bill and handed it to her with a flourish. "Don't you worry," he said as she winced. "Your late aunt managed to get by spendin' only twelve hundred dollars for heatin' last winter."

"Only twelve hundred dollars," Elaine repeated weakly.

"That's right." He paused in the door and grinned back at her. " 'Course, not to speak ill of the dead, but I think she had other ways of keepin' warm."

"What do you mean?" At this point any other way sounded better than twelve hundred dollars.

"Well, one time, about, oh, four, five years ago now, I showed up a little earlier than I'd said, and I saw her comin' up out of the basement with the strangest sort of expression on her face. Walkin' a bit funny, too. I think," he leaned forward and nodded sagely, "I think she was down there having a bit of a nip."

Elaine blinked. "But she never drank."

The oilman tapped his nose. "That's what they say. Anyway, merry Christmas, Ms. Montgomery. I'll see you in the new year."

"Yes, merry Christmas." She watched the huge truck roar away. "Three hundred and twenty-five dollars and eighty cents plus G.S.T. merrier for you anyway. . . ."

"Mommy!"

The wail of a four-year-old in distress lifted every hair on her head and had her moving before her conscious mind even registered the direction of the cry. She charged out the back door without bothering to put on a coat, raced around the corner of the building, and almost tripped over the kneeling figure of her daughter.

"What is it, Katie? Are you hurt?"

Katie lifted a tear-streaked face and Elaine got a glimpse of the bloody bundle in her lap. "Sid-cat's been killeded!"

"Ms. Montgomery?"

Elaine moved Katie's head off her lap and stood to face the vet, leaving the sleeping child sprawled across three of the waiting room chairs. There'd been a lot of blood staining the white expanse of his ruff but Sid-cat had not actually been dead—although his life had been in danger a number of times during the wild drive in to the vet's. There are some things Fords are not meant to do on icy back country roads.

Dr. Levin brushed a strand of long dark hair back off her face and smiled reassuringly. "He's going to be all right. I think we've even managed to save the eye."

"Thank God." She hadn't realized she'd been holding her breath until she let it out. "Do you know what attacked him."

The vet nodded. "Another cat."

"Are you sure?"

"No doubt about it. He did a little damage himself and the fur caught in his claws was definitely cat. You've moved into your aunt's old place, haven't you?"

"Yes . . ."

"Well, I wouldn't doubt there's a couple of feral cats living in what's left of that old barn of hers. You're isolated enough out there that they've probably interbred into vicious, brainless animals." She frowned. "Now, I don't hold with this as a rule, but house cats like Sid don't stand a chance against feral cats and you've got a child to think of. You should consider hiring someone to clear them out."

"I'll think about it."

"Good." Dr. Levin smiled again. "Sid'll have to stay here for a few days, of course. Let's see, it's December 20th today, call me on the 24th. I think we can have him home for Christmas."

When they got back to the farmhouse, a line of paw prints marked the fresh snow up to the porch door and away. In spite of the bitter cold, they could smell the reason for the visit as soon as they reached the steps.

"Boy pee!" Katie pronounced disdainfully, rubbing a mittened hand over her nose.

Every entrance to the house had been similarly marked.

The house itself was freezing. The wood stove had gone out. The furnace appeared to be having no effect.

Elaine looked down at her shivering daughter and seriously considered shoving her back into the car, cramming everything she could into the trunk and heading back to the city. *At least in the city I know what's going on.* She sagged against the cellar door and rubbed her hand across her eyes as a hopeful series of notes rose up from below. *At least in the city, I wasn't hearing things.* But they didn't have a life in the city anymore.

Come and play, said the music. *Come and . . .*

I can't! she told it silently. *Shut up!*

"Mommy? Are you okay?"

With an effort, she shook herself free. "I'm fine Katie. Mommy's just worried about Sid-cat."

Katie nodded solemnly. "Me, too."

"I know what we should do, baby. Let's put up the Christmas tree." Elaine forced a smile and hoped it didn't look as false as it felt. "Here it is December 20th and we haven't even started getting ready for Christmas."

"We go to the woods and chop it down?" Katie grabbed at her mother's hand. "There's an ax in the shed."

"Uh, no sweetheart. Mommy isn't much good with an ax." Chopping wood for the stove had been a nightmare. "We'll use the old tree this year."

"Okay." The artificial tree and the box marked decorations had been left by the dining room table and Katie raced toward them, stopped and looked back at her mother, her face squeezed into a worried frown. "Will Santa be able to find me way out here? Does he know where we went."

Elaine reached down and laid a hand lightly on Katie's curls. "Santa can find you anywhere," she promised. Katie's presents had been bought with the last of her severance pay, the day she got the call that her aunt had left her the family farm. No matter what, Katie was getting a Christmas.

The six-foot fake spruce seemed dwarfed by the fifteen-foot ceilings in the living room and even the decorations didn't do much to liven it up although Katie very carefully hung two boxes of tinsel over the lower four feet.

"It needs the angel," she said stepping back and surveying her handiwork critically. "Put the angel on *now,* Mommy."

"Well, it certainly needs something," Elaine agreed, mirroring her daughter's expression. Together, very solemnly, they lifted the angel's case out of the bottom of the box.

Carefully, Elaine undid the string that held the lid secure.

"Tell me the angel story again, Mommy."

"The angel was a present," Elaine began, shifting so that Katie's warm weight slid under her arm and up against her heart, "from my father to my mother on the day I was born."

"So she's really old."

"Not so very old!" The protest brought a storm of giggles. "He told my mother that as she'd given him an angel . . ."

"That was you."

". . . that he'd give her one. And every Christmas he'd sit the angel on the very top of the Christmas tree and she'd glow." When Elaine had been small, she'd thought the angel glowed on her own and had been more than a little disappointed to discover the tiny light tucked back in between her wings. "When you were born, my parents . . ."

"Grandma and Grandpa."

"That's right, Grandma and Grandpa . . ." Who had known their granddaughter for only a year before the car crash. ". . . gave the angel to me because I'd given them another angel."

"Me." Katie finished triumphantly.

"You," Elaine agreed, kissed the top of Katie's head, and folded back the tissue paper. She blew on her fingers to warm them, then slid her hand very gently under the porcelain body and lifted the angel out of the box. The head wobbled once, then fell to the floor and shattered into a hundred pieces.

Elaine looked down at the shards of porcelain, at the tangled ruin of golden-white hair lying in their midst, and burst into tears.

Come and play! called the music. *Be happy! Come and . . .*

"No!"

"No what, Mommy?"

"Never mind, pet. Go back to sleep."

"Did you have a bad dream?"

"Yes." Except it had been a very good dream.

"Don't worry, Mommy. Santa will bring another angel. I asked him to."

Elaine gently touched Katie's cheek then swiped at her own. *Isn't it enough we're stuck in this freezing cold house*—only the bedroom was tolerable—*in the middle of nowhere with no money? I thought we could make this a home. I thought I could give her a Christmas at least . . .*

But when the angel had shattered, Christmas had shattered with it.

"I'm tired of eating pigs."

"I know, baby, so am I." Porky and Petunia had become the main course of almost every meal they'd eaten since they arrived. Elaine had thought, had hoped they could have a turkey for Christmas but with the size of the oil bill—not to mention oil bills yet to come—added to the cost of keeping the cat at the vet for four days it looked like a turkey was out of the question.

"I don't *want* pigs anymore!"

"Well, there isn't *anything* else."

Katie pushed out her lower lip and pushed the pieces of chop around on her plate.

Elaine sighed. There were only so many ways to prepare pigs and she had run out of new ideas. Her aunt's old cookbooks had been less than no help. They were *so* old that recipes called for a pennyweight of raisins and began the instructions for roasting a chicken with a nauseatingly detailed lesson on how to pluck and gut it.

"Mommy. Mommy, wake up!"

"What is it, Katie?"

"Mommy, tomorrow is Christmas!"

Elaine just barely stopped herself from saying, *So what?*

"And today we bring Sid-cat home!"

And today we pay Sid-cat's vet bill. She didn't know what she was looking forward to less, a cold Christmas spent with Porky and Petunia or the emptying out of her checking account.

Bundling a heavy wool sweater on over her pajamas, she went out to see if the fire in the wood stove had survived the night and if maybe a cup of coffee would be possible before noon.

Not, she thought as a draft of cold air swirled around her legs through the open bedroom door, *that I have very high hopes.*

"Katie!" A layer of ash laid a gray patina over everything within a three-foot radius of the stove. "Did you do this?"

A small body pushed between her and the counter. "You said, stay away from the stove." Katie swung her teddy bear by one leg, the arc of its head drawing a thick, fuzzy line through the ash on the floor. "So, I stayed away. Honest truly."

"Then how . . . ?"

Teddy drew another arc. "The wind came down the chimney whoosh?"

"Maybe. Maybe it was the wind." But Elaine didn't really believe that. Just like she didn't really believe she saw a tiny slippered footprint right at the point where a tiny person would have to brace their weight to empty the ash pan. Heart in her throat, she stepped forward, squatted, and swiped at the print with the edge of her sweater. She didn't believe in it. It didn't exist.

The sudden crash of breaking glass, however, couldn't be ignored.

Slowly she turned and faced the cellar door.

"That came from downstairs," Katie said helpfully, brushing ash off her teddy bear's head onto her pajamas.

"I *know* that, Katie. Mommy has ears. Go sit in the chair by the window." She looked down at her daughter's trembling lip and added a terse, "Please."

Dragging her feet, Katie went to the chair.

"Now stay there. Mommy's going down to the cellar to see what broke the window." *Mommy's out of her mind. . . .*

"I want to go, too!"

"Stay there! Please. It's probably just some animal trying to get in out of the cold." The cellar door opened without the expected ominous creak and although Elaine would have bet money against it, a flick of the switch flooded as much of the cellar as she could see with light. *Of course, there's always the part I can't see.*

The temperature dropped as she moved down the stairs and she shivered as she crossed the second step; until this moment the farthest she'd descended. From the bottom of the stairs she could see the cistern, the furnace, wheezing away in its corner, and the rusted bulk of the oil tank. An icy breeze against her right cheek pulled her around.

Probably just some animal trying to get in out of the cold, she repeated, taking one step, two, three. *A lot it knows. . . .* By the fourth step she was even with the window and squinting in the glare of morning sun on snow. *Oh, my God.* The glass had been forced out, not in, and the tracks leading away were three pronged and deep. She whirled around, caught sight of a flash of color and froze.

The feather was about six inches long and brilliantly banded with red and gold. She bent to pick it up and caught sight of another, a little smaller and a little mashed. The second feather lay half in shadow at the base of the rough stone wall. The third, fourth, and fifth feathers were caught on the stone at the edge of a triangular hole the size of Elaine's head.

Something had forced its way out of that hole and then out of the cellar.

Barely breathing, Elaine backed up a step, the feather falling from suddenly nerveless fingers.

"Mommy?"

She didn't remember getting to the top of the cellar stairs. "Get dressed, Katie." With an effort, she kept her voice steady. "We're going in to get Sid." *And we're going to keep driving. And we're not going to stop until Easter.*

*   *   *

". . . I don't expect anyone to have that kind of cash right at Christmas." Dr. Levin smiled down at Katie who had her face pressed up against the bars of the cat carrier. "I'll send you a bill in the new year and we can work out a payment schedule."

"You're sure?" Elaine asked incredulously.

"I'm very sure."

The vet in Toronto had accepted credit cards but certainly not credit. Under the circumstances, it seemed ungracious to suggest that they might not be around in the new year. Elaine swallowed once and squared her shoulders. "Dr. Levin, did you know my aunt?"

"Not well, but I knew her."

"Did she ever mention anything strange going on in that house?"

Ebony eyebrows rose. "What do you mean, strange?"

Elaine waved her hands helplessly, searching for the words. "You know, strange."

The vet laughed. "Well, as I said, we weren't close and the only thing I can remember her saying about the house is that she could never live anywhere else. Why? Have *strange* things been happening?"

"You might say that. . . ."

"Give it a little while," Dr. Levin advised sympathetically. "You're not used to country life."

"True . . ." Elaine admitted, slowly. *Was that it?*

"If it helps, I know your aunt was happy out there. She always smiled like she had a wonderful secret. I often envied her that smile."

Elaine, scrabbling in the bottom of her purse for a pencil, barely heard her. Maybe she just wasn't used to living in the country. Maybe that was all it was. "One more thing, if you don't mind, Doctor." She turned over the check she hadn't needed to fill out and quickly sketched the pattern of tracks that had led away from the basement window. "Can you tell me what kind of an animal would make these?"

Dr. Levin pursed her lips and studied the slightly wobbly lines. "It's a type of bird, that's for certain. Although I wouldn't like to commit myself one hundred percent, I'd say it's a chicken."

Elaine blinked. "A chicken?"

"That's right." She laughed. "Don't tell me you've got a feral chicken out there as well as a feral cat?"

Elaine managed a shaky laugh in return. "Seems like."

"Well, keep Sid inside, make sure you give him the antibiotics, call me if he shows any sign of pain, and . . ." She reached into the pocket of her lab coat and pulled out a pair of candy canes. ". . . have a merry Christmas."

"Mommy?" Katie poked one finger into her mother's side. "Sid-cat doesn't like the car. Let's go home."

Elaine bit her lip. Home. Well, they couldn't sit in the parking lot forever. Dr. Levin had said it was a chicken. Who could be afraid of a chicken? It had probably been living down in the basement for some time. It had finally run out of food so it had left. There was probably nothing behind that hole in the wall but a bit of loose earth.

Her aunt had never said there was anything strange about the house and she'd lived there all her adult life. Had been happy there.

Where else did they have to go?

The fire in the wood stove was still burning when they got home. Elaine stared down at it in weary astonishment and hastily shoved another piece of wood in before it should change its mind and go out. The kitchen was almost warm.

Very carefully, she pulled Sid-cat out of the carrier and settled him in a shallow box lined with one of Katie's outgrown sweaters. He stared up at her with his one good eye, blinked, yawned, gave just enough of a purr so as not to seem ungracious, and went back to sleep.

Katie looked from the cat to her half-eaten candy cane, to her mother. "Tomorrow is Christmas," she said solemnly. "It doesn't feel like Christmas."

"Oh, Katie. . . ."

Leaving her daughter squatting by the box, *"standing guard in case that federal cat comes back,"* Elaine went into the living room and stared at the Christmas tree. If only the angel hadn't broken. She thought she could cope with everything else, could pull a sort of Christmas out of the ruins, if only the angel still looked down from the top of the tree.

Maybe she could glue it back together.

The ruins lay on the dining room table, covered with an ancient linen napkin. A tiny corpse in a country morgue. . . .

That's certainly the Christmas spirit, Elaine. . . . She bit her lip and flicked the napkin back. One bright green glass eye stared up at her from its nest of shattered porcelain. *Oh, God. . . .*

"MOMMY!"

She was moving before the command had time to get from brain to feet.

"MOM-MEEEE!"

Katie was backed into a corner of the kitchen, one arm up over her face, the other waving around trying to drive off a flock of . . .

Of pixies?

They were humanoid, sexless, about eight inches

tall with a double pair of gossamer wings, and they glowed in all the colors of the rainbow. Long hair in the same iridescent shades streamed around them, moving with an almost independent life of its own. Even from a distance they were beautiful but, as Elaine crossed the kitchen, she saw that her daughter's arms were bleeding from a number of nasty looking scratches and a half a dozen of them had a hold of Katie's curls.

"Get away from her!" Elaine charged past the kitchen table, grabbed a magazine, rolled it on the run, and began flailing at the tiny bodies. She pulled a pink pixie off Katie's head and threw it across the kitchen. "Go back where you came from you, you overgrown bug!" It hit the wall beside the fridge, shook itself, buzzed angrily, and sped back to Katie.

"Mom-meee!"

"Keep your eyes covered, honey!" They swarmed so thick around the little girl that every swing knocked a couple out of the air. Unfortunately, it didn't seem to discourage them although they did, finally, acknowledge the threat.

"Be careful, Mommy!" Katie wailed as the entire flock turned. "They bite!"

Their teeth weren't very big, but they were sharp.

The battle raged around the kitchen. Elaine soon bled from a number of small wounds. The pixies appeared to be no worse off than when they'd started even though they'd each been hit at least once.

A gold pixie, gleaming metallically, perched for a moment on the table and hissed up at her, gnashing blood-stained teeth. Without thinking, Elaine slammed her aunt's old aluminum colander over it.

It shrank back from the sides and began hissing in earnest.

One down . . . The kitchen counter hit her in the

small of the back. Elaine smashed her wrist against the cupboard, dislodging a purple pixie that had been attempting to chew her hand off, and groped around for a weapon. *Dish rack, spatula, dish soap, spray can of snow.* . . .

Katie had wanted to write Merry Christmas on the kitchen window. They hadn't quite gotten around to it.

Elaine's fingers closed around the can. Knocking the lid off against the side of the sink, she nailed a lavender pixie at point-blank range.

The goopy white spray coated its wings and it plummeted to the floor, hissing with rage.

"HA! I've got you now, you little . . . Take that! And that!"

The kitchen filled with drifting clouds of a chemical blizzard.

"Mommy! They're leaving!"

Although a number of them were running rather than flying, the entire swarm appeared to be racing for the cellar door. With adrenaline sizzling along every nerve, Elaine followed. They weren't getting away from her *that* easily. She reached the bottom of the stairs just in time to see the first of the pixies dive through the hole. Running full out, she managed to get in another shot at the half dozen on foot before they disappeared and then, dropping to her knees, emptied the can after them.

And may all your Christmases be white!" she screamed. Then she sat back on her heels and panted, feeling strong and triumphant and, for the first time in a long time, capable. She grinned down at the picture of Santa on the can. "I guess we showed them, didn't we?" Patting him on the cheek, she set the empty container down—"Good thing I got the large economy size."—and turned her attention to the hole.

The rock that had fallen out, or been pushed out, wasn't that large and could easily be maneuvered back into place. She'd come down later with a can of mortar and . . .

Now that she really took the time to look at it, the hole actually occupied the lower corner of a larger patch in the wall. None of the stones were very big and although they'd been set carefully, they were obviously not part of the original construction. Squinting in the uncertain light, Elaine leaned forward and peered at a bit of red smeared across roughly the center stone.

Was it blood?

It was Coral Dawn. She had a lipstick the same color in her purse. And the shape of the smear certainly suggested. . . .

"Sealed with a kiss?"

Frowning, she poked at it with a fingertip.

The music crescendoed and feelings not her own rode with it. Memories of . . . She felt herself flush. Sorrow at parting. Loneliness. Welcome. Annoyance that other, smaller creatures broke the rules and forced the passage.

Come and play! Come and . . .

A little stunned, Elaine lifted her finger. The music continued, but the feelings stopped. She swallowed and adjusted her jeans.

"I think she had other ways of keeping warm. Walkin' a bit funny, too."

"She always smiled like she had a wonderful secret."

"A wonderful secret. Good lord." It was suddenly very warm in the cellar. If her aunt—her old, fragile aunt who had obviously been a lot more flexible than she appeared—had accepted the music's invitation. . . .

The scream of a furious cat jerked her head around and banished contemplation.

"*Now* what?" she demanded scrambling to her feet and racing for the stairs. "Katie, did you let Sid-cat outside?"

"No." Katie met her at the cellar door, eyes wide. "It's two other cats. And a chicken."

Elaine gave her daughter a quick hug. "You stay here and guard Sid-cat. Mommy'll take care of it."

The pixie trapped under the colander hissed inarticulate threats.

"Shut up," she snapped without breaking stride. To her surprise, it obeyed. Grabbing her jacket, she headed out through the woodshed, snatching up the ax as she went. She didn't have a clue what she was going to do with it, but the weight felt good in her hand.

The cats were an identical muddy calico, thin with narrow heads, tattered ears, and vicious expressions. Bellies to the snow and ragged tails lashing from side to side, they were flanking the biggest chicken Elaine had ever seen. As she watched, one of the cats darted forward and the chicken lashed out with its tail.

Up until this moment, Elaine had never seen a chicken that hadn't been wrapped in cellophane but even *she* knew that chickens did not have long, scaled, and apparently prehensile tails.

The first cat dodged the blow, while the second narrowly missed being eviscerated by a sideswipe from one of the bird's taloned feet. Elaine wasn't sure she should get involved, mostly—although the chicken had obviously come from her cellar—because she wasn't sure whose side she should be on.

Growling low in its throat, the first cat attacked again, slid under a red and gold wing, and found itself face-to-face with its intended prey. To Elaine's surprise, the bird made no attempt to use its beak. It merely stared, unblinking, into the slitted yellow eyes of the cat.

The cat suddenly grew very still, its growl cut off in mid-note, its tail frozen in mid-lash.

All at once, choosing sides became very easy.

Still buzzing from her battle with the pixies, Elaine charged forward. The not-quite-a-chicken turned. Eyes squeezed shut, knuckles white around the haft, she swung the ax in a wild arc. Then again. And again.

The blade bit hard into something that resisted only briefly. Over the pounding of the blood in her ears, Elaine heard the sound of feathers beating against air and something stumbling in the snow. Something slammed against her shins. Opening her eyes a crack, she risked a look.

The headless body of the bird lay, not entirely still, at her feet. She leapt back as the tail twitched and nearly fell over the stone statue of the cat. Its companion glared at her, slunk in, grabbed the severed head, and, trailing blood from its prize, raced into a tangle of snow laden bushes.

"I am not going to be sick," Elaine told herself sternly, leaning on the ax. Actually, the instruction appeared unnecessary, for although she was a little out of breath she felt exalted rather than nauseous. She poked at the corpse with her foot. Whatever remaining life force had animated it after its head had been chopped off, appeared to have ebbed. "And it's really most sincerely dead," she muttered. "Now what?"

Then the crunch of small bones from the bushes gave her an idea and she smiled.

Elaine watched Katie instructing Sid-cat in the use of her new paint box and decided that this could be one of the best Christmases she'd had in years. The wood stove seemed to be behaving, throwing out enough heat to keep the kitchen and the living room warm and cozy. She'd found a bag of frozen cranberries jammed under one of Porky's generous shoulders and a pot of cranberry sauce now bubbled and steamed on top of the stove. Thanks to the instructions in her aunt's old cookbooks, the smell of roasting . . . well, the smell of *roasting*, filled the house.

Her gaze drifted up to the top of the tree. Although the old angel had been an important part of her life and she'd always feel its loss, the new angel was an equally important symbol of her fight to make a new life and find a new home for herself and her daughter. Tethered with a bit of ribbon, its wings snow-covered in honor of the season, the pixie tossed glowing golden hair back off its face and gnawed on a bit of raw pork.

"Mommy?"

"Yes, Katie."

"Didn't Santa bring *you* any presents?"

"Mommy got her present early this morning. While you were still asleep."

"Did you like it?"

"Very, very much."

On the stereo, a Welsh choir sang "Hosannas." Rising up from the cellar, wrapping around a choirboy's clear soprano, a set of pipes trilled out smug hosannas of their own.

BIRTHNIGHT

by Michelle M. Sagara

On the open road, surrounded by gentle hills and grass strong enough to withstand the predation of sheep, the black dragon cast a shadow long and wide. His scales, glittering in sunlight, reflected the passage of clouds above; his wings, spread to full, were a delicate stretch of leathered hide, impervious to mere mortal weapons. His jaws opened; he roared and a flare of red fire tickled his throat and lips.

Below, watching sheep graze and keeping an eye on the nearby river, where one of his charges had managed to bramble itself and drown just three days past, the shepherd looked up. He felt the passing gust of wind warm the air; saw the shadow splayed out in all its splendor against the hillocks, and shaded his eyes to squint skyward.

"Clouds," he muttered, as he shook his head. For a moment, he thought he had seen . . . children's dreams. He smiled, remembering the stories his grandmother had often told to him, and went back to his keeping. The sheep were skittish today; perhaps that made him nervous enough to remember a child's fancy.

The great black dragon circled the shepherd three times; on each passage, he let loose the fiery death of his voice—but the shepherd had ceased even to look, and in time, the dragon flew on.

*   *   *

He found them at last, although until he spotted them from his windward perch, he had not known he was searching. They walked the road like any pilgrims, and only his eyes knew them for what they were: Immortal, unchanging, the creatures of magic's first birth. There, with white silk mane and horn more precious to man than gold, pranced the unicorn. Fools talked of horses with horns, and still others, deer or goats—goats!—but they were pathetic in their lack of vision. This creature was too graceful to be compared to any mortal thing; too graceful and too dangerously beautiful.

Ahead of the peerless one, cloaked and robed in a darkness that covered her head, the dragon thought he recognized the statue-maker from her gait. Over her, he did not linger.

But there also was basilisk, stone-maker, a wingless serpent less mighty than a dragon, and at his side, never quite meeting his eyes, were a small ring of the Sylvan folk, dancing and singing as they walked. They did not fear the basilisk's gaze; it was clear from the way they had wreathed his mighty neck in forest flowers that seemed, to the sharp eyes of the dragon, to be blooming even as he watched.

And there were others—many others—each and every one of them the firstborn, the endless.

"Your fires are lazy, brother," a voice said from above, and the dragon looked up, almost startled, so intent had he been upon his inspection. "And I so hate a lazy fire."

No other creature would dare so impertinent an address; the dragon roared his annoyance but felt no need to press his point. It had been a long time since he had seen this fiery creature. "I was present for your last birth," he said, "and you were insolent even then—but I was more willing to forgive you; you were young."

"Oh, indeed, more insolent," the phoenix replied, furling wings of fire and heat and beauty as he dived beneath the dragon, buoying him up, "and young. My brother, I fear you speak truer than you know. You attended my last birth—there will be no others."

The dragon gave a lazy, playful breath—one that would have scorched a small village or blinded a small army—and the phoenix preened in the flames. But though they played, as old friends might, there was a worry in the games—a desperation they could not speak of. For were they not immortal and endless?

"They do not see me," the unicorn said quietly, when at last the dragon had chosen to land. The phoenix, alas, was still playing his loving games—this time with the harpies, who tended to think rather more ill of it than the dragon had. They screeched and swore and threatened to tear out the swanlike fire-bird's neck; from thousands of feet below, the dragon could hear the phoenix trumpet.

"Do not see you? But, sister, you hide."

"I once did." She shook her splendid mane, and turned to face him, her dark eyes wide and round. "But now—I walk as you fly, and they do not see me. I even touched one old woman, to heal her of her aches—and she did not feel my presence at all."

Dragons are proud creatures, but for her sake, he was willing to risk weakness. "I, too, am worried. I flew, I cast my shadows wide, I breathed the fiery death." He snorted; smoke cindered a tree branch. Satisfied, he continued. "But they did not even look up."

"And," one of the Sylvan folk broke in, "my people

cannot call them further to our dance without the greatest of efforts.''

The dragon turned his mighty head to regard the small, slender woman of the fey ones. And what he saw surprised even he. He lowered his head to the earth in a gesture of respect for the Queen of all Faerie.

"Yes," she said, with a smile that held the ages and used them wisely, "I, too, have come out on this road. Something is in the earth, my friend—and in the air. There is danger and death for all of us." She reached out and placed a perfect hand between his nostrils. He felt a thrill of magic touch him.

He snorted again, and the fire passed harmlessly around her. "I am no foolish mortal."

Her smile held all the beauty and danger of the reaver of mortal men. "Ah? No, I see you are not, mighty brother." She turned, swirling in a dress made of water and wood, fire and wind, and walked away to where her people waited to pay court.

"She is not without power," the unicorn whispered, long after her presence had faded.

"No, little sister, she is not. Nor will ever be, I feel. But she, too, is worried." He walked slowly and sinuously by the unicorn's delicate path until the sun splashed low upon the horizon; the wound of the sky, and the beginning of day's death. Then, he took to air, that his wings might hide the stars and bring the lovely night to those below.

And in the sky, shining as it had been for these past few days, a star burned low and impossibly bright. There was magic in it, and a fire that the dragon envied and feared. And he had been drawn to it, as had all the immortal kin.

Although they all, in their way, could move more quickly than mortal man can imagine, they chose the road that only they could see, and followed it in a procession not seen since magic's first birth. The harpies became hungry and vexed, and in time even the good-natured bird of fire grew weary of their company. He never landed, although occasionally he elected to skim the surface of grass and tree alike, touching just enough to curl, never enough to singe.

The unicorn and the dragon kept company on the road during the day; only at night did the dragon yearn for, and take to, the open air. For there, hovering by the strength of his great wings, he could see the star that never wavered and never twinkled. Days they traveled, and those days became weeks for any who cared—or knew enough—to mark time's passage, but the star never grew closer, never larger.

Others joined them in their strange, unspoken quest; the hydra with his nine mighty heads, the minotaur with his one, and Pegasus, creature of wind and light—a rival to the unicorn's beauty and grace; a thing of air. Each asked, in whispers, why the others walked, but no one had any answer that they cared to give; immortals seldom speak of their own ignorance.

Last came the Sphinx, with her catlike gait and her inscrutable features. For so mighty, and so knowledgeable a personage, the dragon came down to earth, although it was starlit night.

"Sister," he said, touching ground with a beard of scale.

"Brother," she answered. "What is old as time, yet newly born; brings life to the dying and death to the living; is born of magic and born to end magic's reign?"

The dragon sighed; many years had passed since he'd last seen the Sphinx, and he had forgotten how she chose to converse. Still, her riddles held answers for those skilled enough to see them, and the dragon had lived forever. The game of words distracted him for many hours—well into the sun's rise and renewal, before he at last shook his great head. "A masterful riddle, sister. That is the one you should have asked."

She glared at him balefully, and he did not further mention the single failure that marred her perfect record.

"What is the answer?"

But she did not speak it; instead she looked up and into the daylight sky. There, faint but unmistakable, the aurora of a single star could be seen; pale twin to the sun's grace.

"But what does the riddle mean?" The unicorn asked quietly; she did not have the black dragon's pride behind which to hide her lack of knowledge. "And what was the answer?"

"The answer?" He snorted; he did that often, and the trees bore the brunt of his mild annoyance. "She does not give answers for free—and only mortals have the coin with which to pay her."

"Oh." The unicorn cantered over to the unfortunate tree that had stood in the path of the dragon's fire. Very gently, she laid horn to burnt bark—and slowly, the black passage of his breath was erased. "Maybe mortals have the coin with which to pay us all?"

It was a foolish question—one unworthy of an immortal. But as it was she who asked, he thought on it—and when night returned, and the sky beckoned, he was no closer to a comfortable answer than he had been to the sphinx's riddle. But he felt that he preferred the latter's game to the unicorn's open vulnerability.

The night brought answers of a sort, although not in the way that the dragon had expected or hoped for.

As he flew, he watched the road below—and saw, at the farthest reach of his vision, three men on camelback. They were dressed against the chill of the night, and they passed between the trees of the road-made-real by the Queen of Faerie, as if those majestic trees did not exist. They had retainers who traveled on foot; at their beck and call were wagons and caravans fit solely for mortal kings.

Three princes, thought the dragon. *Where do they travel?*

He swept down, outracing the harpies, but his wings did not even panic the camels. The princes did not look up at all from their quiet conversation. The harpies followed; they plunged downward, glinting claws extended, and hit ground before they hit men. Somehow, they had missed, and they rose, shakily, to try, and try again, to make victims out of those who traveled.

But there was no stopping the three and their procession as it came closer and closer to the heart of the traveling beasts. Still, at last, at the break of day, they chose to call a halt to their wandering. Their servants immediately began to set up tents and canvases to protect them from the sun's light.

Only when all was settled and quiet did the Queen of Faerie approach. She wandered, sylphlike but more majestic, into the heart of their gathering, wearing the guise of a mortal maid too beautiful to ignore. Her gathered robe of the elements she disguised as the finest of pure white silks; she looked young, vulnerable—the dream of every foolish youth.

The three princes were seated beneath the largest tent; they drank water from golden goblets, and kept careful watch on the ornate boxes that rested on each man's lap.

Quietly, she approached the most seemly of the men, and ran a gentle finger along the line of his beard. He looked up, his eyes narrowed.

"What is it?" The oldest of the three said, concern and fatigue in his voice.

"I thought I felt something; it must have been the passing wind. It has been a very long journey, and I am tired."

"It has been long, yes," the third man said, "and kings are not used to so arduous a travel—but we are truly blessed, who can undertake this pilgrimage."

The oldest man smiled beatifically. "Yes," he whispered, his hands caressing the inlaid jewel work of his magnificent casket, "we are blessed; for we are mortal kings—but we will see the birth and promise of the king to end all kings—God made flesh." He stood slowly, and walked to the edge of the pavilion. "There—you can still see the star in the sky. We are on the right path, my friends."

If the Queen of all Faerie dared to hold court in such a way that demanded the attention of all the immortals, none cared to complain about it openly. Indeed, when she returned, all ice and cold anger, from her foray into the human encampment, the gathering knew that the unimaginable had come to pass: She had gone, in her own royal person, and failed to call a mortal's attention when she had decided upon it.

The great black dragon lay close to the cool grass, scales in dirt and moss. His head he rested upon his great forepaws; his wings he curled in upon the expanse of his back. His unlidded eyes were fixed upon the fey and delicate fury of the Queen.

"You see," she said softly, in a whisper that might have shaken the underworld, "what we must do, my brethren."

The harpies screeched their agreement. They had passed beyond hunger now, and were ravening; at any moment, the dragon feared that they would begin to attack their kindred.

"We, too, have been drawn onto the course these mortals follow, although we tread the path-made-real at my behest. We, too, have seen the star in the sky— no natural star, nor any magical one that I have encountered before." She lifted a hand, and a ray of light, tinged with an eerie shadow, leapt skyward in her anger. "We are no mortal ephemera, to be called by the whim of a mere godling. Gods have come and gone, and we have remained, steadfast and true, in the darknesses and dreams that they cannot touch."

"Until now, sister," the unicorn said softly. "Can you not feel it?"

No other creature would have dared to correct the Queen of Faerie, and no other creature would have survived it unmarred. But the unicorn was special, dear to the Queen, and earned only a dark frown in return for her question.

"Indeed, dear one, we feel it. But now that we know the cause, we know well what we must do. There is a godling being birthed even now.

"I call for that godling's death." So saying, she raised a second hand and a darkness limned with eerie light also joined her flare in the sky. "This is my curse as Queen undying."

As her words echoed and faded in the near scentless wind, the dragon felt something he had never known before: fear.

They left the three princes—or kings, as the Queen had called them—to the shadows of the mortal realm, with its hot sun, its icy nights, and its endless, barren desert. The star burned brightly, ever brightly, as it laced the sky with shards of cast-off light, and the dragon flew when it was at the height of its brilliance.

He saw the mortal villages pass beneath the shadow of his mighty body, covered now in sleep and silence, now in merriment and celebration, now in mourning and wailing. He saw lives turn beneath him, impossibly fragile, impossibly tiny. He yearned for the breath of fire, for the sounds of their fear and falling bodies— but he knew that until the death of the godling, this grandeur was denied him.

Watching was not.

The phoenix flew beside him in the air, and as the days passed, he grew a little less brilliant, a little less radiant. "The time is coming," he said softly, for the dragon's ear alone, "when the fires will die."

"I will breathe upon you again, little fledgling," the dragon replied, "and you will know new life. You are almost a worthy child to a dragon." It was a lie, of course—no creature would be worthy of that—but he felt compelled to offer it anyway; he did not know why.

"Your fires, I fear," the phoenix replied, all song stilled, "will never again be hot enough to kindle life."

Angered, the dragon roared, startling those below who were in the habit of being taken unaware. He drew a great breath; the wind sailed into his mighty lungs like a storm upon the open sea. His jaws opened wide, and his teeth glittered in the light from the solitary star. Wings flashed black against the sky with so much power the phoenix was driven off course.

The dragon breathed *fire*.

Fire of the firstborn; fire to melt and cinder the very bones of the earth. An endless stream of blue light and heat surged through the air, wilting treetop and grass alike. And when the roaring of voice and fire combined had stilled, the dragon searched the sky for a sign of the phoenix.

It seemed brighter and perhaps just a little renewed.

"That is my fire," the dragon said, with more than a little pride.

"Almost, you give me hope, brother," the magical creature replied.

Satisfied, the black dragon continued to glide, but he roared no more that eve, and although he would not admit it, not even to the gentle one, he was suddenly very weary.

"I have never killed a child before," the unicorn said quietly, as the road stretched on beneath her delicate hooves.

"All mortal men are children," the black dragon replied, equally quietly. "If we sleep, they turn in their season, and wither as trees do. But they emerge into no spring. They are born, they age, they die."

"True," she agreed, but her tone was hesitant.

"What worries you?" The dragon ducked under a playful plume of phoenix fire. He inhaled and returned the volley without changing the nature of the game.

"I remember," she said at last, "when the world was a forest. There were men then, yes, but they were few—and we ruled and played as we desired, teasing their dreams and creating new ones.

"The world is no forest now. Men are harder to reach, harder to touch; instead of seeking us, they have turned away. This invisibility," she added, as she trailed her horn across the air, "is new—but is it so very different? We are already fading."

The dragon thought long on this, but not deeply—although depth was usually his way. "When we kill the child, all will be as it was."

"So you believe the Queen?"

"Of course." He paused. "Do you doubt her?"

"I have never killed a child before."

*   *   *

Starlight trailed down the spirals of her horn like pale, silver liquid. Although he longed to take to the skies, he remained at her side. He felt an odd tremor, a strange desire, as he looked at her silhouette in the night sky. Gold and jewels and magical things had once inspired him—but in time they had lost their luster and importance, and become just another cold, hard bed, undifferentiated from the rocks of his cavern.

She was different, and although he did not desire to possess her or hoard her, he felt something that reminded him of his . . . youth. The star flared suddenly brilliant, and his eyes were drawn to it. Before he understood why, he had opened his great jaws; the sound of his trumpeting filled the quiet night with yearning.

And as he turned the corner of the bending path-made-real, the forest suddenly ended in mid-tree. A blanket of cold, dry sand lay underfoot, and beyond it, so far away that even his eyes could make out no details, lay a small mortal town. High above it, a heart exposed, the star burned in beautiful relief.

They were almost upon it.

There was nothing but for the Queen of Faerie to lead the regal procession through the uncomfortable desert. The cold, of course, bothered no one—but the disappearance of her magically called trees displeased her. She bore the circlet of silver across her flawless face, and her hair, pale and fine, draped from her shoulder to the hem of her magnificent cloak. Her people attended to her in their own way; they played beautiful, haunting melodies on pipes and harps and chimes; they danced and whispered her praises in their soft, fey voices. It did not lighten her mood.

At night, the streets were still; the animals slept away from the cold of the night air in tight little boxes that no dragon would have fit in, had he cared to try. People—and the town had the look of a busy, crowded place—had also disappeared into their dwellings, which were, for the most part, even tinier than those built for their animals.

They tread the road in silence; even the voices of the Sylvan folk dropped away into a hush. The phoenix hovered an inch or two above the ground, which was as close to earth as he ever came, except for dying; the harpies' endless stream of abuse and obscenities had run dry. The unicorn spoke once, and no one would have urged her to be silent.

"Can you feel it?" she whispered as her hooves did a delicate little dance, "can you feel it?"

There was something in the air; something familiar—a word that hovered close to the tongue without quite being caught and uttered. The dragon shook his mighty head, as if to clear it, but before he could answer, the stable came into view.

It was as the other buildings to the eye; straw strewn about the wood and mud floor; ox and mule within stabled walls, sheep and goat without, in a fenced enclosure. But above it, the star burned bright, burned direct; and there was a tingle in the eyes and heart of any who viewed this humble building that was undeniable. One door, a ramshackle old eyesore, was off its hinge, and it swung in the wind, creaking.

Except that there was no wind. The air was dead and cool.

They had come to kill a child. The child waited. His parents—the black dragon could not think of who else the haggard, sleeping couple could be—lay to either side of him, faces buried in their dirty, tired arms. They slept. But He did not.

He eyes were wide, unblinking—as beautiful and deep as a dragon's unlidded eyes. His face was peaceful; he wanted no milk, no food, no sleep. He stared out upon them, as if they had come to pay him court.

The black dragon lost his breath a moment, as he viewed this perfect, tiny child. No gold, no jewel from the earth's bowel, had ever been so flawless. He felt a tug, like hunger, and knew a pang that he had not felt since his early days in a younger world. He almost rushed forward, to pluck the babe from matted straw and carry it off in a rush of wings to the safety of his caverns.

And then the child spoke. "Welcome."

It was the voice of magic's birth. The babe lifted his hands in no infant's gesture. Palms up, in offering or welcome, he greeted them all from his coarse throne of straw and hay, in his rough robes of peasant infancy. He did not ask why they had come.

"Changeling," whispered the Queen of Faerie, a tremor in her voice.

"No," the child answered. "I am born of a mortal parent."

From behind the ranks of her court, she came. Her face was fair and pale—as perfect and blemishless as his—yet her walk seemed stiff and oddly ancient; there was no grace left in it.

The child looked up at her.

She did not speak of what she saw in his eyes, but she froze; meeting the gaze of the basilisk or the Medusa would have had less effect. She could not move forward, and at last retreated, with just a whisper of forest darkness in which to veil her failure.

And she was not without power; calling upon the green, she whispered a single word as she made her passage. "Sister."

The unicorn bowed her head; her horn touched

ground, gleaming in the unnatural light. She approached the child, taking delicate, hesitant steps; the weight of the Queen's request was tangible, terrible.

And because she could not lift her ageless, open eyes, she met the child's gaze, and her horn shuddered to a stop, an inch away from his covered breast.

"Sister," he said, and his delicate, tiny fingers touched the tip of the golden spirals. "We do not war among ourselves."

"You are not of our number," the Queen of Faerie replied, before the trembling unicorn could speak.

"He is." It was not the child who answered, but the Sphinx. She was large, although not so magnificently vast as the dragon, and she could not approach the newborn godling, but nonetheless she made her presence felt by the side of his ephemeral cradle.

The dragon turned an eye to the side to catch her inscrutable profile; he listened carefully, to better hear the word-game that was certain to follow.

For the first time in the Sphinx's long history, no riddle came. "He is the last of our number; there will be no more."

Not even a whisper disturbed the stillness that followed her pronouncement. The star flared suddenly; the sky turned the charred gray of misted day. The godling began to rise, to float in the air as if it were a solid and fitting throne. His fingers still held to the unicorn's horn, and her head rose as he did, until all could see the anchor that she unwittingly formed.

"He said that he was born of mortal parents," the Queen protested. "He did not lie." But she stared, transfixed.

"Mortal parent and endless magic," he answered softly. "I have come to show you rest and peace, if you will have it."

"What peace?" the Sphinx asked.

"There is a garden that waits for you, as new and green and perfect as this world once was. Sister," he said, gazing down upon the unicorn's face, "there are still pools and endless forests; there is silence and beauty; there is a home that waits your presence. Will you walk it?"

"And what of this world?" she asked in a voice so tremulous even the dragon barely heard it.

"It is old and tired, as are you, who echo it. You have become the dreams and the nightmares of mortal, dying men. Wake, and walk free."

She gazed up at him; the black dragon tried, and failed, to catch her expression. "I will walk in your garden."

"Then go," he said, and suddenly, the unicorn began to fade.

Startled, the dragon roared. His breath plumed out in a cloud of red fire and wind. It disturbed nothing.

The godling floated away from the manger, and came next to the Sphinx. "You knew," he said quietly, and she nodded, lifting her face for his infant's touch.

"I have grown tired of riddles and endless questions. My thanks for the final answer." And she, too, faded from view.

To the harpies, he gave the promise of comfort and lack of hunger. To the phoenix, he gave the heart of his star—youth eternal, perfect glory. One by one, the immortals gave ground, until the streets were nearly empty.

The Queen of Faerie stood among her people; the black dragon stood alone. It was to the court of the Queen that the child went.

"What do you have to offer me?" she said proudly, a hint of fear in her eyes. "For this world of mortals is my world, and their dreams are my life. Will you take them from me?"

"No, greatest of my sisters," he said, and his voice grew stronger, fuller; his eyes were the color of starlight. "I am born of mortals, and to them I offer my garden as well. They will dance at your behest, live and love at your side, and know . . . paradise. You will have circles wider and greater than any, but you will never lose these loves to death and decay."

"It is their dying that makes them interesting," she answered coldly.

"It is now; it was not always so. Their death has tainted you."

"And you would give me death to relieve that taint?" Her lips turned up in something that was not even close to a smile.

"Yes," was the stark reply, for no one with mortal blood can lie to the most terrible of Queens. "The choice is yours."

"And if I refuse?"

He shrugged, but his face showed pain. "You refuse. But they will go, in the end, to those gardens—and you will never know them. You will dwindle; the forests will shrink and die at the coming tide of man."

She closed her eyes, knowing as always the truth of what she heard. "I . . . will go."

The black dragon thought her more beautiful, then, than she had ever been, as she preceded her people into the unknown.

"There is only you, now." It was true; but for the black dragon and the godling, the streets were empty, and the first rays of dawn were turning the skies. "Will you go?"

"Yes," the dragon answered quietly. There was no

hesitation in his voice. "But why have you left me for last?"

The little godling made no answer. But he seemed frail now, as if the passing of each immortal had robbed him of substance.

"What will you be, when we are gone?"

"Mortal," the child answered, in an oddly still voice.

"Mortal?"

"Yes. But not to other mortals. I will be their light and their darkness. I will give them hope, and I will be the cause of their despair. I will be miracle and mundanity; I will be magic and the law that ends all magic. You have killed thousands, brother—numbers undreamed of will die in my name. The peerless one healed hundreds, and numbers greater will also find healing. You were their dreams; I shall take your place."

"And what will your dream be?"

The child laughed at the gleam in the dragon's eyes. "There will be gold for you in paradise; it was hard to manage." But the dragon was not to be put off by humor, and the laughter faded into stillness. "My dream? Paradise." He looked at his own tiny palms and perfect feet. Shivered.

"And how," the dragon asked quietly, "will you reach paradise? Who will give you passage?" Dragons think deeply, when they choose to think at all.

"You were not listening," the godling said sadly. "I will be mortal, and I will die. My people will kill me slowly." The starlight faded from his eyes, and left a film in its wake. "Will you—will you wait for me there?" It was the first and last time that he sounded like a child.

The dragon took a deep breath, and a hint of smoke

curled round his nostrils. "Will I have true fire again?"

"Forever."

"Then I will wait."

The child reached out with a shaky hand, but the dragon shied from his touch. "No, no, little godling. I will wait here."

"You can't," was the flat answer. "When the sun crests the horizon, there will be no immortals left."

"Then you lied to the Queen!" The dragon's roar was the breath of a chuckle.

"I lied."

"What will happen at full sunrise?"

"You will be mortal."

"Human?"

The child nodded, his gaze intent.

"I will die as you do, then. But still . . . I will wait."

"You will remember me; I can promise that much, but I think I will forget this as I grow." Again fear touched his features, and he spoke quickly; sunrise was almost upon them both. "Remember what it was like to be old and tired—to be only dream, with no reality. Remember that, and when the time comes, do what must be done to free me."

The dragon bowed his mighty head, and the child touched his nostril. Where once a huge, black serpent had towered above the ground, there now stood a very young boy. He caught the child carefully in his arms as the sun came, and gazed up to see the dying, and the birthing, of an age. Then he crept into the manger, kissed the quiet child's forehead, and laid him back down against the straw.

Three decades later, for thirty pieces of silver—a metal he had always disdained—the dragon found a way to bring the last of the immortals home.

OX AND ASS BEFORE HIM BOW

by Mark Aronson

Come warm yourself before the fire, friend. We who travel the roads to bring the benefits of commerce to our fellow man must take our comfort where we can.

The innkeeper? Pay him no mind. His demeanor is sour, but his wine is sweet. And no matter what dank corner he has overcharged you for, you have paid for the warmth of this hearth.

Besides, I am in a mood to celebrate, and you must be my guest. Innkeeper! (Watch as I perform a miracle; you shall see the heaviest frown become the lightest smile.) Innkeeper! Two flagons of your best Greek wine, and water enough to tame it!

See how he hops! Soon there will be flame of another kind to warm us. Yes, it is too cold for the season, I agree. But as the prophet says, all men speak of the weather, yet do nothing about it. Or perhaps it was a Judge.

Ah, no. I see you squirming to count the coins in your purse. You are my guest, I insist. I see how many seasons have laid themselves against your robe, and . . .

Sit! Sit! Please take no offense, for I meant none! It has been but a year since I myself was as poor as you and poorer. I could not then afford to stand a man to a round; surely you would not now deny me that pleasure.

—Thank you for your understanding. Yes, it makes a story fit for telling . . . but here is the wine at last. Let us first drink to a year of prosperity.

To Abraham the father, David the king, and Solomon the builder, may our business flourish and the Romans perish!

An excellent vintage.

I remarked on your robe—at least it is whole. Mine was tattered and barely fit for public wear. The bindings of my sandals were shredded and torn. And my purse, ah, my poor purse—as empty as the desert sky in midsummer.

Did you arrive on foot? A mule? Oh, my prosperous friend! I had but the small gray ass stabled in back . . . yes, the one with the gold-embroidered blanket. He is called Katan, the Small One, he whom I now prize above all other animals, the creator of my luck.

Oh yes, those other animals are mine as well, through good fortune. But last year . . . last year! A miserable year! May the Lord curse new governors!

Indeed, it is all the fault of Quirinius, the governor sent by Augustus. He, of course, assumed his predecessor was a criminal of the highest order—and naturally wished to exceed him in villainy. So he ordered a census, as you recall, the better to assess taxes of honest merchants like you and me, and required all to register in the cities of their ancestry.

Have you ever seen the roads so full? Entire families uprooted themselves to make the journey from Joppa to Jarash, or from Engedi to Tiberias, that they might be counted under the Imperial edict. That they might be privileged to fill the cedar treasure chests of Quirinius in his fortress on the sea.

At first I was amused by these petty comings and goings—I who have spent a lifetime wandering to offer goods of surpassing quality at prices so . . . forgive me; habits are not easily broken.

But soon I was not so amused. Entering Apollonia, I inquired after Avi the potter, who buys from me rare sands for his glazes and sells me vessels much in demand at the governor's court. "Gone to Ascalon, the place of his birth," came the reply. "And Elazar the weaver?" I asked. "To Hebron," said his neighbors.

At every stop on my route I searched for my web of customers and suppliers. In truth, they were even more my stock in trade than the goods I carried. And at every stop the words changed, but not the tale. "Where are Yonah, Zvi, Yitzchak?" "Gone to Jerusalem, Nazareth, Bethlehem."

And so in one season was the work of a lifetime undone. With every step along my long-traveled route my prosperity slipped into the sand beside the road. Yet what choice had I but to trace my well-worn path? From this spot in Bethlehem through Jerusalem to Nicopolis, Diospolis, Joppa, and Apollonia, thence to the provincial capital at Caesarea Maritima, where I had none of Avi's fine pottery to sell to the court. And feeling the need for food, I was forced to dispose of the sands I carried for Avi at distressed prices to whomever would buy.

On to Vejjun, Nazareth, Tiberius, and Gadara, where, having sold far too many of my goods at a mournful loss, I was forced to sell three of my pack beasts in order to feed myself, Katan and my one remaining donkey.

In truth, I would have sold my little Katan, but who would buy so plainly unburdenable a beast of burden?

And so I continued east to Adraa and Bostra, where in happier times I would trade for delicacies and curiosities from Babylon and the empires of the east, making the long trip to the city of the Amonites, which the Romans call Philadelphia, most profitable. But now, alas, I was not burdened by excess profit, but instead by excess hunger.

My luck seemed to turn in Jarash and Pella, where my web of trade remained intact. But in my reduced circumstances, there was little of mutual profit to be undertaken, even among sympathetic friends, and I must needs be satisfied to avoid a loss.

In Scythopolis I was forced to sell my better clothing, which in past times had lent me stature as I bargained with agents of the nobility. And so I trod the road to Samaria, Neapolis, and Jericho, where my total of goods comprised my winning smile, the robe on my back and one small brick of frankincense from the ovens of Ubar. And Katan, of course, to whom I spoke endlessly, for I no longer had the price of companionship.

The road *to* Bethlehem is, perforce, the road *from* Bethlehem. Yet I recalled the latter to have been paved with far happier stone than the former. As I walked the last league, eyes cast down, scanning the pebbles lest one turn to gold undiscovered, I realized that I had for some time been in the company of three men of stern visage and fanciful garb.

Though my goods were lacking, my wit was not, and I recognized them to be Persians of high rank. I hailed them in their own tongue . . . oh, yes, my new friend, it is wise to learn as many tongues as you are able. Besides our own and Greek, I suggest Latin and Parthian at least, together with the speech of the Bedouins and Persians. Attempt to speak with your customer in his own speech and he will feel flattered; feeling flattered, he will deal more softly. Or so it has always proved for me.

I hailed them, as I said, in their own tongue, and learned they were astrologers and magicians of note in their own land, bound for Bethlehem on a quest incomprehensible to me. They attempted to show me charts of the stars and calculations of time and place by way of explanation. I nodded wisely, but the arithmetic of profit and loss is sufficiently arcane for my poor intellect.

One of the three was in obvious distress. He showed me a chart—Lord of Hosts!—there was more ink on that scroll than water in the Great Sea! It purported to show—and I did not offer refutation—that he was to have brought with him a gift of incense, as the others had brought gold and spices, in fulfillment of the conditions of their calculations. But he had none.

I reached into the small bag laid across Katan's narrow back and brought forth my brick of frankincense. "Take this," I said, "my gift to you. May it bring you the good fortune you seek."

Mad? Perhaps I was, a little. Where were you, oh magicians, when the price of this fragrant block would have made a difference! For I had already decided to trust my fate to chance, and the purity of my poverty was intoxicating in the manner of the visions one sees when fasting.

Arriving at last in Bethlehem, at this very inn, I attempted to secure a sleeping space—a space for which I had paid in advance, as is my custom, at the start of my ill-starred journey. The inn was full, and more than full, as was the whole town, packed tight as grapes in a winepress. For this is a city of David, and across the land there are many who claim him as ancestor, rightfully or not, and so returned here to be counted.

Me? I claim Bethlehem as the city of my birth, and no more. Our host, though close with his wine measure, is an honest man . . . yes, I speak of you! Friend, another flagon? Good, good.

An honest man, as I said, and he found me a space near to the door on the upper floor. But sleep did not embrace me, for I had paid but one night's lodging and so must leave on the morrow. I descended quietly to the stable to seek out Katan, who, though rarely offering an original thought, manages yet to demonstrate the wisdom of silence.

A lamp glowed in the stable, and I witnessed a curious sight. The three Persians of whom I have spoken knelt before the hay trough, in which lay a newborn child. Before them were strewn their gifts, including my frankincense, now displayed on cloth of gold; plainly this child was the object of their quest.

His appearance? The child's, you mean? He seemed to be well formed in the usual way; there was nothing remarkable about him. His arms wheeled in the manner of birds on a current of air, as babies do, and for a moment he touched Katan, who was sniffing at the hay, and rubbed his nose, just as I do when Katan asks for attention.

Not wishing to intrude myself into so singular a tableau, I stole away silently. As I turned to leave— though I cannot be certain of this—I seemed to catch the eye of the magician to whom I had given my last stock of goods. There could have been the slightest hint of a smile beneath his beard. I cannot swear to it either way.

In time I slept, and in time I woke. Resolve was my breakfast; I could afford nothing more substantial. And though it presented a ludicrous sight, I climbed atop Katan and spoke to him.

"For countless leagues have I led you in search of prosperity. And I have failed. From this day hence there shall be no reins; I will not lead you. You shall lead and I shall follow."

As if he had the power of understanding, Katan trotted briskly, following the road south to Hebron.

We dwell upon our misfortunes and touch but lightly upon our triumphs. So let it be with the remainder of my tale.

For five days we traveled to the south, I upon Katan, the reins draped slack across his mane. Each step along the path brought greater misgivings. Should I abandon this foolishness, seize the reins and hurry back to my accustomed path in hopes of building anew the trade I had worked so long to cultivate? Surely the census was done. Surely Mordecai or Jephiah or even Radaak the Babylonian would lend me capital to establish again a business of benefit to so many.

As I contemplated these choices, lost in thought, Katan stopped. I looked about me. We were near to the Dead Sea, between Engedi and Eleutheropolis, at the mouth of a small valley where fat sheep dotted the hillsides. Despite prodding, Katan refused to go farther. I climbed down, and taking in hand his reins for the first time in five days, led Katan to the gate of the nearby shepherd's cottage. The door opened, and I was struck down by lightning.

Twice.

First by the soft eyes and great kindness of the beautiful Rachel bat Tziyon, widow of Nahum, who owned the sheep and the valley they grazed in. And second by the bolts of cloth in every corner of her dwelling, with patterns of great complexity and colors of great subtlety in fabrics of wondrous smoothness.

Nahum had been a practical man, I learned, and even after his passing his enterprise ran itself. The shepherds and shearers did their jobs with commendable efficiency, while factors and traders of my calling paid handsomely for the fine wool of the valley.

Rachel, however, saved for herself the most choice

fleeces, and from them spun fine thread and wove her fanciful creations—for her own amusement, there being little recreation in her secluded valley. To my great surprise, none knew of her avocation beyond her personal servants.

All this I learned over the simple yet delicious supper she prepared for me with her own delicate hands. And while the custom of hospitality is strong among those who live far from the centers of commerce, I sensed in her an attraction to me similar to that which I felt for her.

My friend, a toast with the last of our wine to the fair Rachel! And another to Katan, most magnificent of beasts, who led me to her!

Within the hour, we had struck a bargain. I would take three bolts of her glorious fabric to a certain merchant of my acquaintance in the marketplace at Ascalon, there to prove its value. Rachel was amused, certain that the fanciful products of her boredom were of little worth.

In Ascalon, where I was scarcely known, my goods caused great turmoil. Merchants clamored to discover their provenance, but I merely smiled and spoke of the weather. In short order I had sold Rachel's fabric for the price of three mules and gold sufficient to make my purse burst its strings, and amassed orders for cloth enough to cloak Jerusalem.

I returned in triumph to Rachel, who from a bolt of her finest cloth had prepared for me a robe of unrivaled richness—yes, yes, this very robe which glows so brightly in the fire's flicker.

Her dark, gentle eyes opened wide in amazement and amusement at my success—and in humility at finding the work of her hands so treasured by so many. It was then for the first time that I touched her soft skin and took her to me. . . .

Well.

Suffice it to say that with laden animals I traveled again to Ascalon, Katan as always in the lead, then on to Caesarea Maritima by ship, where the women of the court of Quirinius murdered one another for scraps of Rachel's fabric.

And always at deeply satisfying prices.

The court of Herod, not to be outdone by Quirinius, now clamors as well for my goods, and I have with me requisitions that will keep Rachel busy for a goodly time to come.

Or, should I say, Rachel's servants, for I myself intend to keep Rachel busy—Rachel the Widow, who upon my return has promised to become Rachel the Wife.

All this in the space of a year. From despair to delight, from solitude to serenity. And all because of the wanderings of a small gray ass.

To Katan! Who bore me on the path to Eden—for no earthly reason!

No earthly reason at all.

FATE

by Kristine Kathryn Rusch

She held a deck of cards in her left hand and cut it easily, sliding the top of the deck to the bottom. Her skin was pale white, her hair even whiter, and she wore a backless white evening dress. Grif could almost imagine her in the glassed-in cage on the lower levels, astride the white tigers.

Around him, the clink, clink of coins echoed from the slot machines. Occasionally a buzzer would ring and a red light would flick on and off. The murmur of conversation almost covered the Christmas muzak. The casino had stuck mistletoe to the plants running along the ceiling, but no one noticed. Not even the hotel patrons who wandered through the casino, following a wide swatch of carpet leading to the elevators. The rooms above, several thousand of them, were all done in jarring jungle motifs. Outside a fake volcano spit fire at sunset, and inside half a dozen animals paced the basement waiting for their turns in the glassed-in cages so that bleary eyed patrons could go to the zoo without leaving the hotel.

She seemed impervious to the bizarre surroundings. She didn't fit, despite her expertise with the cards.

Grif pushed past an obese man clutching a bucket full of nickels. She sat on a stool just outside the ring of blackjack tables, watching the patrons play. The casino was nearly empty tonight—only the hard-core gamblers and the loners haunted a casino on Christmas Eve—and would remain so until the New Year's crowd started to appear on December 27th.

Grif liked to think he didn't belong in either category—hard-core gambler or hard-core loner—yet here he was, on the strip in Vegas, as if it were any other Friday night.

He tugged the sleeve of his tux over his shirt cuffs, and rounded a row of one-armed bandits. She was still sitting there, cutting the deck over and over with her left hand.

He put his palm on her back, found the skin cooler than he imagined. "That's a great way to tip off the guys upstairs that you know your way around cards."

She didn't jump. Instead she looked up at him, a slow luxurious movement that sent a tingle through him. Her eyes were pale blue, almost colorless, but her features had a rounded Mediterranean cast. Her gaze continued past him to the camera lens hidden in the plants above him.

"I'm not hiding anything," she said. He half expected an accent, and was surprised when he didn't hear it.

"How come you're not playing?" he asked. He didn't take his hand off her back.

She smiled, revealing an even row of white teeth. "I'm waiting for someone."

He sighed, touched the nape of her neck, then removed his hand. She took his wrist between her fingers. Her grip was surprisingly strong. "But he's not here. Perhaps I could go with you, and be your luck."

The tingle ran through him again, a wave of desire so thick he could hardly stand. "Maybe—" he stopped himself. His apartment was on the other side of town. He hadn't made the bed in weeks, and dishes filled the sink. Once it had been an impressive place to take women, but since his losing streak this fall, he let almost all appearances go.

Except the tux. It remained important for him to play Vegas casinos as if he were in Monte Carlo. It lent an air of dignity to a life with little dignity left.

"What's the lady's preference?" he asked.

She dropped the deck of cards into the small beaded clutch purse she was carrying. "Craps," she said.

And that time he did hear it. A faint lilt that spoke of romance languages and ancient cities beside the sea, of years gone by when casinos were more than a hobby, more than a place to spend Friday nights. He had quit the circuit with two million dollars in several banks. Investments had built that up to five million, and last fall's losing streak brought him down to four. One fifth of all he owned, gone in a heartbeat. That happened to careless men, not to Grif Petrie.

He touched the wad of bills in his pocket—more than enough to impress a lady—then extended his arm. She took it, her touch sending a chill through him. Maybe after a bit of luck, he would get lucky. He smiled a little to himself. On Christmas Eve, the hotel was nearly empty. He would get a high-roller's suite on the twenty-fifth floor. They were garish too, but impressive garish with a view of the entire city.

Grif led her to the only operating craps table, where a tall man wearing a stetson and cowboy boots played with a row of five-dollar chips, and a woman beside him hid in a puff of smoke. Occasionally she would snake an arm out and place a dollar chip on a sucker bet, swearing as she lost. Grif pulled ten hundred dollar bills from his money clip and tossed them in front of the dealer. He spread them out, then counted ten hundred dollar chips, and set them on the table. The stickman shoved them over to Grif and Grif put one on the pass line, and placed the others in the groove above the table. The boxman gave Grif an odd glance. The boxman usually handled the late-night poker tables; he had never seen Grif play anything but cards.

The stickman pushed the dice in front of Grif. He offered them to the lady, but she shook her head. Then he tossed them at the end of the table. He rolled three sevens before rolling a ten and placing some of his winnings on the come line. Then he upped his bet, rolled five tens, a nine and a six, placing the winnings beside his original stash.

"You are my luck," he said to her, his hands shaking.

The cowboy at the end of the table was following Grif's betting strategy. The woman lost her pile of dollar chips and left. The noise from the table attracted a few other players, and Grif continued his streak, with the stickman calling him the hottest shooter of the night.

Finally, after he had turned his thousand dollar stake into five thousand dollars with only hundred dollar bets, he rolled another seven, and lost the point. The collective groan around the table echoed through the casino. The cowboy lost five hundred on the bet, pocketed the rest of his earnings and left. A young man with the intensity of a compulsive gambler plucked the dice off the table. Grif cashed in his chips, took his lady's arm, and left.

"Quitting so soon?" she asked.

"I don't want to press my luck." Craps were fun, but not a professional's game. The dice were as fickle as a woman.

She smiled and shrugged. "Little blackjack?"

"Maybe later." He put his arm around her back. "First we got some winnings to celebrate."

She seemed to understand his meaning. She accom-

panied him through the lush greenery to the registration desk.

"This'll only take a minute," he said.

She nodded. He went up to the desk, asked for,
and got a suite. While the registration clerk gathered
all the pertinent information, Grif stared at the aquar-
ium covering the wall behind the desk. Fish moved at
a leisurely pace, not caring that it was Christmas, not
caring that people were making or losing money in
the rooms beyond. He wondered what it was like
working here, with the heat of the fish tanks adding
humidity to the air, and then decided he didn't want
to know. He had never held a real job. His father had
taught him to count cards at the age of ten. By the
time he could legally go into a casino, he was already
an experienced high stakes poker player, and a successful card counter. He had gotten out, as his father
had trained him to, when he had enough to live on
for the rest of his life, but the boredom got to him.
And that was why he came to Vegas, why he returned
to the casinos, and probably why he had been losing.
Losing was a treat.

The clerk used a little machine to punch the room
combination in a pair of plastic room cards. Maybe
he thought losing was a treat because he could find
no other rationale for his behavior. He had been away
from the tables for six months, and in that time his
hands shook and nothing interested him. Clarisse,
when she left him, called him a sick fuck and a compulsive gambler, but compulsive gamblers don't earn
and save over five million dollars in the space of ten
years. He had told her that and she had laughed at
him, and continued to move out.

He took back his gold Visa card, and the room
cards the clerk slid to him. Then he turned. His lady
was talking to a tall, broad-shouldered man wearing

south-of-the-border denim. Grif's shoulders tensed, all the good feeling from the win disappearing under a layer of panic.

"Found him," she said.

Grif nodded and was about to step away when she put her hand on his arm.

"Cal Dooley," the big man said, extending his hand.

"Grif Petrie." Grif took the man's hand, noting the firmness of the grip, the calluses on the fingers. Somehow he couldn't picture this woman with this man.

"Good," she said. "Now that we have introductions, I'm going to the ladies room. I'll meet you gentlemen in the bar beside the blackjack tables."

Grif slipped the room cards in his pocket beside the full money clip.

"Some woman, hey?" Cal said. "I told her I always come here Christmas Eve, and what does she do but fly across an entire ocean and half a continent to meet me."

Grif swallowed, and nodded, unable to see the attraction. She was slender and aristocratic. He was rough and crude, an LBJ Texas farmer. Money probably. Grif had seen enough women over the years hang onto men with money so that the women could travel to exotic places, lose lots of cash at sucker craps or roulette, and wear expensive clothes.

Cal started through the breezeway leading to the back portion of the casino. "Met her in Italy last summer. One hell of a drink of woman. Alli's short for Alcina, did she tell you that? Give you one of those lines about the fates?"

"She said she'd be my luck," Grif said, trying to keep the misery from his voice.

"She can be that, too. Damn if I didn't win close

to a million dollars last summer having Alli by my side."

"We had a good run at the crap table tonight," Grif said.

They entered the bar and took a table without a video poker display on top. The chairs were leather and Grif sank into his as if all the energy had left him. Usually winning highs stayed with him, but he was striving for a sexual high—and he knew he'd missed it by the space of a few minutes.

"Glad to see her here," Cal said. "She'll add a touch of spice to my holiday. Sure as hell surprised me."

"She said she was meeting you."

"Hmm." Cal signaled a waitress. "She didn't let me know. Just appeared here, sure as you please. Always knew that girl came from money. But between us, I didn't expect to ever see her again—and especially not smiling. We didn't part on the best of terms—"

"I see you're making yourselves at home." Alli slipped into the chair between them. Her skin seemed fresher, her eyes sparkled more. Grif sank deeper in the leather. A woman in love.

"You fucked up, hon. You didn't tell poor Grif here about the fates."

She looked at Grif, then took his hand and played with his fingers. Cal watched, smile remaining. Grif felt himself grow hard. He couldn't pull away. "We've only known each other a short time." She let go of his hand and put hers on his thigh, her fingers tracing the sensitive skin. "Cal got sick of me talking about it. Why do you want me to tell Grif?"

"So I don't have to hear it the rest of the holiday." Cal got up. "I'll go see what's keeping that waitress."

Alli watched him go. "When I met Cal, I told him my name was Alcina, like the Fate, but that people called me Alli. He thought I meant the Greek fates, and so one afternoon, he was explaining that to a group of his friends and I corrected him. He didn't like that."

"I didn't know there were other fates."

Alli shook her head. "You Americans should really rebel against your school systems. You get such a poor education. A fate, in my country, is like a dryad or a sprite. A wood or water spirit of great beauty and kindness, who will bestow good fortune on those it favors. But if someone treats it cruelly, well, the fate will exact revenge—taking either that person's health, beauty, or good luck. Cal didn't like hearing that. I had embarrassed him in front of his friends. He has quite an ego."

Her fingers had moved up his thigh. Grif caught her hand in his. "If that's true, you'd better quit."

She smiled. "Oh, no. You'll see just how big soon. He doesn't mind other men because he believes that no one can take his place."

"I know that no one can take my place." Cal set the drinks down—a rum-and-coke for Alli, a beer for himself, and a martini for Grif. "You didn't look like a man who went for a brew," Cal said.

Grif nodded, and took the martini. He needed something strong. The entire evening was making him feel odd.

"I saw you slip those room cards into your pocket," Cal said. "And Alli's got her eye on you. How's about we take these drinks upstairs, and see if we can keep the little lady occupied?"

Grif glanced at Alli, but she was already standing, drink in hand. Grif stood too, feeling wobbly. He thought he had done everything in his years gambling, but never had a couple approached him with such ease and assurance. He didn't want Cal there, but he did

want Alli as bad as he used to want a win. He suspected without Cal, he wouldn't get her at all.

They said nothing as they took the elevator to the
twenty-fifth floor. The suite was at the end of a long
hallway painted in white, with green leaves and orange
accents rising from the floor. The carpet was green
and the room doors were done in a fake white wicker,
giving everything a cool 1940s jungle look.

Grif opened the door to the suite and stepped inside. A row of floor to ceiling windows faced him,
giving him a view of the city's lights. Wicker furniture
covered the mirrored floor. To his left, a door opened
to a huge bathroom complete with a jacuzzi that sat
ten. To his right, he could see into the bedroom. The
bed was jumbo king-sized and rimmed in mirrors.

Not a suite made for sleeping.

Alli came in behind him and put her hand on his
bottom. Desire made Grif dizzy. Cal closed the door
and locked all the locks. "You got style, bud," he
said.

On the table near the windows, a fruit basket sat
with an unopened bottle of champagne beside it. Alli
rubbed her body against Grif's, ran her hands forward
along his hips, and cupped him, feeling his hardness.
She made a small purring noise, then pushed him
away.

"Why don't you turn down the bed, Grif?" she said.
"Cal and I will pour the champagne and join you in
a minute."

They needed their privacy. They hadn't spoken
alone since they linked up. Grif knew that he was
being dismissed and didn't care. He wandered into the
bedroom and Alli closed the door behind him. He
jumped a little but didn't lose the horniness that almost consumed him. He tugged off his shoes,

cummerbund, and jacket, then ran a hand along the satin coverlet.

The smoothness of the fabric made him harder. He couldn't picture what they would do there, the three of them, but he knew he would enjoy it, even though he usually didn't like sharing women. For a moment he hesitated, then he stretched himself full length on the bed. He wanted them to hurry. He wanted to feel her, all of her, naked against him—

A scream echoed from the front room, followed by a thud, and then another shout. The sounds shot through the haziness Grif felt. He sat up, heard another bang, and yanked the door open.

Blood coated the mirrored floor. Cal sprawled against the bar in the far corner, a bar stool toppled across his lap. His throat was a bloody pulp and his eyes were open, staring, unseeing.

A white tiger paced the room, blood on its muzzle. Grif's heart stopped for one panicked instant, then he forced himself to move. He grabbed the edge of the door and was about to slam it, when the tiger transformed itself into Alli.

She was naked. Her body was slender, perfect, with melon sized breasts, and long legs that tapered into a pair of beautiful feet. Grif's desire returned so powerfully that he nearly dropped everything and went to her. Then she wiped the blood from her mouth with the back of her hand, and the moment was gone.

"Sorry," she said. "I owed him."

Grif swallowed. "That? You owed him that?"

"All we ask is a little gratitude," she said. "And all he did was take."

"We?" Grif's mind was beginning to function again. He looked for the tiger, didn't see it. His grip on the door frame tightened.

She smiled and sat on the couch, crossing those delicious legs and giving him a view of her backside. "You Americans have no appreciation for subtlety. I'm a Fate, darling. We appreciate a little warmth in return for our kindness."

"The tiger?" he asked, unwilling to let go of the door until he knew what happened to the beast.

"What did your eyes tell you?" she asked.

He didn't respond. He had seen the tiger, and then he had seen her. And he hadn't believed it.

At his blank look, she sighed. "We're shapeshifters. A white tiger was a bit more useful to me at that moment than a human woman."

It made some kind of crazy sense: the odd run of luck at a game he rarely played; the deep desire that controlled him more than any other he'd ever experienced; her knowledge of Cal's whereabouts even though Cal hadn't spoken to her in six months; the blood on the back of her hand.

Cal's head slumped to the side. A trickle of blood ran down the stairs leading to the doorway.

Grif didn't move. Shutting the door wouldn't matter. She could change into some kind of bug and crawl underneath it. His heart was pounding in his throat.

"What did I do to you?" he asked.

"Took my luck," she said.

He could hardly breathe. He wished he still carried a gun. She had to be a living creature, something he could kill. "What are you going to do to me?"

"Depends," she said. "I could leave now and call security. There's no way you could hide Cal. I wonder how many men still kill each other over beautiful women?"

"But I wasn't going to hurt you," he said. His voice had a whine in it he had never heard before. "I was going to bring you up here and—"

"Enjoy me, for your own sexual pleasure." She

stretched out on the couch, her body even more beautiful in repose.

The blood was beating in his head. He was trying not to move, trying not to go to her. The desire was back, stronger than ever, but he wouldn't let it swallow him. "When I first saw you," he said, "I warned you about your actions. I was afraid the men upstairs would throw you out."

Something ran across her face, something that made her eyes brighter for just an instant. "So you did," she said, and sat up. "So you did." She got up and came over to him. He could smell Cal's blood on her, but he didn't care. She tilted her face to his, and as he leaned into the kiss, she caressed his mouth with her fingers.

"How very unusual," she murmured. "You gave first."

They made love through that night and into the next morning. He wanted to continue, but she stopped, afraid that she would hurt him. "No," she said. "We have something else to take care of first."

She led him into the living room, and he stopped when he saw Cal. Grif had forgotten about Cal, forgotten, in the depths of his passion, about the strangeness of the night before.

His mouth went dry, and all the fear returned.

"We need to clean up," she said.

Grif stood for a moment, and stared at Cal. What had the man done to deserve a death like this? Did anyone deserve to die for being insensitive? Grif wanted to reach out to the other man, to talk to him, to convince him to change his ways. But it was already too late.

"Got a razor blade?" Alli asked.

"Hmmm?" Grif turned to her, feeling vulnerable without clothing.

"Never mind." She walked over to her clutch purse and removed a package of razors from it. Then she wiped the razor clean, placed it in Cal's fingers and ran it through the gape in his neck. His hand fell, the razor blade skittering from it. "Holiday time," she said to Grif over her shoulder. "Lots of suicides. No one will think twice."

He watched the deftness with which she moved. All the desire had fled him, and he was left with a deep tiredness and growing repulsion. "It's still my room. They're going to know—"

"No, they're not," she said. She pulled the dress over her body, then grabbed Cal's wallet from his jeans. As Grif watched, her body transformed into his, her clothes becoming his clothes, her skin becoming his. Only her eyes remained unchanged. "See?" Her voice was deeper—Cal's voice.

Grif began to shiver. He retreated into the bedroom and pulled on his clothes. He had seen strange things in casinos, but this was the strangest.

"Hurry," she called from out front.

As he went into the living room, he found her on the phone requesting that housekeeping skip the room today. "I'm entertaining and don't want to be disturbed." Seeing two Cals, the dead one and the imposter, was almost more than Grif could bear. Alli put down the phone and took Grif's arm. He resisted the urge to pull away. He didn't want her angry at him, too.

"Now," she said, "we need to get you out of this. Just come with me."

She took his arm and led him out of the room. They walked side by side, silently, two men leaving a suite where they had shared—something. Something horrible. Grif made himself stare ahead.

They took the elevators down, and once they were in the casino, Alli became completely Cal. She greeted people she didn't know with loud hellos. She spoke to stickmen and dealers, promising to return and to haul off most of the casino's money. She led Grif to the registration desk, and leaned over it.

"We got a room in my buddy's name," she said, "and he's leaving. I want to take it over."

The woman behind the desk punched a few numbers in the computer, asked Alli questions, and she answered them all.

"You're Mister Petrie?" she asked Grif.

He nodded.

"And you didn't want maid service today?"

"It was a late night. One of my friends is still asleep." His voice was rough. He had to struggle to force it through his throat.

"All right, sir. Whose name will this be under?"

Alli pushed forward one of Cal's credit cards. As she signed the documentation, Grif started to leave. She grabbed his arm. Her grip was surprisingly strong. He remembered the blood on her hand.

"There we go," the registration clerk said. "Thank you for your patronage, Mr. Petrie, and Merry Christmas!"

The words startled him. He nodded in response, then let Alli lead him outside. The volcano was silent. A group of Japanese tourists took pictures from the bridge over the small moat around the volcano.

"I frighten you, don't I, Grif?" Alli asked, no longer speaking in Cal's voice.

He turned. She stood beside him, still wearing Cal's south-of-the border denim, but in the female body that had attracted him and started this whole mess.

He didn't know how to answer her. If he lied, she would probably know it, and yet he didn't want to be rude.

He would never be rude to anyone again.

"I—I don't know what to think about all this."

She smiled, and tucked a loose strand of his hair behind his ear. "You and I have flirted since you were ten years old, and you gained a lot from me. But it's time to let go, Grif."

He blinked, feeling the same confusion he had felt the night before.

"If you don't let go, you'll start expecting luck, and then demanding it, and then—" she shrugged, a graceful movement, "—well, look at Cal."

Grif had looked at Cal. He would never forget. "Is that why you brought me here? To warn me?"

"So human. So egocentric." She smiled. "You brought yourself here. And you came to me, the attraction so deep you would do anything for me. Doesn't that scare you, Grif? There's a dead man in your room."

She leaned forward, kissed him, and even through his exhaustion, he would gladly have carried her back inside. But she pulled away, slid into Cal's body again, and disappeared through the revolving door.

Grif started after her, then stopped. If he chased her, she said, he would end up like Cal, dead on a mirrored floor in an anonymous hotel, an apparent suicide, alone for the holidays. Grif's hands were shaking like those of a man who had gone too long without a drink.

Behind him, the volcano exploded. He ducked and covered his head with his hands, then rose slowly, relieved that no one on the sidewalk had seen his action. A shower of flame and sparks rose in the morning sky. He had never seen the volcano go off in the daytime before. It must have been a Christmas thing.

He glanced at the door, then turned away from it. Maybe next year, he would be on some Hawaiian beach with some beautiful woman—a real woman—away from any cards, away from any temptation. He still had a lot of money. He could do whatever he wanted—within reason.

He already knew he would never again do anything that would test his luck.

THE LAST SPHINX

by Barbara Delaplace

It was the last of its kind. The once proud wings were now bedraggled and torn, with many missing feathers. The mane that had formed a noble frame around the creature's face was snarled and matted, and the supple tail that once had been so expressive in every mood showed no more life than a piece of rope. It limped on three legs, and every rib showed. But the dulled eyes were the worst of all. A Sphinx's eyes should reveal all the cunning wisdom of that ancient race, but this one's eyes showed only unutterable weariness.

The Dog was the first to be aware of its approach, for he was guarding his master's property. (Even on a night of bitter cold like this, he made his rounds faithfully.) Normally he would have barked a fierce warning at the Sphinx, for dogs and sphinxes are two very different kinds and they share no love for one another.

But this was not a normal night. On this one midwinter night each year, the Dog—and all the animals in home and barn—could speak.

"Who are you? Why are you here? You should go away!" said the Dog sharply.

But the Sphinx only looked at him and made no answer.

"What do you want? Why are you here?" demanded the Dog again.

245

And again the Sphinx did not reply.

The Dog was apprehensive because sphinxes are powerful creatures and could easily kill even a tough, shaggy-coated guard like him—though he had no thought of abandoning his post. But when he looked more carefully, he realized this sphinx was not whole and sound; that, in fact, *he* could probably kill *it*. And the Sphinx looked at him without hope of mercy.

Somehow that made a difference to the Dog. To attack, and kill if necessary, those who threatened his master's family or home, that was the proper order of life. But it wasn't right to slaughter a creature obviously walking its final road to the End of All Things. Because he was a dog, he did not know "compassion" was the word for what he was feeling, but he knew it seemed fitting to offer what help he could: a warm shelter and water, maybe food. (Though he did not know what food a sphinx ate.)

So he spoke again. "Are you cold?"

No reply, but somehow he sensed that, yes, the Sphinx was very cold. "Come with me to the barn," he said, and turned away. The Sphinx limped slowly after him.

When the Dog pushed open the door, the Ox, master of the barn, greeted him. (Animals have their own rankings among species, and the oxen with their dignity, strength, and habit of slow, careful thought, were respected by all.) But when he saw the Sphinx enter behind him, he flung up his head in alarm and bellowed.

"Who is this? Why have you brought it here?" The other animals in the barn—the Cow and her Calf, the Donkey, the Cat, the Rooster and his Hens—were startled from their rest and gazed in fear or awe or hatred at the Sphinx. For they were all servants, each in their own way, but sphinxes have never served any but themselves.

The Dog stood his ground, for though he respected the Ox, he never feared him. "The Sphinx is weary and cold. It needs shelter and food. And it is hurt."

The Ox looked carefully at the Sphinx, as the Dog had done before, and saw the Dog was right. This creature was on the Last Road. Still, it was a sphinx, and they were well-known as a dangerous race. Therefore he spoke to it. "If I let you stay in the barn, you must not hurt us. Do you agree?"

But the Sphinx did not answer the Ox.

The Ox waited, then said, "You must agree, or I will not let you stay." (He felt his strength was a match for a sphinx, at least this one.)

The Sphinx still did not answer.

The Cat, always quick in thought and deed, spoke. "Why do you not speak? *We* all can."

No reply.

The Dog said to the Cat, "Perhaps the Sphinx is wounded and so cannot speak."

The Cat replied sharply, "It is not wounded. See how its throat is sound and untouched. Speak!" she commanded the Sphinx. At this encroachment of his authority, the Ox lowered his head and eyed her, but she was unabashed.

And the Sphinx was mute before the barn's inhabitants.

The Dog said, "We cannot turn it away. We should not leave any creature homeless in the cold. We can share the warmth of the barn."

"But what if it hurts my daughter?" said the Cow. "She is still young. I will not let anyone harm her. And sphinxes are killers." She stamped her hoof in angry fear.

The First Hen spoke in fear also. "My sisters and I

are each barely a mouthful for so great a creature. Look how thin the Sphinx is—it must be hungry. I do not want it to stay." The Rooster and the other Hens murmured their agreement.

"You see how some here are afraid, and not without reason," the Ox said to the Sphinx. "You must agree, or leave."

The Sphinx said nothing. It stood, head held high, looking the Ox squarely in the face. The Ox began to gather himself in case he had to force it to leave. For a long moment the tension grew as the other animals watched fearfully. And then slowly, with obvious pain, the Sphinx bowed its head and knelt before the Ox.

So the Sphinx was permitted to stay in the barn, though the Cow still rolled her eye toward it, and made her body a barrier between it and her Calf. And the Rooster led the Hens to the farthest corner of the barn away from it.

The Dog guided the Sphinx to an empty stall well-bedded with straw, and the Sphinx lay down stiffly with a sigh. He was about to ask if it wanted water, when a distant howl came on the night air. All the animals lifted their heads to listen carefully, judging how far away the pack was, and the Dog's hackles stood up—he hated wolves. He said to the Sphinx, "I must go back outside and stand guard, for the Man and his family are away tonight. Donkey, will you help the Sphinx?"

The Donkey replied, "I will." So the Dog trotted to the door and slipped outside. The Donkey turned to the Sphinx and said, "I know you do not speak, but if you are thirsty, I will share my water with you." So saying, he took the handle of his water bucket between his teeth, and carried it over beside the Sphinx.

The Sphinx looked at the Donkey, then tried to

reach the water in the bucket. It was too stiff and unable to bend its neck, so it got clumsily to its feet. But it stumbled, knocking the bucket over, and the water flowed over its paws and into the straw. It looked at the Donkey again, seeming apologetic for its awkwardness.

The Cat jeered at the Donkey. "Now you have lost your water, and to what purpose?" The Sphinx looked sharply at the Cat, who had leapt up to the stall's rail.

"It doesn't matter. I can drink from the Cow's trough, or share with the Ox," replied the Donkey. "But the Sphinx is still thirsty."

"It cannot share my water!" said the Cow quickly, while her Calf looked on with alarm in her eyes. "But you are welcome, Donkey."

The Ox said to the Sphinx, "If you come here, you can drink from my trough." Which the Sphinx did, and after quenching its thirst, it bowed its head to the Ox. Then it returned to the stall, where the Cat still sat on the rail.

Now cats do not love sphinxes either. For though cats have been worshiped by men as though they were gods, the cats always remember that sphinxes come of a far more ancient lineage that has been long revered. And like many younger siblings, they are never secure in their place, but wonder if one day the eldest will demand it as well. So they pay close attention to their rights and comforts, to be sure others are always aware of them. For if they do not protect their rights, who will?

Thus, the Cat was displeased, because the stall was one of her favorite resting places, warm and free of drafts. She was sure the Dog knew this. (And perhaps the Dog did and had chosen the place deliberately, for dogs like to tease cats, whom they regard as far too self-important.) But because the Sphinx was so much larger than her, she could not make it leave her place. So she tried to assert her position another way.

She said, "Again I ask you, why do you not talk? On this night, all animals can speak."

The Sphinx simply looked at her.

She persisted, "Only say one word. Then I will know that you were found worthy of being given the gift of speech for one night, as we all were."

The Sphinx's brow lowered, and the Donkey hastily spoke. "Cat, we do not know why the gift was given to us. I do not know if I am worthy, but I am grateful."

"I am worthy," said the Cat. "My kind is worthy, for we have been worshiped. We know what it is to have people watch in excitement and awe as we walk before them."

The Donkey replied, "I know what that is like too, Cat."

"*You*?" the Cat scoffed. And even the others looked on in surprise, since the Donkey was normally quiet and unassuming.

"Yes. For once I bore a burden greater than even those the powerful Ox has borne—a Man. And people threw palm branches down in my path for me to walk upon."

"But that was not to honor *you*," insisted the Cat.

"No, it was not. It was to honor the Man on my back. I was not important. Still, I know what it is like. And I will never forget."

The barn was still, and even the Cat was subdued for a moment. For though her ancestors had been worshiped, she herself never had experienced anything like the Donkey. (Nor would she have ever guessed he had, because he was unpretentious.)

In the silence came again the howling of the wolves, much closer than before. All ears pricked up, listening. But the animals knew they were safe in the barn and that the Dog was outside guarding them.

Then the Cat sought to regain face. "Still, I have never heard before of one who could not speak on this night. Sphinx, again I ask you to say only a word."

The Sphinx looked at her, then yawned. This angered the Cat, for among her kind yawning in the face of another is an insult. She hissed, "Perhaps you were denied the gift. Perhaps you have done something evil and thus are punished. Perhaps you are evil!"

The Sphinx's eyes suddenly blazed in the unlit barn. Somehow it found strength and was on its feet with the awful speed of its kind, tail lashing around its haunches, a heavy paw raised to strike. The Cat crouched on the rail, fluffed in fear, realizing she looked at death. The Ox moved quickly toward the stall. And the Dog, who heard the Cat's hissing from outside, came into the barn and followed the Ox.

But before they reached the stall, the Sphinx lowered its paw and turned away from the Cat. It looked at the two approaching animals, then looked away, as if ashamed of losing control.

"You promised you would not hurt anyone here," said the Ox to the Sphinx.

But the Donkey spoke on the Sphinx's behalf. "You know the Cat goaded it."

"Yes, I know. But a creature that is so strong must also have strong self-control."

"It showed self-control. It turned away from the Cat."

"Because we were coming to stop it."

"The Sphinx could have struck the Cat long before we could have stopped it. It *did* show self-control," insisted the Donkey.

"It is evil! It should be driven away," snarled the Cat.

The Dog was about to speak, when there was a howl, closer again than before. And suddenly the First Hen cried, "Our youngest sister is gone!"

"What?" said the others. The Rooster said, "She strays foolishly, thinking only to find the next morsel of food. And with the Dog on guard, she felt safe."

A cry full of fear came from outside. "Help me, sisters! Help me, my lord!" (For so hens call their rooster.)

And there was an unmistakable wolfish howl of triumph, "There, pack-mates! See our prey!"

The Dog lunged outdoors, shouting as he ran, "I come! I come! Go away, you wolves! Go away! Go away or I will kill you!"

And to the astonishment of all, the Sphinx followed the Dog in deadly silence, drawing on some last reserve of strength.

There followed a dreadful noise of snarling, scuffling bodies, and cries of pain. The Ox stood by the door in case the Dog failed to hold off the pack and its members tried to enter. And each animal wondered what role the Sphinx was playing.

Then the Dog gave a terrible scream of pain. There was the sound of paws moving away. And the Youngest Hen crying in pain and fear, each sound becoming fainter as she was carried off.

The Cat slipped between the legs of the Ox and through a gap in the door. After a moment she called to the others, "The wolves have gone." They came out of the barn and looked at the bloody moonlit scene.

The Dog was lying on his side, horribly wounded, his throat torn open. His eyes flickered toward them, but it was obvious he was leaving them behind to go down the Last Road. He had made the wolves pay dearly to send him on that journey, though, for three of them had gone ahead of him, their bodies already lifeless. There was no sign of the Sphinx.

"So that is how we are repaid for giving it shelter," said the Cat. "It took the Hen and ran away, leaving the Dog to face the wolves alone."

"I cannot tell what happened," said the Ox. "The ground is too hard to hold tracks well, and the frost has been scuffed because of the fight."

"What of our sister?" asked the First Hen.

"She is probably filling the belly of the Sphinx," said the Cat with spiteful satisfaction. The Rooster replied angrily, "We all heard her calling us. We must go to her aid."

"We cannot, Rooster. It is too dangerous," said the Ox. "There were more wolves in the pack than these. We must stay here. We will mourn for the Dog, and I think you must mourn for your youngest sister." At this the Hens began to weep.

The animals stood vigil over the body of their loyal friend for the rest of the night, and it was a long, cold night indeed. But it was made a little easier because they could talk together and share memories of the Dog and the Youngest Hen, and thus share their sorrow as well. So the gift of speech was a most welcome gift that night.

At the first light of dawn, their voices were stilled, and they were alone again, isolated by their silence. (Though animals have ways of communicating without words, those ways are not as rich and precise as speech.)

And the Donkey set out to follow the trail left by the remainder of the pack, for he did not believe what the Cat said about the Sphinx abandoning the Dog and devouring the Hen. The trail went a long way up into the hills, and the Donkey realized the Ox had been right—they could not possibly have gone safely in the perilous night for such a distance.

Finally he came to a small gully, and at its entrance were a few scattered feathers and some bloodstains. He entered it sadly, for now he feared he was going to find exactly what the Cat had foretold.

But here in front of him was the carcass of a wolf, killed by the blow of a huge clawed paw, the gashes ripping across its body. And there, a few feet away, was a second dead wolf. The Donkey trotted deeper into the gully.

Whereupon he heard the clucking of the Youngest Hen! There she was, very much alive (though missing some feathers) between the paws of the Sphinx. She refused to move as the Donkey approached.

The Sphinx was alive, though grievously hurt, and the Donkey could see it would not live much longer. Since he could no longer speak, the Donkey lowered his head and touched his muzzle to the Sphinx's face.

And the Sphinx spoke! "Greetings, my friend." Its voice was weak. "You see, I did not betray your trust. . . ." It saw the astonishment in the Donkey's eyes and answered the question there. "Yes, I can speak, though last night I could not." It paused, and the Donkey could see it gathering what little remained of its strength. "I come of an ancient race under the dominion of an ancient and perhaps crueler god, and I am ruled by different commandments than you. Thus, on the night you and your brethren were given the gift of speech, I was bound in silence." The Sphinx paused again, and now its voice was very weak. "But our time has passed, and the God you serve rules now. . . ."

Its head drooped and it collapsed on its side, and the Donkey saw how the dark blood had flowed from the many wounds the wolves had inflicted. So the

Youngest Hen and the Donkey waited together as the Sphinx took its remaining steps on the Final Road.

And as they waited, the Donkey considered what the Sphinx had said. Are we that different? We both are living creatures. The Sphinx responded to the Dog's kindness and the Ox's trust as any of us would have. And it had the courage and honor to defend one of the least of us to the death. But because he was a donkey, he did could not find a sure answer, ponder though he might. All he could do was stay by the Sphinx, with the Youngest Hen, so that it would not be alone. So died the last Sphinx. Then the Donkey and the Youngest Hen returned to their home, and the Rooster and the other Hens rejoiced to see their sister alive.

But the Cat never knew the truth of what happened, for the Donkey and the Youngest Hen could not tell her. Nor did she ever learn what the Donkey knew, that it is unwise to judge others solely by appearance. For one never knows what lies in the heart, except God.

THE BEST LAID SCHEMES

by Jack Nimersheim

"It's all that goddamn Tinkerbell's fault! Sucking up to that Peter Pan faggot the way she did." God, how I had grown to hate Maug Moulach's voice—real fingernails-on-a-blackboard stuff, to quote an overused analogy. "And then, going all soft on those two useless brats . . . what the hell were their names, Wendy and something? No wonder people don't respect us anymore."

Broonie from Shetland nodded silently, which was about all he ever did. Glen Eitli expressed his agreement a bit more emphatically, making guttural noises and slamming his hand down on the glass tabletop—an odd sight, indeed, given that he only had one . . . hand, that is. The others around the conference table found equally eccentric ways to indicate their support for Moulach's position.

Obviously, I needed to regain control of the meeting somehow. If I didn't, it would soon degenerate into utter chaos.

"Please," I interjected, trying to keep my voice calm. (Or, at least, as calm as possible, given the situation.) "Let's try, if we can, to focus our attention on the topic at hand? It's been my experience that merely assigning a scapegoat to an already existing problem rarely contributes to its resolution."

"I propose we listen to the pink one, brothers . . . and, of course, to Sister Maug. His observation is not without merit."

The rich, baritone voice startled me. These were the first words I'd ever heard Broonie utter. Prior to this comment, I did not even know whether he counted speech among his abilities. Judging from the stunned silence that greeted the ancient Trow's suggestion, I wasn't the only one thrown off balance by his intervention.

All eyes turned toward me, measuring my response. Glen Eitli's cyclopean stare unnerved me somewhat, to be sure; a one-eyed Fachan tends to have this effect on mere mortals. Nevertheless, I took a deep breath and forged ahead. With luck, I figured I might be able to capitalize on the opening my unexpected ally had provided me.

"Thank you, uh, Mr. Broonie. If I were you folks, I wouldn't give a tinker's damn about Tinkerbell. Or any other renegade fairy, for that matter. The way I see it, what's done is done. You can't change the past. Our top priority now should be figuring out exactly where we stand today. That will allow us to come up with some ideas on how to go about meeting your objectives for tomorrow."

Damn! A golden opportunity to assert myself and all I could manage were a few cliches—feeble ones, to boot. The pressure was getting to me. Hell. Why shouldn't it? In over two decades of advertising, I'd never handled an account that even remotely resembled this one. I still remember the day Steve dumped this pile of crap on my lap.

*   *   *

"Hey, Billy boy, what's happening? I see you're working on the Burger Prince campaign. How are things going?"

Steve's Cheshire-Cat grin should have sent up a red flag. It didn't.

"Great. Just great. In the past six hours I've come up with ten new and creative ways to convince the masses that a steroid-laden glob of dead cow and a handful of potatoes, fried in coconut oil and then drenched with sodium, not only tastes good, but is good for them, too."

"Is that a note of cynicism I hear in your voice?"

"More like an entire symphony." I went back to sketching in the Ultra-Super BigBurger I'd been working on when Steve interrupted me. Over the years, I've mastered the fine art of talking and drawing at the same time.

"Ah, this is just the Autumn of your discontent, buddy boy. You'll snap out of it." Paraphrasing Shakespeare was one of my partner's more obnoxious habits.

"I wouldn't bet my next commission check on that, Steve. We've had this agency for, what, fifteen years now? I originally got into this business because I thought it would be fun, exciting. And it was . . . at first. But lately, I don't know, everything's changed. Day in, day out, it's the same old stuff. Sure, one minute we might tell America that its hair is falling out, the next we may try to convince everyone that their teeth are rotting, or that their pits smell. When you get right down to it, though, the melody never changes, only the words to whatever chorus we happen to be singing at the time.

"I'm bored, Steve. B-O-R-E-D. What I need is some kind of new and different project to recharge my batteries."

What's the old saying? "Be careful what you wish for; it may just come true." The way I figure it, Steve must have had this axiom tattooed on the insides of his eyelids.

"You want 'new and different,' my friend? Well, allow me to introduce you to the answer to your prayers. Billy boy, meet Glen Eitli. Mr. Eitli, this is William O'Brian, the more industrious half of our little enterprise."

I don't know what I expected to see when I looked up from my drawing board. Probably another fat-cat V.P. of Marketing from still another fast-food franchise or cosmetics conglomerate—all decked out in your basic Republican three-piecer and flashing a disdainful smirk that says, "Trust me about as far as you can throw me, pal." Whatever I anticipated, it certainly didn't include Glen Eitli, the Son of Colin.

My partner is neither tall nor particularly handsome. Compared to his companion, however, Steve looked like a cross between Robert Redford and Larry Bird. I mean, we're talking a terminal case of the short-and-uglies, here. The creature standing next to him hit the tape at about the three-foot mark. It's not that I have anything against little persons, mind you, but Glen Eitli satisfied only half of the qualifications normally associated with this particular politically correct euphemism. Little he may have been, but he was definitely not a person.

A good indication of Glen Eitli's decidedly nonhuman pedigree surfaced when he extended his hand in greeting. Covered with thick, matted fur, it protruded from the ridge of his chest like some obscene, cancerous growth. A lone eye staring out from the middle of his furrowed brow offered further testimony to Eitli's somewhat unusual lineage. Compared to these oddities, the fact that he somehow managed to maintain his balance on but one gnarled and thickly veined leg descending from the center of his body hardly deserves mention.

"It's pleased I am to be makin' your acquaintance, Mr. O'Brian. You wouldn't by any chance be kin to the Dundee clan of that fine Scottish family, would ye?"

I responded to this polite inquiry the same way I believe any experienced and dedicated professional would have under similar circumstances: I fainted.

"What in the hell do you mean, he's our newest client? That thing is a goddamned alien!"

"Glen Eitli is not an alien, Billy boy. He's a fairy."

"I'm not interested in his sexual preferences, Steve."

"Not that kind of fairy. He's the real thing. One of the 'Wee Folk' that dominate the lore and legends of England, Ireland, and Scotland. To be more precise, Glen Eitli claims to be a Fachan, which he described to me as a type of fairy that inhabits the Scottish West Highlands—the very place, if I recall correctly, that your own father's father emigrated from."

"Right. And I'm the Prince of Whales."

"Whatever you say, Your Highness."

"Don't yank my chain, Steve. Just explain to me what the hell this is all about."

"What it's about, pal, is the future. And the way I see it, that admittedly odd-looking creature cooling his heels—pardon me, his heel—in your office right now is our ticket to a very prosperous one."

"I see your mouth moving, Steve, but I'm not hearing any words I understand."

"Okay, buddy, here's the scoop. It seems that the fairies aren't too thrilled with the way our modern society perceives them. I haven't had time to scope out the whole picture yet—I only talked with Eitli a few minutes before bringing him in to meet you—but my initial impression is that he and his . . . um . . . cousins, so to speak, are worried about what they view as an erosion in their power base."

"I'm only going to ask you this one more time, Steve: What the fuck are you talking about? And see if you can respond in plain English this time. If you don't, you'll find out exactly how strong my Scottish heritage is."

"Hey, pal, calm down, or you'll pop an artery for sure. From what I gather, based on my brief conversation with Eitli, there was a time when the fairies demanded our respect. They intimidated and, in the case of certain radical factions, terrorized a lot of people. Mention fairies today, however, and most folks react the same way you did. More likely than not, they'll think you're talking about a bunch of guys who share an affinity for sibilance standing around holding hands with one another, waiting for the next Johnny Mathis tune to turn up on the jukebox."

"The point, Steve. Get to the goddamn point!"

"Well, it seems that the fairies are fed up with their current situation—I'm talking about Eitli and his crew here, not the Mathis fans. The way they figure it, they're in need of a major image overhaul. And guess which advertising agency they've selected to help them regain their former glory?"

That's how O'Brian and Fitch came to represent Glen Eitli and Associates—or the "Wee Folk," as Steve still insists on calling them.

Glen Eitli's "associates" consisted of an odd assortment of bizarre creatures representing the various branches of the fairy community. I've already mentioned Broonie and Maug Moulach. Whoever came up with the word "opposite" must have had these two in mind when they did so.

Broonie was the King of the Trows, a clan of fairies from the Shetland islands that still claimed ancient but strained ties to the Scandinavian trolls. He also happened to be quiet, considerate, and always willing to evaluate an idea based on its own merits. Moulach, on the other hand—or Hairy Meg, as her compatriots called her, after first making sure she was nowhere within earshot—was outspoken and combative. The wrong word at the wrong time (or the right word at the wrong time, for that matter) could cause Moulach to go nova. On a good day, her anger was held in check by what might best be described as a hair trigger.

Maug Moulach's mercuric temperament proved a constant source of amusement to Dunnie, a shapeshifting goblin from Hazelrigg on Belford Moor. Dunnie seemed more interested in playing practical jokes on his companions than in coming up with any practical solution to their shared dilemma. His efforts in this area provoked endless and creative competition from a second, equally determined prankster, Fear Dearg. Even immersed in this esoteric crowd, the latter cut an unusual figure. Barely six inches tall, Fear Dearg always dressed in a long scarlet coat and similarly colored sugar-loaf hat. So far as I could tell, he never took them off. (I remember one meeting during which the thermostat in our office malfunctioned. Even as the temperature in the crowded conference room approached ninety degrees, the tiny Cluricaun from Munster did not remove either of these items.)

Given his admiration for Shakespeare, Steve responded enthusiastically to the news that Robin Goodfellow had also been named to the advisory council. He was terribly disappointed when, due to a

prior commitment, Goodfellow arrived late for our
initial meeting. Steve was so excited by the time the
most famous of fairies entered the room, that I fully
expected him to commit some kind of faux pas. (A
predilection toward social gaffes is another one of my
partner's endearing qualities.) However, even I could
not have anticipated the speed with which he would
fulfill my expectations. Goodfellow had barely cleared
the door when Steve was out of his chair bounding
toward him, arms outstretched as if he were greeting
a long-lost friend.

"Puck! Puck, my good fellow! Hey, that's a joke.
Goodfellow, as in Puck. Get it? Oh, well, never mind.
Anyway, Puck, you have no idea how long I've looked
forward to meeting you."

Steve's first mistake was to assume that Shakespeare
had adequately researched fairy lore, prior to writing
A Midsummer's Night Dream. His second was to act
upon this assumption.

It turns out that Robin Goodfellow despised the
nickname the Bard had bestowed upon him. As Glen
Eitli explained to me later, the reason for Goodfellow's reaction was related to a little-known historical
fact of which I—and, obviously, Steve, also—was unaware. According to Eitli, in pre-Victorian times the
word Puck was commonly used to identify the Devil.
No wonder Goodfellow found it offensive. To his
credit, the son of Oberon did not reciprocate with
malice; mischief might be a more appropriate word to
describe his subsequent actions.

I can still hear Goodfellow bellowing his characteris-
tic "Ho! Ho! Ho!" immediately after administering
what he no doubt perceived to be just retaliation for
Steve's insolence. I can only imagine how this retort
must have sounded in the donkey ears my partner
suddenly found himself sporting.

With Goodfellow's arrival, our little group was complete. Glen Eitli the Son of Colin, Broonie, Maug Moulach, Dunnie, Fear Dearg, and Robin Goodfellow—whom Steve never again referred to as Puck. It was a strange and strangely wondrous cast of characters. And I faced the unenviable task of forging a consensus among them.

My mother, rest her soul, always wanted me to be a doctor. Looking around the conference table during that initial meeting, I suddenly found myself wishing that I had followed her advice.

Maug Moulach launched her attack against Tinkerbell in early November, during our ninth weekly meeting with Eitli and the others. Steve and I had poured almost all our creative energies into this project for over two months, and still found ourselves unable to deliver a proposal acceptable to all parties involved.

Frustration was beginning to fray everyone's nerves, including mine. Clearly, it was time to put the cliches out to pasture (if you'll forgive me once more) and come up with some kind of major brainstorm. If we failed to close this account, things would be awfully bare under my Christmas tree this year.

Suddenly, an entire strategy popped into my head. It was an unorthodox approach, to be sure, one fraught with potential pitfalls. Furthermore, I knew Steve would be justifiably upset with me for making a major presentation to a client without running it by him first. Still, if I could pitch the concept properly—which, in this case, my hustler's instincts told me involved letting everything pour out of my subconscious spontaneously, rolling with the flow as inspiration struck—I felt certain I could sell Eitli and the others on the idea.

It was a gamble, to be sure. But as they say, desperate times call for desperate measures. And if I've learned one thing during my twenty years in advertising, it's that, more often than not, desperation is the midwife to inspiration. Besides, it's not like Steve and I had a wealth of alternatives to fall back upon. When you get right down to it, we had two choices: Put up or shut up. What the hell did I have to lose?

I cleared my throat before starting into my spiel.

"Gentlemen, and Maug, I think I've come up with the perfect solution to our problem. . . ."

We kicked things off two weeks later with a ten-second teaser. Nothing fancy, mind you. Just a color slide of an actor dressed up in a Santa Claus suit, lying in a pool of blood. A voice-over as it faded to black offered a simple warning: "Parents, prepare your children for a real Christmas surprise this year."

We placed this spot on the number-three station in fifteen secondary markets. Our choices weren't random. Each was a network affiliate. It was a calculated risk, but I felt fairly certain that some greedy stringer somewhere would alert the national news desks to our minimalist and somewhat macabre presentation.

Human nature being what it is, I wasn't disappointed. NBC and ABC called the second day the spot aired. CBS was on the phone twenty-four hours later. (We subsequently discovered that the delay was caused by the fact that both Rather and Wallace wanted the story. Rumor has it that these two journalistic giants engaged in an impromptu wrestling match on the floor of the commissary in CBS's New York headquarters before some Vice President of News Programming finally gave the nod to Rather. It would have been nice to crack 60 Minutes that early in the campaign, to be sure. But what the hell? Beggars can't be choosers.)

Not a bad beginning. Through adroit manipulation, we'd managed to leverage a minor investment into network exposure. Even more important to our ultimate goals, the enigmatic nature of that initial spot piqued the nation's interest. The challenge now was not to reveal too much, too quickly. It was crucial that we keep the rubes on the hook—a strategy both Steve and I had had grilled into us *ad nauseum,* way back in Advertising 101.

To this end, we never let our clients go before the cameras. In fact, we provided no clues whatsoever to their identity. Instead, Steve and I responded to all inquiries and interview questions with a carefully orchestrated series of cryptic comments designed to keep people talking, but not disclose anything of real substance for them to talk about.

Phase two of our strategy kicked in during the first weekend of December, fourteen days after the initial airing of the "Dead Santa" spot, as it had been dubbed by the media. Our basic theme remained unchanged. We merely fleshed it out with considerably more, and more graphic, details.

"I don't mean to be questioning the wisdom of a fellow Scotsman, William, but . . ."

"Ah, pipe down, Broonie! I don't want to miss this. I've dreamed about knocking off that pompous son-of-a-bitch for centuries. This may not be the real thing, but it's still pretty damn satisfying. Explain to me again how you accomplished it, O'Brian." Maug was sitting on the floor of the conference room staring at the television, an activity with which she occupied much of her time these days.

"It's called a matte shot, Maug. The actual process

is extremely complicated. Basically, however, I took
the sequence we filmed of you in the studio and combined it with pictures shot from a real airplane flying
over the Arctic. Then, using miniatures . . ."

"Quiet! Here comes my favorite part—the 'strafing,'
I believe you called it, didn't you, O'Brian?"

"That's right, Maug."

"Check out the look of terror on that fat bastard's
face! He knows I've got him dead in my sights, another quaint expression you taught me, O'Brian."

Maug couldn't get enough of seeing herself play out
this bloodthirsty scenario. Neither could the rest of
America, if our marketing surveys were reliable.

People were fascinated with the sixty-second vi-
gnette showing Maug Moulach picking off Santa Claus
from the pilot's seat of an F-15 fighter jet. So much
so, in fact, that the three major networks, Fox, and
more than two hundred independents asked permis-
sion to run it, free of charge, in their *primest* prime-
time slots. We accepted all offers—after an appropriate delay designed to imply indecision, of course.
The only request we couldn't satisfy came from the
NFL, which was disappointed as hell when we informed them that this spot was but one element of an
integrated Christmas campaign, and that it would be
pulled from the schedule long before SuperBowl
Sunday.

"William, if I may?"

"What? Oh, I'm sorry, Broonie. Did you have
something you wanted to discuss with me?"

"Indeed I do, laddie. As I was saying before being
so rudely interrupted, I don't mean to question the
wisdom of a fellow Scotsman, but I'm not sure I feel
comfortable with the direction this 'advertising campaign,' as you call it, is taking."

"What is it you disagree with, Broonie?"

"While it's true that we fairies have always been a mischievous lot, violence is something the vast majority of us shy away from. I was wondering why you feel it's necessary to portray us in such a brutal fashion."

"It's really quite simple. Look up at that television set, Broonie. What do you see?"

Maug was once again cheering her performance, which at any given time was almost guaranteed to be running on some channel.

"That's easy, William. I see Maug Moulach—a spiteful creature, if ever there was one—fulfilling one of her favorite fantasies. I've long been aware of the hostility that exists between Maug and ol' Kringle. It all started, I believe, with a lump of coal she found in her stocking one Christmas morn. I'd be willin' to bet me last lucky clover that the old fellow meant it as a joke. But Maug, being Maug, failed to see the whimsy in Kris' little prank. To finally be able to pay him back—even if it is all an 'electronic hoax,' as I believe you once described it—gives her no end of glee.

"What I fail to see is how revealin' to the world Maug's violent tendencies—an aberration among the Wee Folk, I assure you—will help us achieve our ultimate goal."

Broonie and I had become close friends in the weeks since he'd risen to my defense at that November meeting. In part, this was because of his gentle nature. Honesty forces me to admit, however, that a certain amount of the comfort I took from Broonie's company could be traced to the fact that he was the most *human* member of the fairy delegation. He suffered none of the grotesque physical deformities that characterized his companions. Nor did he display a penchant for outrageous behavior, a trait in which the others seemed to take great pride. In fact, except for his small stature, Broonie reminded me of my grandfather. His white hair and beard may have framed a gray and wizened face, but his bright green eyes projected the same wit and wisdom that I idolized in Grandpa O'Brian before he died.

Broonie possessed another quality I found refreshing: his naîveté. The tiny Trow may have been several hundred years old, but he understood little about how life worked beyond the boundaries of his isolated community north of Sumburg Head.

"Let me see if I can explain, Broonie. There was a time, I admit, when mischief and harmless pranks sufficed to intimidate the local peasants. But the world has changed since then. So, too, has humanity.

"It's a jungle out there, my friend, not the lush, green landscape of the Scottish hillsides that you're accustomed to operating in. Once upon a time, to quote a million fairy tales, rearranging a woodpile or stealing some larder in the dark of night may have been enough to convince us of your existence. Try that today, however, and chances are some bozo who thinks he has a God-given right to protect his property from derelicts and dope-heads any way he sees fit will be standing guard on the front porch with a high-caliber, semi-automatic rifle, complete with an infrared scope, just waiting to blow your Scottish ass off.

"What we have to do is persuade a cold, callous, and overly analytical world that, even in these harsh times, fairies are a force to be reckoned with. What better way to accomplish this than to depict you as totally ruthless creatures who lack even a shred of decency?"

"But to show us slaughtering ol' Kris Kringle the way ye have, William. Don't you feel that this might be takin' things just a wee bit too far?"

"Not at all, Broonie. It's perfect. In fact, it was

thinking about the upcoming Christmas holidays that provided the original inspiration for this entire campaign, back in our November meeting.

"Think about it. Who's the sweetest, most harmless individual, man or myth, that you know? Barring a few major deities and various other religious figures whom, for obvious reasons, I felt it best to disregard— after all, I didn't want to hand the world another sanctimonious martyr; God knows, we have enough of those already—I decided it had to be Santa Claus. I mean, here's a dude who spends the entire year preparing for one special night on which he delivers a little bit of magic, not to mention some pretty impressive booty, to an eagerly waiting world.

"We're talking about a major do-gooder, here. The guy's an icon. The fact that Maug already had a bone to pick with him was an incredible stroke of luck. It saved us a bundle on coaching fees. When the time came to shoot that second commercial, I simply put Maug in the fake cockpit, outlined the basic story line to her, and started the cameras rolling. After viewing the first rushes, I realized that even De Niro couldn't have brought as much passion to the part.

"Trust me on this one, Broonie. Once we convince people that the fairies are capable of shooting down Santa Claus in cold blood without a hint of remorse, your image problems will be over."

"Of course, I'm willin' to stick with ye, William, me lad. But I can't help recallin' the immortal words of me friend and fellow countryman, Robert Burns, when he warned, *'The best laid schemes o' mice and men gang aft a-gley.'* That's strikes me as a sage bit of counsel, m'boy. One that's worth ponderin' over, if only a wee bit."

* * *

I must admit, a "wee bit" was about all the consideration I gave Broonie's suggestion. What the hell could there possibly be to worry about? Things were working out even better than I had originally thought they would. After that second spot revealed the identity of our mysterious clients, more—and more impressive—opportunities opened up for the Wee Folk to deliver their message.

Geraldo's people contacted us, begging for exclusive interview rights. We promptly maneuvered then into a head-to-head bidding war against Oprah, who had called from Chicago only hours earlier. (Sally Jesse and Maury also put in a request, but inside sources informed us that their coffers weren't quite up to the task.) Although the final offer from the Midwest included a slightly higher talent fee, we opted for the kid from the East Coast.

Why? To be honest, it was another calculated risk.

Figuring Geraldo was at least as pretentious as Steve, we sent Robin Goodfellow, along with Maug and Dunnie, to participate in the special live show his producers arranged at our request. As we suspected, the talk-show circuit's boy wonder couldn't resist exploring the Shakespearean connection.

"Thank you, Maug Moulach, for that candid account of one woman's brush with the darker side of Saint Nick. When we come back, you'll meet a man who claims to be Robin Goodfellow, although he's probably better known to you by the name that's made him England's most illustrious and easily recognized hobgoblin: Puck."

From my vantage point backstage I saw Robin Goodfellow grimace, then grin, then wink, once. Voila! Instant media exposure . . . again.

Geraldo making an ass out of himself may have become such a common occurrence that it no longer

warranted national coverage, but the report of someone else turning him into one—literally, this time, in
front of what the Nielson overnights estimated to be a
twenty-three share audience—was the lead story that
evening on all three networks, CNN, *and* the MacNeil/
Lehrer News Hour. When you make it onto PBS, you
know you've arrived.

"Well, we did it, pal." Steve raised his beer can and
tilted the top of it toward me in a mock toast.

The goddamn thermostat was on the fritz again.
Opening the window lowered the temperature in my
office to an almost bearable eighty-two degrees. Steve
had shown up at my door about an hour ago, just
before quitting time, carrying a six-pack and a bag of
pretzels. Normally, I enjoyed these impromptu bull
sessions with Steve. Tonight, I couldn't wait for him
to leave.

So far as I could tell, the two of us were the only
ones still in the building. Everyone else had already
left. Headed home, I guess. Or gone wherever it is
that people go who don't go home on Christmas Eve.

"Yeah, I suppose we did."

"You *suppose* we did? Shit, Billy boy, we just
made advertising history!"

"Uh-huh."

"You certainly don't act like somebody who just
clinched a Cleo. Did I say *a* Cleo? Hell. We're bound
to win at least three or four of those babies. Who
knows? We may just sweep the awards this year.

"We should get a special display case built for them,
don't you think? Put it behind Sally's desk in the main
reception area. That'd certainly brighten up the old
waiting room, wouldn't it?"

"Maybe."

"What do you mean, maybe? Oh, I get it. You're

thinking we should move into bigger, more modern offices. Well, hell. Why not? Come the New Year, we'll have potential clients lining up around the block, begging to be represented by O'Brian and Fitch. We'll put finding some new digs at the top of our agenda. We can start looking right after the holidays.

"Speaking of which, I should get going. I promised Marge I wouldn't be too late tonight. The kids have been acting kind of strange lately. It's the damnedest thing. Try as they might, they just can't seem to get into the holiday spirit. Usually by tonight, Brenda's bouncing off the walls with excitement and Billy's rummaged through every closet in the house, looking for where we stashed the gifts. This year, it's like they don't give a damn.

"Marge seems to think that a big family dinner, followed by Midnight Mass at the Cathedral, will snap them out of their lethargy. I'm not sure I agree, but what can it hurt? Anyway, I'd better be heading home."

Steve stood up, finished his beer, dropped the empty can into the trash, and started out of the room. Just before he reached the hall, he turned around, smiled, and winked at me.

"We done good, buddy boy. By the way, merry Christmas."

"Yeah, right, Steve. Merry Christmas."

The sound of a Salvation Army bell drifted up from the sidewalk. Somewhere down the street, someone was whistling "Santa Claus is Coming to Town." At least, I think that's what it was. The melody sounded familiar, but the tempo was all wrong—too slow, almost like a funeral dirge.

The outside door slammed shut a few seconds later. Putting my feet up on the desk, I leaned back in the

chair and closed my eyes. I was alone at last . . . or
so I believed.

"You can sense it, can't ye, laddie?"

As it had the first time I heard it, the deep and
resonant voice startled me. My eyes shot open and I
damn near fell backward. I caught myself just in time
to avoid falling flat on my ass.

"Broonie!"

The grizzled, old Trow was sitting in the chair Steve
had vacated only moments earlier, staring across the
top of the desk at me.

"Aye, William, t'is I."

"What the heck are you doing here?"

"I just thought I'd drop by and see if I could help
a friend."

"I appreciate the thought, Broonie, but I wasn't
aware that I needed any help. Hell, why would I? It's
Christmas Eve and everything's right with the world.
Peace on Earth, good will toward men—and all those
other holiday platitudes."

"Ye don't fool me, laddie. Like I said, you can
sense what's happenin'. And I don't think you like
it." His eyes held no mischief, nor even a trace of wit.
The wisdom, however, still shone through.

"You're right, Broonie," I sighed. "I can, and I
don't. We really fucked up, didn't we?"

"Well, now, I'd say that depends."

"On what?"

"On who y'mean by 'we' and what you're referrin'
to with that quaint little colloquialism you humans
seem so fond of."

"I mean *we*, Broonie, Steve and me."

"I wouldn't be too hard on yourself if I were you,
laddie. After all, you did have a wee bit of help in
your efforts, if you know what I mean. Besides, I
seem to remember you sayin' once that finding some-

one to blame for a problem rarely contributes to its solution."

"Yeah, I did say that, didn't I?"

"That you did, m'boy. And you were right. Understanding the 'what' of a problem is much more important than figurin' out who's responsible for it—an observation that brings me back to my second question. Just what is it that you're thinkin' you 'fucked up,' to quote your own somewhat crude description?"

"You know, the . . . I don't know . . . the *magic,* the special feeling that's always made this a special time of the year. It's gone, isn't it?"

This time it was Broonie's turn to sigh.

"Aye, laddie, I'm afraid it is."

"Steve's still too busy contemplating the megabucks we'll rake in as a result of this campaign to realize it, even though his own kids have been affected. But you're right. For some reason, I can sense it.

"This wasn't what I set out to accomplish. You believe that, don't you, Broonie?"

"I do, William, not that that changes anything."

"What went wrong, old friend? Do you have any idea?"

"I think it has to do with what you once told me about how humanity has changed, down through the ages. Once upon a time, to revive the phrase you used on that occasion, people looked out upon the world and saw a wondrous place, a place filled with magic and mystery.

"We, the Wee Folk, thrived back then, as did many other so-called mythological creatures. Thunder was not the consequence of billions of charged particles shattering the sound barrier. T'was the fury of a god. Thus was born Thor—a brutish and blustering oaf, if ever I met one. Spirits, not microscopic entities, were thought to have invaded the bodies of the sufferin' and the infirm.

"Over time, however, science has replaced magic at the heart of your convictions. And as this happened, little by little, one by one, you discarded your myths, until only a handful survived. The story of Santa Claus—or Saint Nicholas, or Father Christmas, or whatever—was one of these.

"Maybe Kris endured because he personified something that wasn't cosmic in scope, or earth-shattering in its expression. He was merely a kind and gentle man who set aside one night of the year to bring joy and happiness to the children of the world. When you slaughtered the man, you shattered the myth."

"But that was just a commercial, Broonie. A trick of technology. Surely, no one believed it was real."

"They didn't have to believe, William. They reacted. And in their reaction, I have a feeling they saw a side of themselves they didn't like very much. Truth to tell, I'd be willin' to bet that a part of you also enjoyed watching that lovable old man chopped to bits by Maug's vicious attack. Am I correct?"

I didn't respond. Nor did I want to. I didn't need to.

THE GIFT OF THE MAGICIANS, WITH APOLOGIES TO YOU KNOW WHO

by Jane Yolen

One gold coin with the face of George II on it, whoever *he* was. Three copper pennies. And a crimped
tin thing stamped with a fleur de lis. That was all.
Beauty stared down at it. The trouble with running a
large house this far out in the country, even *with* magical help, was there was never any real spending
money. Except for what might be found in the odd
theatrical trunk, in the secret desk drawer, and at the
bottom of the pond every spring when it was drained.
Three times she had counted: one gold, three coppers,
one tin. And the next day would be Christmas.

There was clearly nothing for her to do but flop
down on the Victorian sofa, the hard one with the
mahogany armrests, and howl. So she did. She howled
as she had heard him howl, and wept and pounded
the armrests for good measure. It made her feel ever
so much better. Except for her hands, which now hurt
abominably. But that's the trouble with Victorian
sofas. Whatever *they* were.

The whole house was similarly accoutered: Federal,
Empire, Art Deco, Louis Quinze. With tags on each

explaining the name and period. Names about which she knew nothing but which the house had conjured up out of the past, present, and future. None of it was comfortable, though clearly all of it—according to the tags—was expensive. She longed for the simpler days at home with Papa and her sisters when even a penniless Christmas after dear Papa had lost all his money meant pleasant afternoons in the kitchen baking presents for the neighbors.

Now, of course, she had no neighbors. And her housemate was used to so much better than her meager kitchen skills could offer. Even if the magical help would let her into the kitchen which they—it or whatever—would not do.

She finished her cry, left off the howling, and went down the long hallway to her room. There she found her powder and pouffs and repaired the damage to her complexion speedily. He liked her bright and simple and smelling of herself, and magical cosmetics could do *such* wonders for even the sallowest of skins.

Then she looked into the far-seeing mirror—there were no windows in the house—and saw her old gray cat Miaou walking on a gray fence in her gray backyard. It made her homesick all over again, even though dear Papa was now so poor, and she had only one gold, three coppers, one tin with which to buy Beast a present for Christmas.

She blinked and wished and the mirror became only a mirror again and she stared at her reflection. She thought long and hard and pulled down her red hair, letting it fall to its full length, just slightly above her knees.

Now there were two things in that great magical house far out in the country in which both she and Beast took great pride. One was Beast's gold watch because it was his link with the real past, not the

magical made-up past. The watch had been his father's
and his grandfather's before him, though everything
else had been wiped away in the spell. The other thing
was Beauty's hair for, despite her name, it was the
only thing beautiful about her. Had Rapunzel lived
across the way instead of in the next kingdom, with
her handsome but remarkably stupid husband, Beauty
would have worn her hair down at every opportunity
just to depreciate Her Majesty's gifts.

So now Beauty's hair fell over her shoulders and
down past her waist, almost to her knees, rippling and
shining like a cascade of red waters. There was a magical hush in the room and she smiled to herself at it,
a little shyly, a little proudly. The house admired her
hair almost as much as Beast did. Then she bound it
all up again, sighing because she knew what she had
to do.

A disguise. She needed a disguise. She would go
into town—a two day walk, a one day ride, but with
magic only a short if bumpy ten minutes away—in
disguise. She opened the closet and wished very hard.
On went the old brown leather bomber jacket. The
leather outback hat. She took a second to tear off the
price tags. Tucking the silk bodice into the leather
pants, she ran her hands down her legs. Boots! She
would need boots. She wished again. The thigh-high
leather boots were a fine touch. Checking in the mirror, she saw only her gray cat.

"Pooh!" she said to the mirror. Miaou looked up
startled, saw nothing, moved on.

With a brilliant sparkle in her eyes, she went out of
the bedroom, down the stairs, across the wide expanse
of lawn, toward the gate.

At the gate she twisted her ring twice. ("Once for
home, twice for town, three times for return," Beast
had drummed into her when she had first been his

guest. Never mind the hair. The ring was her *most* precious possession.)

Ten bumpy minutes later she landed in the main street of the town.

As her red hair was tucked up into the outback hat, no one recognized her. Or if they did, they only bowed. No one called her by name. This was a town used to disguised gentry. She walked up and down the street for a few minutes, screwing up her courage. Then she stopped by a sign that read MADAME SUZZANE: HAIR GOODS AND GONE TOMORROW.

Beauty ran up the steep flight of stairs and collected herself.

Madame Suzzane was squatting on a stool behind a large wooden counter. She was a big woman, white and round and graying at the edges, like a particularly dangerous mushroom.

"Will you buy my hair?" Beauty asked.

"Take off that silly hat first? Where'd you get it?" Her voice had a mushroomy sound to it, soft and spongy.

"In a catalog," Beauty said.

"Never heard of it."

The hat came off. Down rippled the red cascade.

"Nah—can't use red. Drug on the market. Besides, if . . . He . . . knew." If anything, Madame Suzzane turned whiter, grayer.

"But I have nothing else to sell." Beauty's eyes grew wider, weepy.

"What about that ring?" Madame Suzzane asked, pointing.

"I can't."

"You can."

"I can't."

"You can."

"How much?"

"Five hundred dollars," said Madame Suzzane, adding a bit for inflation. And for the danger.

Beauty pulled the ring off her finger, forgetting everything in her eagerness to buy a gift for Beast. "Quickly, before I change my mind."

She ran down the stairs, simultaneously binding up her hair again and shoving it back under the hat. The street seemed much longer, much more filled with shops now that she had money in her hands. Real money. Not the gold coins, copper pennies, and crimped tin thing in her pocket.

The next two hours raced by as she ransacked the stores looking for a present for Beast and, not unexpectedly, finding a thing or two for herself: some nail polish in the latest color from the Isles, a faux pearl necklace with a delicious rhinestone clasp, the most delicate china faun cavorting with three shepherdesses in rosebud pink gowns, and a painting of a jester cleverly limned on black velvet that would fit right over her poster bed.

And then she found Beast's present at last, a perfect tortoiseshell comb for his mane, set with little battery-driven (whatever *that* was) lights that winked on and off and on again. She had considered a fob for his grandfather's watch, but the ones she saw were all much too expensive. And besides, the old fob that came with the watch was still in good shape, for something old. And she doubted whether he'd have been willing to part with it anyway. Just like Beast, preferring the old to the new, preferring the rough to the smooth, preferring her to . . . to . . . to someone like Rapunzel.

Then with all her goodies packed carefully in a string bag purchased with the last of her dollars, she was ready to go.

Only, of course, she hadn't the ring anymore. And no one would take the gold coin or the copper pennies or the crimped tin thing for a carriage and horse and driver to get her back. Not even with her promise made, cross her heart, to fill their pockets with jewels once they got to Beast's house. And the horse she was forced to purchase with the gold and copper and tin crimped thing began coughing at the edge of town and broke down completely somewhere in the woods to the North. So she had to walk after all, all through the night, frightened at every fluttering leaf, at every silent-winged owl, at all the beeps and cheeps and chirps and growls along the way.

At near dawn on Christmas day, Beast found her wandering alone, smelling of sweat and fear and the bomber jacket and leather hat and leather boots and the polished nails. Not smelling like Beauty at all.

So, of course, he ate her, Christmas being a tough hunting day since every baby animal and every plump child was tucked up at home waiting for dawn and all their presents.

And when he'd finished, he opened the string bag. The only thing he saved was the comb.

Beauty was right. It *was* perfect.

THE BLUE-NOSED REINDEER
A John Justin Mallory Story

by Mike Resnick

"Bah," said Mallory, as he entered the office with a *Racing Form* tucked under his arm. "And while I'm thinking about it, humbug."

Winnifred Carruthers turned to him and dabbed some sweat from her pudgy face.

"You don't like the way I'm decorating the tree?" she asked.

"Christmas trees are supposed to be green," said Mallory.

"Just because they were green in *your* Manhattan doesn't mean they have to be green everywhere, John Justin," replied Winnifred. "Personally, I think mauve is a much nicer color." She pushed a wisp of white hair back from her forehead and stepped back to admire her handiwork. "Do you think it needs more ornaments?"

"If you put any more ornaments on it, the damned thing will collapse of its own weight."

"Then perhaps some tinsel," she suggested.

"It's just the office tree, Winnifred," said Mallory. "If people need a detective agency, they'll come here whether we decorate the place or not."

"Well, it makes *me* feel better," she said. "I'd string

rows of popcorn, but . . ." She glanced at the remarkably human but definitely feline creature lying langorously on a windowsill, staring out at the snow.

"Yeah, I see your point," said Mallory. "Though she'd probably prefer that you string up a row or two of dead mice."

"I'd rather kill them myself," purred the creature. "You do it too fast. That takes all the fun out of it."

"We're feeling bloodthirsty this holiday season, aren't we, Felina?" said Mallory.

"I feel the same as always," said Felina without taking her eyes off the falling snow.

"I think that's what I meant," said Mallory sardonically.

"I'm going to sit down for a minute or two," announced Winnifred. "I'm not the woman I was fifty years ago."

"You want me to put the star on the top?" asked Mallory. "My arms are longer."

"If you would," said Winnifred gratefully.

"You don't want to do it now," said Felina.

"Why not?" asked Mallory.

"Because you're about to have a visitor."

"You see him outside?"

She shook her head and smiled a languorous feline smile. "I hear him on the roof."

"A visitor or a thief?" asked Mallory.

"One or the other," said Felina.

Mallory walked to his desk and took his pistol out of the top drawer, then walked to the front door and waited.

"He's not coming that way," said Felina.

"Which window?" demanded Mallory.

"None."

"There isn't any other way in," said Mallory.

"Yes there is," said Felina, still smiling.

Mallory was about to ask her what it was, when he heard a thud and an *"Oof!"* coming from the fireplace. He walked over and trained his gun on the huge figure that sat there, dusting soot off his bright red coat.

"Is that any way to greet a client?" said the man, staring at Mallory's pistol.

"Clients come through the front door," replied Mallory, still pointing the gun at him. "Thieves and intruders slide down the chimney."

"Slide is hardly the word," said the man. "They're building 'em narrower and narrower these days."

"Maybe you'd better explain what you're doing in my chimney in the first place," said Mallory.

"It's traditional. Now, are you going to keep aiming that gun at me, or are you going to give a fat old man a hand and maybe talk a little business?"

Mallory stared at him for another minute, then shoved the pistol into his belt and helped the huge man to his feet.

"Ah, that's better!" said the man, brushing himself off and smoothing his long white beard. "You're the guys who found the unicorn last New Year's, and exposed that scam at the Quatermain Cup, aren't you? They say that the Mallory & Carruthers Agency is the best detective bureau in town."

"It's the *only* one in town," replied Mallory. "What can we do for you?"

"Who am I speaking to—Mallory or Carruthers?"

"I'm John Justin Mallory, and this is my associate, Colonel Winnifred Carruthers."

"And *that*?" asked the man, pointing to Felina.

"The office cat," said Mallory. "And who are you?"

"I doubt that you've heard of me. I'm from out of town."

"We still need your name if we're to write up a contract," said Winnifred.

"Certainly, my dear," said the man. "My name is Nick."

"Nick the Greek?" asked Winnifred.

He smiled at her. "Nick the Saint."

"What can we do for you, Mr. Saint?" asked Winnifred.

"Call me Nick. Everybody does."

"All right, Nick—how can we help you?"

"Something was stolen from me," said Nick the Saint. "Something very valuable. And I want it back."

"What was it?" asked Mallory.

"A reindeer."

"A reindeer?" repeated Mallory.

"That's right."

"We're talking a real live one?" continued Mallory. "Not a ceramic, or a jade statue, or . . ."

"A real live one," said Nick the Saint.

"I knew it," muttered Mallory. "Unicorns, pink elephants, and now this. Why is it *always* animals?"

"I beg your pardon?" said Nick the Saint.

"Never mind," said Mallory. "His name wouldn't be Rudolph, would it?"

"Actually, his name is Jasper," answered Nick the Saint.

"Not that there are a lot of reindeer in Manhattan," said Mallory, "but it would help if you could describe him, and perhaps explain what makes him so valuable."

"He looks like any other reindeer," said Nick the Saint. "Except for his blue nose, that is."

"He doesn't like dirty books?"

"This is hardly the time for humor, Mr. Mallory," said Nick the Saint severely. "I absolutely must have him back by Christmas Eve. That's only four nights off."

"This nose of his," said Mallory. "What does it do—glow in the dark?"

"You know the way redshifts measure how quickly astronomical objects are moving away from you?" asked Nick the Saint. "Well, blueshifts measure how fast they're approaching. There's a lot of garbage up there where I work—satellites and space shuttles and such—and old Jasper's nose lets me know when they're getting too close. The brighter it gets, the sooner I have to change my course to avoid a collision."

"He smells them out?" asked Mallory.

"I don't know *how* it works, Mr. Mallory. I just know that it *does* work. Without Jasper, I'm a target for every heat-seeking missile that picks me up on radar."

"I see," said Mallory. "Where did you keep Jasper? The North Pole?"

"Too damned cold up there," replied Nick the Saint. "I just use it as a mail drop. No, Jasper was stabled at the Sunnydale Reindeer Ranch just north of the city, up in Westchester County."

"How long has he been missing?"

"About three hours."

"So you haven't received any ransom requests?"

"Not yet," said Nick the Saint.

"Who runs the Sunnydale Reindeer Ranch?"

"An old Greek named Alexander."

"Have you had any disagreements with him or his staff recently?"

"Nothing that would make him want to steal a reindeer."

"Anything that might make him want to kill one?" asked Mallory.

"Bite your tongue, Mr. Mallory! Without Jasper I'm a sitting duck up there!"

"Aren't you exaggerating the danger a bit?" asked Mallory. "I always heard flying was the safest way to travel."

"Try flying over Iran and Iraq and then tell me that," said Nick the Saint.

"I'll take it under advisement," said Mallory. "And you're sure you can't think of anyone who might want the reindeer?"

Nick the Saint shook his head. "Why would anyone want to steal anything from me? I'm the friendliest guy in the world. Always got a ready ho-ho-ho, always a cheery smile, I'm the first one to put a lampshade over my head at our Christmas party . . . No, I can't think of anyone who doesn't like me."

"Well, then Jasper is probably being held for ransom," said Mallory. "Colonel Carruthers and I will see what we can do from this end, but I strongly suggest you sit by your phone. I wouldn't be surprised if you got a call in the next twenty-four hours, telling you how much they want for him and where to make the drop."

"The drop?"

"The payment."

"Then you're taking the case?" said Nick the Saint. "Excellent! I'll go right home and wait for a call."

"Try using the door when you leave," said Mallory.

"You have no sense of style, Mr. Mallory," said Nick the Saint.

"No, but I have a sense of economic survival," said Mallory. "We'll require a retainer before you go."

"A retainer? And here I thought we were getting along so well."

"We'll get along even better once I know we're getting paid for our efforts."

"How much?" asked Nick the Saint.

"Five hundred a day plus expenses, and a ten percent bonus if we get Jasper back to you before your deadline."

"That's outrageous!"

"No," answered Mallory. "That's business."

"All right," muttered Nick the Saint, pulling a wad of bills out of his pocket and slapping them on the desk. "But don't be surprised if all you get for Christmas is a lump of coal."

*   *   *

"Well, I suppose the first thing I'd better do is contact the Grundy," said Mallory.

Felina hissed.

"Must you, John Justin?" asked Winnifred. "He's so frightening."

"He's the most powerful demon on the East Coast," said Mallory. "He's the logical place to start."

"You're not actually going to his castle, are you?"

"No, I thought I'd invite him here."

"I don't want anything to do with this," said Winnifred, walking to the closet and grabbing her coat and hat. "I *hate* dealing with him. I'll do some shopping."

"He was our first client," remarked Mallory.

"I didn't trust him then, and I don't trust him now," said Winnifred, walking out of the office and slamming the door behind her.

"How about you?" Mallory asked Felina. "You going or staying?"

"Staying," said the cat girl.

"Good for you."

"Oh, I'll desert you in the end, John Justin," she added. "But I'll stay for a little while."

"How comforting."

Mallory picked up a phone, dialed G-R-U-N-D-Y, and waited. A moment later a strange being suddenly materialized in the middle of the room. He was tall, a few inches over six feet, with two prominent horns protruding from his hairless head. His eyes were a burning yellow, his nose sharp and aquiline, his teeth white and gleaming, his skin a bright red. His shirt and pants were crushed velvet, his cloak satin, his collar and cuffs made of the fur of some white polar animal. He wore gleaming black gloves and boots, and he had two mystic rubies suspended from his neck on a golden chain. When he exhaled, small clouds of vapor emanated from his mouth and nostrils.

"You summoned me, John Justin Mallory?" said the Grundy.

"Yeah," said Mallory, as Felina spat and backed away into a corner. "Ever hear of Nick the Saint?"

"A high roller from up north?" asked the Grundy. "Owns the Kringleman Arms Hotel?"

"That's the one."

"What about him?"

"His most valuable reindeer just turned up missing," said Mallory. "I thought maybe you might know something about it."

"Of course I do."

"You've got power, money, jewels galore, everything a being devoted to Evil Incarnate could want," said Mallory. "What the hell do you need an old man's reindeer for?"

"I did not steal it, John Justin," said the demon. "I said I knew something about it."

"*What* do you know about it?"

"I know who stole it, of course."

"Okay," said Mallory. "Who?"

The Grundy smiled. "I'm afraid it isn't that easy, John Justin," he said. "It is your function in life to detect, and it is my function in life to exalt the evildoers and hinder the moralists."

"Do you always have to sound like a professor of Philosophy 101?" asked Mallory.

"It is my nature."

"Fine, it's your nature. Now are you going to tell me who's got the reindeer or not?"

"Certainly not."

"I'm going to find it with or without your help," said Mallory. "Why not make my life easier and I'll split the fee with you."

"Making your life easier is not part of my job description, John Justin Mallory," said the Grundy. He began laughing, and as he laughed his body grew more tenuous and translucent, then transparent, and finally vanished entirely, as the last note of his laughter lingered in the air.

"Well," said Mallory, "it was worth a try."

He poured himself a drink and waited until Winnifred returned.

"Did he show up?" she asked.

"He wasn't any help."

"Is he ever?"

"I have a grudging admiration for him," responded Mallory. "Except for you, he's the only person in this Manhattan who's never lied to me."

"Well, what do we do next, John Justin?" asked Winnifred.

"I should think Nick the Saint will be getting a ransom call any minute now," said Mallory. "I mean, what the hell else is a blue-nosed reindeer good for? Still, I suppose it can't hurt to start doing a little legwork, just to prove we're earning our fee."

"Where to?"

"The Sunnydale Reindeer Ranch seems the logical starting point," said Mallory. "I'll drive up there myself. You stay here and keep in touch with Nick the

Saint. Let me know as soon as someone contacts him with a demand for ransom."

*   *   *

"Welcome to the Sunnydale Reindeer Ranch," said the old man as Mallory walked up to the barn. "My name is Alexander the Greater."

"Greater than what?" said Mallory.

Alexander frowned. "I *hate* it when people ask me questions like that!"

"Well, actually I'm here to ask you some other questions," said Mallory. "I'm a private investigator, working for Nick the Saint."

"Ah," said Alexander. "You're here about Jasper."

"Right."

"Follow me," said Alexander, leading him into the barn. "There are fifty stalls, as you can see. Jasper was in Number 43, up the aisle here. When I came out to feed him this morning, he was gone."

"It snowed last night," said Mallory. "Were there any signs of footprints or reindeer tracks?"

Alexander shook his head. "Nope. It's like he disappeared right off the face of the earth."

"Has this ever happened to you before?"

"Have I ever lost Jasper before? Of course not."

"Has anyone ever robbed you before?"

"No. Most people don't even know this place exists."

"You mind if I look around?"

"Help yourself," said Alexander.

Mallory spent the next few minutes walking up and down the barn, looking into each stall. There were forty-nine reindeer, but none with a blue nose. He considered checking the surrounding area for tracks, but it had snowed again since morning and he was sure any sign of Jasper's departure would be covered by now.

Finally he returned to the old man. "I may want to ask you some more questions later on," he said.

"Happy to have the company," said Alexander. "There's just me and my reindeer here." Suddenly there was a loud screech. "And an occasional banshee living in the rafters," he added.

*   *   *

Mallory sat at his desk, taking a sip from the office bottle.

"Where do you look for a reindeer?" he said. "Who's got the facilities to keep it while they're negotiating a price?"

"The zoo?" suggested Winnifred.

"The racetrack," said Felina.

"The dog pound?" offered Mallory.

"I suggest that we split up," said Winnifred. "We can cover more ground that way. I'll take the zoo and you take the racetrack."

"*I'll* take the zoo," said Mallory. "Felina and I are no longer welcome at the track since our last little experience there."

"All right," said Winnifred, checking her wristwatch. "We'll meet at the dog pound in, shall we say, three hours?"

"Sounds good to me."

Felina suddenly leapt across the room and landed on Mallory's shoulders, almost knocking him through the wall.

"I'm going with you, John Justin," she said happily.

"Why am *I* so blessed?" muttered Mallory.

*   *   *

"All right," said Mallory as they walked into the zoo. "I want you by my side at all times."

"Yes, John Justin," purred Felina.

"I mean it," he said. "If you cause any trouble, you're out of here."

"Yes, John Justin," purred Felina.

"Do you even know what a reindeer looks like?"

"Yes, John Justin," purred Felina.

"Why don't I trust you?" he asked.

"Yes, John Justin," purred Felina.

They passed the sphinx and the griffin, which both looked chilly in their open-air confinements, and then came to a number of students, some of them human, some goblins, a few reptilian, who were picketing the gorgon house, demanding that the four gorgons on display be returned to the wild.

"Come on, Mac," said one of the picketers, a greenish goblin about half Mallory's height. "Will you and your lady friend sign our petition?"

"She's not exactly my lady friend," replied Mallory.

"This is no time for technicalities," said the goblin. "Surely you don't approve of keeping gorgons caged up?"

"I hadn't given it much thought," admitted Mallory.

"Well, it's time to *start* thinking about it, Mac," said the goblin. "Sign our petition to return 'em all to the wild."

"Where's their natural habitat?" asked Mallory. "Africa? Asia?"

"Grammercy Park, actually," said the goblin.

There was a huge, building-jarring roar from inside the gorgon house.

"What do gorgons eat?" asked Mallory.

"Oh, you know—the usual."

"What is the usual?"

"People," said the goblin.

"How about goblins?"

"Are you crazy?" demanded the goblin. "You'd put a goblin-eating monster in the middle of Grammercy Park? What kind of fiend are you?"

The goblin glared at him for a moment, then turned and walked away, and Mallory, taking Felina by the hand, continued walking past the harpy and unicorn exhibits. When he found a keeper who had just finished feeding the unicorns, he caught his attention and called him over.

"Excuse me," said Mallory, "but where do you keep your reindeer?"

"Me?" replied the keeper. "I ain't got no reindeer. Got a dog. Got a wife who yells at me all day long. Got three sons who won't look for work and two daughters who won't look for husbands. Even got a 1935 Studebaker roadster. But reindeer? Where would I keep 'em?"

"I didn't mean you, personally," said Mallory. "I meant, where does the zoo keep its reindeer?"

"Don't rightly know that we have any," answered the keeper. "Got a pegasus, if your girlfriend is looking for pretty four-legged-type critters."

"No, we need a reindeer," said Mallory, flashing his detective's credentials. "Are you sure one didn't arrive today?"

"Ain't seen hide nor hair of one," said the keeper. "Got a real nice Medusa in the next building, if that's to your liking."

"Who would know for sure if you had any reindeer?" asked Mallory.

"I would, and we don't," said the keeper. "By the way, you better keep an eye on your girlfriend before she falls down and hurts herself."

Mallory turned and saw Felina some thirty feet up the bole of a large tree that housed a number of banshees, who were screaming and hurling twigs at her. She had a predatory leer on her face, and as the banshees saw that their imprecations were having no effect on her, they flew to higher and lighter branches, with Felina following in nimble pursuit.

Mallory climbed over the fence that surrounded the tree and stood beneath it.

"Felina!" he yelled. "Get down here!"

She glanced down, smiled at him, and continued climbing—and suddenly Mallory heard an angry grunt directly behind him. He turned and found himself facing an enormous, broad-backed, elephantine creature with three heads.

"I say," said the first head, "he looks absolutely delicious. Shall we eat him?"

"He looks like he'd go very well with onions and mushrooms, and possibly a wine sauce," agreed the second head.

"We're all in agreement, then?" said the first head.

"I ain't talking to you guys," said the third head.

"Oh, come on, Roderick," said the first head. "I said I was sorry."

"Don't care," sulked the third head.

"Now see here, Roderick," said the second head. "Reginald has apologized to you. Isn't that enough?"

"No," said Roderick. "We always agree to kill people, and then *he* always ends up eating them."

"It goes to the same stomach," said Reginald, "so what's the difference?"

"If there's no difference, let *me* eat this one all by myself," said Roderick.

"If that's what it will take to get you talking to us again," said the second head with a sigh.

"Now, just hold on a second, Mortimer," said Reginald. "Who gave you leave to make the rules? I saw him first, so it's only fair that I get to eat him."

"It's *not* fair!" complained Roderick. "Just because I'm nearsighted, he always sees them first and gets to do the eating. I've got half a mind to crush this puny man-thing to a pulp so *nobody* can eat him."

"Uh, let's not be too hasty here," said Mallory, backing away toward the fence.

"Didn't anyone ever tell you it's bad manners to interfere in a family argument?" said Reginald. "Now please be quiet while we decide which of us is going to eat you."

"As the potential dinner, I think it's only fair that I have a say, too," persisted Mallory.

"You know, I never looked at it that way before," said Mortimer, "but of course he's absolutely right. He certainly has to be considered an involved party."

All three heads turned to Mallory. "All right," said Reginald. "Which of us would you prefer to be eaten by?"

"It's a hard decision to make on the spur of the moment," said Mallory. "How about if I spend a few minutes thinking about it and get back to you?"

"All right," said Reginald. "But you have to remain in the enclosure."

"Right," chimed in Roderick. "After all, fair is fair."

Just then there was a huge amount of shrieking overhead, and Felina fell through the air and landed nimbly on the three-headed creature's back.

"I told you not to leave my side," said Mallory.

"But they looked so tasty."

"You broke your word. If I survive the next couple of minutes, you're in big trouble."

"It's not my fault," said Felina.

"Then whose fault is it?" asked Mallory.

"Uh . . . I hate to interrupt," said Mortimer, "but

weren't we deciding which of us was going to eat you?"

"She's the reason I'm here," said Mallory disgustedly. "Eat *her*."

"Eat her? We can't even reach her."

"I'll get her for you," said Mallory, walking around the creature and climbing onto its back via its tail.

"Well, no one ever said they were bright," he whispered. "Can you jump over the fence from here?"

"Of course," said Felina. "Jumping is one of the very best things cat people do."

"Then would you please jump over it and bring back some help?"

"I thought you were mad at me," said Felina.

"We'll talk about it later," he said. "Right now staying alive and uneaten is more important."

"First you have to say you're not mad at me," said Felina stubbornly. "Then I'll get help."

"All right," said Mallory, wondering what his blood pressure reading was at that very moment. "I'm not mad at you."

She shook her head. "You have to say it with sweetness and sincerity."

"Hey! What's going on back there?" demanded Roderick.

"I'm just telling her I'm not mad at her," said Mallory.

"What's that got to do with anything?" said Reginald. "We're hungry."

"Felina, they're *hungry*!" hissed Mallory. "It's not going to take them very long to figure out that if they roll over, I'm dead meat."

"Oh, all right," she said, leaping lightly over the fence.

"Hey, she's running away!" said Roderick.

"That's all right," said Mallory. "You've still got me."

"But we can't reach you!"

"I can't tell you how sorry I am about that," said Mallory, looking across toward the unicorn house, where Felina was talking to the old unicorn keeper. Finally he nodded and trudged across the sidewalk after her.

"Okay, you guys," he said when he arrived. "Let the detective go."

"Aw, we were just having a little fun with him," whined Roderick.

"And maybe a little lunch," added Reginald.

"You know what I've told you," said the old man. "If you keep eating the customers, pretty soon we ain't gonna have none, and then where will we all be?"

"How about if we just eat a leg or two?" asked Roderick.

"You let him go, or there will be no PBS documentaries about your mating habits for a week," said the old man.

"No! We'll let him go!" cried Mortimer. "Get off our back *now*!"

Mallory slid down to the ground and raced to the fence.

"He looks kind of stringy anyway," said Roderick.

"Besides, he's a detective," added Mortimer. "Did you ever try to clean one of those?"

Mallory scrambled over the fence while the three heads were busy rationalizing their loss and telling dirty stories about the last documentary they had seen.

"Thank you," he said to the unicorn keeper.

"It's people like you that give carnivores a bad name," said the old man, turning on his heel and walking away.

Mallory checked his watch, saw that he just had time to meet Winnifred at the dog pound, and started walking toward his car, half-hoping Felina would stay behind. A moment later he felt a ninety-pound weight on his back and heard a loud purring in his ear.

"I'll say this for my luck," he muttered. "It's consistent."

*   *   *

"No luck at the track?" asked Mallory as he met Winnifred in front of the dog pound.

"None," she said. "How about the zoo?"

"The only luck I had there is that I'm still alive."

"By the way," added Winnifred, "I checked in with Nick the Saint, and he still hasn't received a demand for ransom."

"That's damned strange," said Mallory, frowning. "What the hell else can you *do* with a reindeer?"

"Eat it," suggested Felina.

"What do you think, John Justin?" asked Winnifred.

He shook his head. "If that was the motive, why steal the most valuable one? No one's going to eat his nose."

"Then I suggest we stop wasting time out here and check out the pound," said Winnifred.

"Just a minute," said Mallory. He led Felina back to his car, sat her down in the back seat, secured the safety belt, and then locked all the doors.

"She created problems at the zoo?" asked Winnifred when he had rejoined her.

"Not half as many as she can create at a dog pound," answered Mallory. "I know that trouble is our business, but she seems bound and determined to turn it into our hobby as well."

They walked up to the main office, where a large

shaggy man with a face resembling a Saint Bernard got up from his desk and greeted them.

"Good afternoon, dear friends," he said, drooling slightly from the corner of his mouth. "Welcome to the Manhattan Dog Pound. How may I help you?"

"We're looking for a reindeer," said Mallory.

"One with a blue nose," added Winnifred.

The man growled deep within his throat. "Why would you expect to find a reindeer here?"

"Just a hunch," said Mallory.

"Well, you're certainly welcome to inspect our premises, but I guarantee you won't find what you're looking for," said the man, starting to pant slightly. "Let me get one of our employees to accompany you." He pressed a button on his desk, and a moment later a lean man with chalk-white skin and black spots all over it entered the room. "Tyge," he said, "please give these two visitors a tour of the premises."

"Rrrright," said Tyge. He turned to Winnifred. "Pleased to meet you, ma'am."

"Likewise, I'm sure," said Winnifred, extending her hand. Tyge took it in his own hands, held it to his nose, and took a deep sniff, then repeated the same procedure with Mallory.

"*Arf*ter me," said Tyge, leading them through a door at the back of the office.

They found themselves in a narrow aisle between two sets of chain-linked runs, and inside each was a man, woman, or child.

"I thought this was a dog pound," said Mallory.

"Yep, it sure is, yep, yep, *yip*," said Tyge. "Each of these people wants a dog for Christmas, so when any stray dogs show up, we send 'em in here and see if they want to go home with any of them."

"Back where I come from, dog pounds hold dogs, not people," said Mallory.

"No dog deserves such *ruff* treatment," said Tyge, barking the word. His upper lip curled back, revealing a row of clean white teeth. "I never heard of anything so brutal. Imagine, putting dogs in cages and letting *people* choose which ones they want!"

"Different strokes," said Mallory. "Do you have any reindeer here?"

"Never heard of a reindeer wanting a dog before," chuckled Tyge. "That's a *larf*!"

"Then we won't take up any more of your valuable time," said Winnifred.

"It's been my pleasure, ma'am," said Tyge. "I wonder if you could do me one little favor before you leave?"

"What?"

He turned his back to her. "Could you just kind of scratch between my shoulder blades a bit?"

Winnifred reached forward and scratched.

"Now under the chin?"

Winnifred scratched again, and suddenly Tyge's left leg began shaking spasmodically.

"That's enough, ma'am," he said. "Thank you."

"My pleasure," said Winnifred, following Mallory back to the exit.

"Well, that was a waste of time," said Mallory. "Maybe we'd better check in with Nick the Saint and see if anyone's contacted him yet."

"Maybe we'd better rescue the car first," said Winnifred, walking out into the open, for Felina had somehow worked her way loose and had three dog pound employees, each more canine in appearance than the last, cowering on the hood of the car while she grinned and displayed her claws to them.

Mallory walked behind her and encircled her with an arm, lifting her off the ground while she writhed and spat. The three employees raced toward the safety of the pound, howling their terror.

"Aren't you ashamed of yourself?" said Winnifred when Mallory had stuffed Felina into the car and started the engine.

Felina licked her forearm and turned her back on them.

"I'm speaking to you, young lady!" snapped Winnifred.

"I think it's going to snow again," said Felina, looking out the window.

"You know," said Mallory, who had been silent since leaving the dog pound, "now that I come to think of it, *my* Manhattan wasn't so bad."

*   *   *

Winnifred hung up the phone. "He still hasn't gotten any ransom request."

"I think," said Mallory, "that it's about time we started considering the fact that the damned reindeer wasn't stolen for ransom, and begin examining other possibilities."

They were back in the office, and Felina had been banished to the kitchen, where she had turned on the tap in the kitchen sink and was watching, fascinated, as the water swirled down into the drain.

"I'm open to suggestions," said Winnifred. "Why else would someone steal a reindeer?"

"Not *just* a reindeer," Mallory pointed out. "But a blue-nosed reindeer with certain talents that none of the others had."

"The military?" suggested Winnifred. "They'd give a pretty penny to get their hands on an animal that could dodge heat-seeking missiles."

"No, I don't think so," said Mallory.

"Why not?"

"Because they *would* give a pretty penny for Jasper," he said. "If they wanted him, they'd simply appropriate the funds to buy him."

"What if Nick didn't want to sell?"

"Then they'd have found some way to confiscate him," replied Mallory.

"All right," said Winnifred. "If not the military, then who?"

"I keep going over it and over it in my mind," said Mallory, "and I keep coming up with the same answer: a competitor."

"He doesn't *have* any competitors, John Justin."

"Well, he does *now*," said Mallory. "He's without a lead reindeer, and someone else has one four days before Christmas."

"Where's the motive?" asked Winnifred. "It's certainly not profit, not if this competitor is giving away presents all over the world." She paused. "And the kind of person who has enough goodness to give them away isn't the type to steal another man's reindeer in the first place."

"What kind of person *does* steal Nick the Saint's reindeer four days before Christmas?" mused Mallory.

"I don't know," said Winnifred.

"I think," said Mallory, "that I'd better pay another visit to Alexander the Greater first thing tomorrow morning."

* * *

Mallory pulled his car up to the barn and got out of it.

"So you're back again?" said Alexander the Greater, walking out of the barn to greet him.

"That's right."

"Got some more questions?"

"Better ones, too," said Mallory. "But first I'd like to take another look at Jasper's stall."

"Be my guest," said Alexander. "You know where it is."

"Thanks," said Mallory.

He entered the barn and started walking past the stalls, peering into each of them. When he came to Number 43, which had belonged to Jasper, he walked right past it and down to the end of the barn, then returned to Alexander.

"You've been doing a little business, I see," said Mallory.

"Not much," answered Alexander. "Things are pretty quiet right before Christmas."

"You're too modest," said Mallory. "Just yesterday you were boarding forty-nine reindeer, and today you've only got forty-one. That means you sold eight of them since I was here."

"Well, they come, they go, you know how it is," said Alexander with a shrug.

"No I don't," said Mallory. "Suppose you tell me how it is?"

"I beg your pardon?"

"Who did you sell the reindeer to?"

"That's none of your business, Mr. Mallory," said Alexander the Greater.

"As a matter of fact, I've got a feeling that it *is* my business," said Mallory. "Was it the same person who took Jasper away yesterday morning?"

"You're guessing, Mr. Mallory."

"I'm a good guesser, Alexander," said Mallory. "For example, I'd guess that you're looking at five to ten years for aiding and abetting in the theft of Nick the Saint's reindeer. I'd also guess that I'd be willing to forget your complicity if you'd supply me with the name I want."

"Not a chance," said Alexander stubbornly.

"Then I guess that I'm going to walk into your office and find it on my own."

"Two out of three ain't bad," said Alexander with a nasty grin. He put two fingers into his mouth and emitted a loud whistle, and suddenly three wiry little figures, each half the size of a grown man, raced out of the barn. "Meet my security team, Mr. Mallory," he said, indicating the three leprechauns. "Team, this is Mr. Mallory, whose presence is no longer desired here."

"We'll kill him," growled the nearest of the leprechauns.

"We'll rip his head off his shoulders," added the second.

"We'll gut him like a fish," said the third.

"There won't be enough of him left to bury," said the first leprechaun.

"We'll slice him to bits with such dexterity that we'll be awarded both ears and the tail," said the second.

"The bigger they are, the harder they fall," said the third. "He'll never know what hit him."

Mallory had been retreating toward his car. Once there, he opened the door and Felina jumped out. She faced the leprechauns, grinned, and stretched out her fingers. All ten of her claws glistened in the morning sunlight.

"Of course," added the first leprechaun, "we could avoid a lot of needless violence and bloodshed and simply discuss the matter."

"Right," said the second. "Maybe we could cut a deck of cards, like gentleman. If he's low, he leaves; if he's high, he gets to inspect your records."

"Besides, my lumbago's been bothering me recently," added the third leprechaun.

"Yours, too?" said the first, as Felina took a step toward them. "Suddenly my rheumatism is acting up. Must be the weather."

"I've got weak kidneys, myself," said the second. "In fact," he added, "now that I think of it, I gotta go to the bathroom." He turned and raced off.

"The door sticks," said the first leprechaun, following him at a dead run. "I'll help you."

"What a bunch of cowards!" said the third leprechaun contemptuously.

"Then you propose to stay and fight?" asked Mallory.

"No, but only because my religion doesn't permit me to fight on Tuesdays. It's a matter of high moral principle."

"This is a Friday," said Mallory.

"It is?" asked the leprechaun.

Felina grinned and nodded.

"My goodness!" said the leprechaun. "It's only four days from Tuesday! I'd better be on my best behavior, just to be on the safe side." He turned to Alexander the Greater. "Sorry, Chief, but I'm off to sacrifice a fatted lamb, if I can find one."

He turned and raced off across the landscape as fast as his muscular little legs could carry him.

"Well?" said Mallory.

"You win," said Alexander with a sigh. "I'll give you the name you want."

"I'd rather see it in black and white," said Mallory. "Somehow I've lost my trust in this place." He turned to Felina. "Keep an eye out for the elves, and warn me if Alexander tries to leave the barn."

He went to the office, which was just inside the entrance, and started thumbing through paperwork that hadn't yet been filed. Within two minutes he found what he was looking for. He put the papers in his pocket, waited for Felina to reluctantly give up waiting for the leprechauns and jump into the back seat, and drove back to town.

*   *   *

"You have a triumphant smirk on your face, John Justin," said Winnifred when he returned to the office.

"Not without cause," he replied.

"What did you find out?" she asked.

"I know who stole Jasper, and I think I know why," said Mallory.

"But?" she said. "It sounds like there should be a 'but' at the end of that sentence."

"You're very perceptive," said Mallory. "I know who stole the reindeer, and I think I know why . . . but I'm not sure that justice will be served by pressing charges."

"It's your job to arrest criminals," said Winnifred.

He shook his head. "It's the police's job to arrest criminals. It's our job to make our client happy, and I think I see a way to do that, but first I'm going to have to confront the thief."

"Is it safe?"

"I've met him once before, the first night I came to this Manhattan," said Mallory. "He didn't kill me than; there's no reason why he should kill me now."

"You probably didn't have information that could send him to jail then," Winnifred pointed out.

"He'll know I'm not stupid enough to have it with me," answered Mallory. "If anything happens to me, I expect you to use it."

"I don't even know what it is."

"I'm about to lay it out to you," said Mallory, removing the papers from his pocket. "And then I'm going to see what kind of deal we can make."

*   *   *

The Old Abandoned Warehouse was practically hidden by the thick fog coming off the East River, but Mallory knew where it was, and he knew—or thought he knew—what he would find there. He parked in a lot about three blocks away, then walked past a row of bars and restaurants catering to goblins and a strip joint promising that Slinky Scaly Sally would shed everything, even her skin, to make her reptilian audience happy, and finally he came to the unmarked door that he sought, and knocked on it.

"Who's there?" demanded a deep voice.

"John Justin Mallory."

"You got an appointment?"

"No," answered Mallory. "You got a good lawyer?"

The door squeaked open, and Mallory found himself confronting a huge blue-skinned man in a purple sharkskin suit, light blue shirt, violet tie, and navy blue shoes and socks. He stood just under seven feet tall, and weighed in the vicinity of five hundred pounds.

"Well, well," said the Prince of Whales. "So the Grundy hasn't killed you yet."

"Have you got some place where we can sit down and talk?" asked Mallory.

"Why do I want to talk to you?" asked the Prince of Whales.

"Because I know all about the blue-nosed reindeer."

"People have died for saying less than that to me," said the Prince of Whales.

"Yeah, I suppose they have," answered Mallory.

"But they were stupid people. They probably didn't tell you up front that whatever they had on you would be turned over to the police if you laid a finger on them."

The Prince of Whales glared at him for a long moment, then shrugged. "All right, shamus," he said. "Follow me."

He led Mallory through the enormous warehouse to a small office built into a corner of it, then ushered him inside.

"Drink?" he said, holding up a bottle containing a blue liquid with scores of small fish swimming around in it.

"I'll take a pass," said Mallory, sitting down.

"Good," said the Prince of Whales. "There's that much more for me, then." He lifted the bottle to his lips and drained its contents, fish and all.

"Do they tickle when they go down?" asked Mallory curiously.

"Not so's you'd notice it," answered the Prince. "Now cut the chatter and let's talk deal."

"What makes you think I'm here to offer you a deal?"

"If you weren't, you'd have sent the cops," answered the Prince. "So let's have it."

"Okay," said Mallory. "Let me start with what I know."

"That shouldn't take long."

"I know that you leased eight reindeer from Alexander the Greater this morning. I know you took them away with you. I know the lease expires in a week."

"And that's it?" asked the Prince.

"Not quite," said Mallory. "I know you're the biggest fence in Manhattan."

"Everyone knows that," said the Prince of Whales, "but they ain't never proved it in court."

"Now let me tell you what I think," continued Mallory.

The Prince of Whales reached into his pocket, pulled out a penny, and tossed it to the detective. "For your thoughts," he said.

"I think that they're getting awfully close to proving it," he said. "I think you've gotten word that sometime shortly after Christmas they're going to raid your warehouse, before you have a chance to hide or unload your merchandise."

"You think so, do you?" said the Prince.

Mallory nodded. "And I think you saw a way to get rid of your inventory right out in the open, where nobody would even dream of trying to stop you." He paused. "I think you stole Jasper and leased the other reindeer so that you could dump all your illegal goods on Christmas Eve. After all, who arrests Santa Claus for giving away millions of presents? And so what if this year there are a few more video recorders and toasters and boom boxes and a few less toys? Most of the people will be just as happy, and when the bust comes in a week or two, your warehouse is empty and nothing can be traced back to you. You won't even have the reindeer, and I've got a hunch that Alexander will suddenly find poor old Jasper grazing in some nearby forest, where everyone will assume he's been living for the past week."

The Prince of Whales stared at him for a long moment.

"You're pretty good," he said. "I'll give you that. You got everything but the tax angle."

"Tax angle?"

"It's the locals who are trying to bust me for fencing. The Feds don't care what I do as long as I pay my taxes. I figured to deduct a couple of billion dollars for charitable contributions after I made the rounds on Christmas Eve. I could carry that forward for the next twenty years on my taxes."

"Maybe you still can," said Mallory.

"Okay," said the Prince of Whales. "You talk, I'll listen. What's the deal?"

"What if I can get my client to agree to drop all charges against you?"

"What's it gonna cost?"

"First, you have to return Jasper today," said Mallory. "I assume he's somewhere in the warehouse?"

"Yeah, he's back there with the others in a bunch of stalls I made up. What else?"

"My client is a tough old bird, and I don't know if simply returning the reindeer is enough," said Mallory. "But if you sweeten the pot by turning over all your goods to him and letting *him* dump them on the market on Christmas Eve, I think he might go for it."

"He'll sign a document certifying that I gave them to him free of charge?"

"I think he will. Anything he doesn't use this year, he can use next time around." He paused. "Do we have a deal?"

"You bet your ass we have a deal, Mallory!" said the Prince of Whales. "The only part of this scam I didn't like was flying around behind those goddamned reindeer. I'm scared to death of heights."

"All right," said Mallory, walking over to the phone. "Let me talk to my client and make sure he's willing."

The deal was official ninety seconds later.

*   *   *

"Bah," said Mallory. "And while I'm at it, humbug."

"What now, John Justin?" asked Winnifred.

"Here it is Christmas Eve, and that old geezer hasn't come up with our expense money or our bonus yet. That's a hell of a note, considering who he is."

"You'd just spend your share betting at the track, anyway," said Winnifred.

"Well, there's an elephant called Flyaway running at Jamaica tomorrow," admitted Mallory. "I've got a hunch."

"Didn't you once tell me that you bet a horse called Flyaway in your Manhattan some ten or fifteen times and never won?"

"Eighteen," admitted Mallory. "But it's such a great name. The name alone is due to win."

"I'm glad you attack our cases with more intelligence than your wagers," said Winnifred.

"He's here," announced Felina, who had been sleeping atop the refrigerator.

"Who's here?" asked Mallory.

"The blue-nosed reindeer."

"How can you tell?"

Felina smiled. "Cat people know things that humans can never know," she purred.

Suddenly there was a small clanking noise in the fireplace, and Winnifred walked over to it.

"Well, it looks like he kept *both* promises," she said, picking up a small parcel.

"What do you mean?" asked Mallory.

"This," she said, holding up a roll of bills, "is for us. I'll take it over to the bank and put it in the night deposit window." She paused. "And *this*," she added, tossing him a small object, "is for you."

Mallory caught it and examined it with a wry grin on his face.

It was a lump of coal.

DAW

FANTASY ANTHOLOGIES

☐ **CATFANTASTIC**   UE2355—$3.95
  edited by Andre Norton and Martin H. Greenberg

A unique collection of fantastical cat tales—original fantasies of
cats in the future, the past, the present, and other dimensions.

☐ **CATFANTASTIC II**   UE2461—$4.50
  edited by Andre Norton & Martin H. Greenberg

More all-new and original tales of those long-haired, furry keepers of mankind, practioners of magical arts beyond human
ken. . . .

☐ **THE NIGHT FANTASTIC**   UE2484—$4.50
  edited by Poul & Karen Anderson

Unforgettable tales of dreams which may become reality—and
realities which may dissolve into dreams. . . .

☐ **HORSE FANTASTIC**   UE2504—$4.50
  edited by Martin H. Greenberg & Rosalind M. Greenberg

Let these steeds carry you off to adventure and enchantment
as they race, swift as the wind, to the magic lands. . . .

☐ **DRAGON FANTASTIC**   UE2511—$4.50
  edited by Rosalind M. Greenberg & Martin H. Greenberg

All-original tales of the magical beasts which once ruled the
skies, keepers of universes beyond human ken.

DAW
Science Fiction Anthologies

DAW

Jennifer Roberson

THE NOVELS OF TIGER AND DEL

Tiger and Del, he a Sword-Dancer of the South, she of the North, each a master of secret sword-magic. Together, they would challenge wizards' spells and other deadly traps on a perilous quest of honor.

SWORD-DANCER	UE2376—$4.99
SWORD-SINGER	UE2295—$4.50
SWORD-MAKER	UE2379—$5.99
SWORD-BREAKER	UE2476—$4.99

CHRONICLES OF THE CHEYSULI

This superb fantasy series about a race of warriors gifted with the ability to assume animal shapes at will presents the Cheysuli, fated to answer the call of magic in their blood, fulfilling an ancient prophecy which could spell salvation or ruin.

SHAPECHANGERS: Book 1	UE2140—$3.99
THE SONG OF HOMANA: Book 2	UE2317—$4.50
LEGACY OF THE SWORD: Book 3	UE2316—$3.95
TRACK OF THE WHITE WOLF: Book 4	UE2193—$4.99
A PRIDE OF PRINCES: Book 5	UE2261—$3.95
DAUGHTER OF THE LION: Book 6	UE2324—$3.95
FLIGHT OF THE RAVEN: Book 7	UE2422—$4.99
A TAPESTRY OF LIONS	UE2524—$5.99

DAW
Tanya Huff

VICTORY NELSON, INVESTIGATOR:
Otherworldly Crimes A Specialty

☐ **BLOOD PRICE: Book 1**   UE2471—$3.99

Can one ex-policewoman and a vampire defeat the magic-spawned evil which is devastating Toronto?

☐ **BLOOD TRAIL: Book 2**   UE2502—$4.50

Someone was out to exterminate Canada's most endangered species— the werewolf.

☐ **BLOOD LINES: Book 3 (*Jan. '93*)**   UE2530—$4.99

Long-imprisoned by the magic of Egypt's gods, an ancient force of evil is about to be loosed on an unsuspecting Toronto.

THE NOVELS OF CRYSTAL

When an evil wizard attempts world domination, the Elder Gods must intervene!

☐ **CHILD OF THE GROVE: Book 1**   UE2432—$3.95
☐ **THE LAST WIZARD: Book 2**   UE2331—$3.95

OTHER NOVELS

☐ **THE FIRE'S STONE**   UE2445—$3.95

Thief, swordsman and wizardess—drawn together by a quest not of their own choosing, would they find their true destinies in a fight against spells, swords and betrayal?

☐ **GATE OF DARKNESS,**
   CIRCLE OF LIGHT   UE2386—$3.95

The Wild Magic was loose in Toronto, for an Adept of Darkness had broken through the barrier into the everyday mortal world. And in this age when only fools and innocents still believed in magic, who was there to fight against this invasion by evil?

DAW

New Dimensions in Fantasy

Sean Russell

☐ **THE INITIATE BROTHER (Book 1)**   UE2466—$4.99
In this powerful debut novel rich with the magic and majesty of
the ancient Orient, one of the most influential lords of the Great
Houses is marked for destruction by the new Emperor and
must use every weapon at his command to survive—including
a young Botahist monk gifted with powers not seen in the world
for nearly a thousand years.

☐ **GATHERER OF CLOUDS (Book 2)**   UE2536—$5.50
Initiate Brother Shuyun, spiritual adviser to Lord Shonto, re-
ceives a shocking message: the massive army of the Golden
Khan is poised at the border, and Lord Shonto is caught
between it and his own hostile Emperor's Imperial Army. Yet
even as this trap closes, Brother Shuyun faces another crisis.
For in the same scroll that warned of the invasion was a sacred
Udumbara blossom—a sign his order has awaited for a mil-
lennium. . . .

Elizabeth Forrest

☐ **PHOENIX FIRE**   UE2515—$4.99
As the legendary Phoenix awoke, so, too, did an ancient Chinese demon—and Los Angeles was destined to become the
final battleground in their millennia-old war. Now, the very earth
begins to dance as these two creatures of legend fight to break
free. And as earthquake and fire start to take their toll on the
mortal world, four desperate people begin to suspect the terror
that is about to engulf mankind.

CAROLE HALSTON
Compromising Positions

Silhouette Special Edition

Published by Silhouette Books New York

America's Publisher of Contemporary Romance

SILHOUETTE BOOKS
300 East 42nd St., New York, N.Y. 10017

ISBN: 0-373-09500-7

First Silhouette Books printing January 1989

Printed in the U.S.A.